INFINITY CREW

ANTHONY J. BUCCI

CONVICTED
PUBLISHING

Published in 2020 by Convicted Publishing

Copyright © Anthony J. Bucci 2020

Anthony J. Bucci has asserted his moral right to be identified as the author of this Work

ISBN Hardback: 978-1-7359112-2-9
Paperback: 978-1-7359112-0-5
Ebook: 978-1-7359112-1-2

A CIP catalogue copy of this book can be found in the Library of Congress.

Published with the help of Indie Authors World
www.indieauthorsworld.com

IndieAuthors
World

Dedication

To my sister Grace. There is not a day that goes by that I don't miss you. We all miss you. No matter how much suffering I went through over the years I never let go of your memory. You were in my heart and soul every step of the way. Thoughts of you, and how brave you were in the end gave me the strength to go on when I did not think I could. It took me a long time to write these few words to you because I don't share my  hurt over you leaving us with anyone. My tears are here now once again, this time for the world to see. I dedicate this book in your loving memory Grace. I hope you're proud of me my beautiful sister.

Acknowledgements

My book is based on the mean streets surrounding Boston where I was born and raised. I am thankful to so many people who have been there for me over the years. These are the only people I owe my loyalty to because they have never made me question theirs.

First and foremost, I'd like to thank my hero, my mother, Rosemarie. With forty dollars in her pocket, my mother took my sister Grace and I out of a mentally and physically abusive household when I was five years old via a state police escort. She raised us on her own and worked three jobs to support us. I put her through hell and back as an out of control kid and adult, yet her unconditional love for me has never wavered. I love you with all my heart mom.

As crazy as it sounds, I'd like to thank the Boston Federal Court System, prosecutors and agents who prosecuted me, twice. My first stint was forty one months on a marijuana charge but that was not enough time to phase a guy like me. Four years later I received a draconian sentence of 21 years for a one day drug conspiracy where no one got hurt. I got that much time because I would not cooperate with the government. That's just not my style. Even though the sentence was way too harsh, believe me, I needed every day of the suffering I endured to reform and evolve into the man I am today. I probably would not be alive had it not been for this sentence.

I'd like to thank my entire circle of support. My children Talena, Tamar, Karissa and Dante. My grandson Landon. My second mom, my amazing aunt Betsy. My cousins: Steve, Chris, Gina, Larry, Ben and my Gemini twin Wendy. My son in-laws Brian and Andrew. My dear friends Brian Phelan, Chris Serino, Michael DiPlatzi, Delia Mele, Karen Zumpfe, Karen Walsh, Stephany, Dorothy, Butchie, Ross, Fab, Bobby S., Aaron & Kim, Tommy Q & Kerstin, Philly & Jen, Terri, N.Y.Bigs, Boston Jay, Big Jerry from the Bronx, New Jersey Rob M, Shamrock Shane, Mikee Q, Mark Lanz, Chris Fox, M.Crooker, Rafco, St. Jude, Nee, R.I. Mike Chunk, Juan, R.I. Ronnie, Albe, Riley, Dennis Petro, Big E, Canadian Richard A., Ace, Big Chris and anyone else that touched my life, and of course those I can't name. Jennifer Carr my magnificent ghost writer. Nataly Garcia who changed my life and also mentored me in my conversion to veganism. I'd like to thank my attorneys Inga Parsons and Stephen Columbus who both went above and beyond for me over the years which they did mostly out of the kindness of their heart. A special shout out to the woman who represented me pro-bono and filed and argued the winning motion that got me home, Attorney Allison Koury. This motion set precedent in federal court and opened the flood gates for inmates to get home home to their families. Above all, Alli is my friend.

My dear friend Paulie Decologero once said to me, to be a hero you need to fight the war. I have never stopped fighting and I will always represent for you. Thank you for giving me the will to fight and persevere. Compassion is now my strength and freedom is my home because of all of you.

Prologue
Otisville, New York
2008

Vinny unbuttoned the khaki pants that matched the khaki shirt, swearing to himself that he would never wear that brand of material or color ever again. He folded the pants and then unbuttoned his shirt. The guard named Santos passed him the new clothes through the slot in the door.

The clothes, sent to R&D, known to civilians as Receiving and Discharge, earlier in the week, were a revelation. The material felt like butter—foreign, that smooth weave of the threads of his button-down shirt, the crisp denim of his designer jeans. Everything was fitted, now, according to the modern style. The last time he put on clothes that were not the standard khaki, the fit was looser, boxier.

Santos took Vinny's khakis through the slot in the door and said, "Maybe we'll have these dipped in bronze and mounted on the wall in here, maybe rename the SHU the 'Vinny Bruno Segregated Housing Unit' for how many times you got sent here."

"The Plant-Based Bruiser," the other guard, Max, said, laughing.

"The toughest sonofabitch I've ever seen, especially for a grass-eater," Santos said.

Vinny laughed. "What do cows eat?"

Santos shrugged. "Grass."

"So, cows are vegetarian. I just cut out the fucking middleman and I spare the animals. Always do the work yourself, fellas." He wagged his finger at them through the rectangle of the door. "Remember that—it's good advice. Besides, I don't eat nothing with eyes. Except, of course, the souls of my enemies."

He laughed as he handed over the khakis and they handed him his belt. Vinny wasn't sure which hole would fit—new belt, new style. Also, in the last twelve years, Vinny had pumped more iron than he had in his whole life, which already had been substantial. He tried a couple before finding the right fit.

"You gained some weight, old man?" Max asked.

Vinny pulled up his shirt, revealing his eight-pack. "I know this gets you off," Vinny said. "Take a good last look, fellas, and all from plants and vegetables, go figure."

They opened the door, and Vinny stepped out, nodding at both Santos and Max. He was half a head taller than they were. He wasn't the tallest man in Otisville, or the biggest, but his overall effect was striking. His shoulders were broad and square, and in his fitted shirt, he no longer appeared like a big hulking box. Vinny knew what effect he had on people, and it pleased him to see the guards taken aback. He was now no longer an inmate number in the Bureau of Prisons. He was Vinny Bruno, free fucking citizen.

As they led him down the hall, in his sharp new duds looking like something out of *GQ*, not the Segregated Housing Unit, the lines of men in their cells on both sides whistled and hollered out to him.

"Hey, Vinny! I'll call you when I'm out!"

"Vinny! Vinny! I'll hit you up! Don't forget about me!"

For someone who kept getting sent to the SHU for fighting, he'd spent a lot more time racking up respect points for settling scores and not being the first one to start shit but definitely being the guy who would end shit. And it had made him a fucking hero at Otisville.

Now, in his own new clothes, he passed through the walls for the last time like something from another world, barely touching the ground. *That* was the effect of Vinny Bruno.

The limo was waiting out front, just as Vinny had requested. Lined up in front of it were his crew, Tommy, Joe, Blaze, and Whispers.

Whispers was the first to step forward. He'd grown his hair out in twists, though there was plenty of premature gray around the crown. "Looking fly, my brother!" Whispers said.

"Vinny Bruno never goes out of style, bro," Vinny said, smiling.

Whispers laughed. "Man, good to fucking see you." They hugged, and then Blaze jumped in from behind, bear-hugging Vinny, who was sandwiched between the two friends. "Fuck, man, you crying?" Whispers asked Blaze.

"Fuck off," Blaze said, wiping his eyes. "I love this guy, stop hating !"

"Come here, *mi hermano*, don't listen to Whispers," Vinny said, hugging Blaze.

Vinny looked at Tommy and Joe. "So good to see you," Tommy said, coming in next for a huge hug. "I missed you so much, bro. Welcome home. You look amazing."

"Not quite fucking home yet, but I'll be there soon. I've missed you more," Vinny said.

Joe was as bougie as ever, in his polo shirt, the black collar flipped up, just grazing the Mexican flag tattoo that stretched a quarter of the way around his neck. "Vinny," he said, reaching out his hand and then pulling him in for the hug, patting his back, then stepping back to look at him. They nodded to each other.

They weren't old at thirty-six, thirty-seven years old, but having not seen them since they were all in their mid-twenties—time hadn't stopped for them the way it had for Vinny. Fuck, how much he had lost. He had to remember to keep his cool, and so he kept the smile on his face.

The limo driver opened the rear door and they all climbed inside, Vinny lagging behind and motioning to the others to get in before him.

"Is everything all set?" Vinny asked the driver, who nodded.

"Yes, sir, everything is just as you requested."

Vinny slid along the leather, stretching out his legs. He reached for the decanter of whiskey sitting on the bar.

"Man, you don't want that shit, only the best for my guy," Blaze said, pulling a bottle of Jose Cuervo Reserva de la Familia out of a bag at his feet.

Even Tommy, who hated tequila, took a shot, though he grimaced afterward.

"Now *that* is no toilet hooch," Vinny said.

"Did you actually drink that shit?" Tommy asked.

"Fuck no, only the best goes into this temple," Vinny said, pointing to his body.

They spent a while shooting the shit, reminiscing about old times. After that, Blaze spoke about Puerto Rico, Mexican Joe about computer technology, Tommy about playing softball, and Whispers about his new Harley. Then the car got quiet. The sky was white, hazy, washing out the trees that extended on both sides of the wide, flat road that led home.

There was a carryon bag under the bar, with a red tag, and Vinny eyed it.

"I don't know whose bag that is," Joe said.

"It's mine," Vinny said, reaching for it and placing it on his lap. On top was a Tupperware full of trail mix, and below that was a backup shirt. Below that, the 9mm.

The limo took an exit off Highway I-90. About a mile off it, they passed a refinery and turned down an unused road lined with abandoned warehouses. The smoke from the refinery disappeared into the thick, heavy air.

"Where the fuck are we going? You got a job for us already?" Whispers asked, laughing.

"Not a job for us, just me. I got one quick stop to make. Wait'll you see it, guys, I bet you're gonna lose your minds. But it'll reconnect us all, make us even tighter as a family."

They watched as the limo pulled onto a small side street between the warehouses, weeds waist-high growing where trucks used to line up. Vinny took turns staring at each of them. "Man," he said. "This has been a long time coming. I don't know what to say, but I've had a long time to think about it, how I got locked up for some bullshit that no outsider could have pinned on me." He shook his head. "You know I had a counselor? It's mandatory. Anyway, she was telling me about this dude Dante, you've probably heard of *Dante's Inferno*, but believe it or not, I'd never read it until a few years ago. Anyway, Dante's lived this messed-up life, and he's still mourning the loss of the woman he loved, and he also got exiled from his hometown because of some political bullshit, and then the poet Virgil, who's dead, takes him on this tour through Hell so he can see what he's in for if he doesn't straighten up. Funny thing, a bunch of people are in Hell for shit that's not that big of a deal. Most of the book has to do with old gripes that only make sense in thirteenth-century Italy, but what I found most surprising is that murderers don't get the worst punishment in Hell. No—it's the traitors to family and people you're supposed to protect that gets you chewed up by Lucifer. And it really got me to thinking about a lot." He looked around and saw the sweat that was beading up on all of them. "Murder's not even the worst." He shook his head again. "I took the fall. It finally made sense when I found out about the rat."

Vinny reached into the bag and pulled out the 9mm.

"Dude, fuck, bro! Watch out with that, there are bumps in the road! What's up?" Blaze asked.

"This is what's up," Vinny said, looking at each person in turn. "I've been waiting for this day. The only thing better than freedom is revenge."

Joe shifted in his seat.

"Time's up. Enjoy the ninth circle of Hell." Vinny took one final look into the eyes of the person who had betrayed him, and fired the shot.

Chapter 1
The Tragic Early Life of Vinny Bruno
East Boston, 1982

His whole life, everyone said Vinny Bruno was built like a linebacker. He'd weighed thirteen pounds at birth, and the nurses said they'd never delivered such a big baby. Fortunately, his mother was of robust, wide-hipped stock, and so she not only survived the birth, but, after a mere twenty-two hours of delivery, she recovered nicely (though never quite enough to repeat the process, quite satisfied with stopping at two, thanks to Vinny's much smaller but older sister, Angela).

Vinny's mother attributed her postpartum recovery to Vinny's natural tendency to be a sweet boy. His father had other ideas, though. A kid like that, who had haunches instead of thighs, that was a kid who was destined to be anything but sweet.

Perhaps both parents got their way.

By the time Vinny was old enough to understand the difference between himself and other people, the sun rose and set for him with Angela. She was only a year and a half older, but once she and Vinny were out of their toddler phase, no one believed that Angela was the older sibling—except Vinny. He deferred to her every opinion and taste. If Angela thought lima beans were better than broccoli, then Vinny was all for that. If *Scooby-Doo* was better without Scrappy, then he too would boycott all new episodes. Sabrina was the best of

Charlie's Angels, and though Superman was Vinny's favorite super-hero, he agreed with Angela that Wonder Woman had the better TV show, although they both were excited when the Superman movie came out.

For Halloween two years running, they dressed as Superman and Wonder Woman, the cheap version, which involved long under-wear with an "S" drawn on the front and a leotard with Mrs. Bruno's gold lamé belt, respectively. With their thick, black hair, the two convinced themselves they really could be the greatest superheroes of all time. It didn't matter that their costumes didn't quite meas-ure up to the neighborhood kids' standards. It didn't matter that their classmates sometimes laughed at the two of them or other-wise ignored them—they were in their own little world, anyway. Superman and Wonder Woman were both good—they represented all that was good and hopeful in the world. Angela told him that after Watergate and Vietnam, the world needed every good force it could get. Then she explained Watergate and Vietnam to him, show-ing him Time magazines she'd picked up from the school library on the subjects.

Their father was less than thrilled that the two of them had their own little world.

"Vinny," his dad would tell him at dinner, "don't spend so much time at school with your sister."

At first, Vinny was horrified that his dad would be so disloyal. Couldn't he see how amazing Angela was? She knew everything. "You don't wanna be called one of those girlie boys," his dad insisted. "Get out there and toss around a football, or get in one of those pickup baseball games the kids play over at the empty lot." Angela would be visibly hurt, and at night in their shared bedroom, she'd tell him she was sorry.

"You don't have to stick with me if you don't want. I know I'm just a stupid girl."

"Hey," Vinny said, "you're my best friend in the world. Ain't no way I'm going to ditch you."

She'd feel better by the end of the talk, and after a while, Vinny stopped arguing with his father and just pretended like he was at least sometimes playing with the other boys in the neighborhood.

∞

When Vinny turned nine, there would be three defining episodes that would put a mark on him so deep that everything that came afterward was a result of these three events.

The first was an Easter holiday that Vinny and Angela spent with their grandfather. Grandpa Bruno sent Vinny outside, saying, "At some point, every boy needs to learn to become a man."

"What about me?" Angela said.

"Don't get smart with me," Grandpa Bruno said. Angela followed Vinny outside anyway, where their grandfather was waiting for them both next to his chicken coop.

"Might as well both learn, it's a basic skill of life," he said.

Their grandfather was holding a brown hen in his hand, bracing it against his stomach while petting its back to keep it calm. "Vinny, why don't you hold this one, and Angela, you can take this Buckeye," he said, while handing her a fluttering dark-brown and black hen. Vinny couldn't get over how heavy the hen felt in his hands.

"Grandpa," Vinny asked, "is this the chicken you got the eggs from this morning?"

"Both of these are. Been good layers, but they've also hit their maturity. Now they're Easter supper."

"What? They're our pets." Angela's eyes were about as big as an egg.

Vinny felt a sick, acid-like dread inside of him. "Actually, Grandpa, I don't think I want to hold this one anymore—" and he tried to set down the light-brown Leghorn, wishing that she would scramble out of reach.

"Boy, where do you think your meat comes from? A package in a grocery store?"

Angela was already sneaking behind their grandfather's back to set her Buckeye back in the coop.

"Hey," their grandfather said, catching her, "get back here," but just as he said it, Angela let the hen fall out of her hands in a rustle of feathers and clucking.

"Dammit, girl," he said while chasing down the bird and then grabbing hold of it tightly, "now I have to calm her back down again. Stand over there," he said, pointing to the shed just behind Vinny. "And Vinny, you watch me and do exactly like I do. There are a couple ways to do it, but I don't know if I trust you with an ax." He gripped the Buckeye in his hands, and then he used his left hand to hold the chicken by the legs. "Now you grab the hen by the head like this, and in a quick motion, you pull the legs up with your left hand and pull the head down with your right, immediately twisting up and back."

Vinny wasn't up for it. "But Grandpa—"

"Like so—" and their grandfather moved both his hands away from each other and the kids heard the crack of the neck. Immediately, the chicken spasmed, its wings flapping. Their grandfather hefted the hen by her legs and then turned to Angela. "Hold out your hand."

"No." She took a step back.

"Dammit, girl, give me your hand, or I'm going to bring your father out here." She held out her hand, and he passed her the chicken's legs. "Now hold it upside-down like that so the blood fills the neck cavity."

Vinny held his Leghorn tight, unwilling to give her up.

"All right," his grandfather said, "now I wanna see you try it."

He couldn't. He couldn't do anything, he just stood there and trembled, watching Angela cry silently while she watched the neck swell with blood.

"Please," Vinny finally said, "isn't one enough?"

"It is!" Angela added, "I'm not going to eat any of it."

"Oh, hell," the old man said, "these aren't your pets, they're food."

"I don't want it," Angela said. "I'm not that hungry, and I can eat the corn that Mom's making."

"You think you're going to go through life a goddamn vegetarian?" the old man asked.

Vinny didn't know what that term meant, and he wasn't sure if Angela did or not, but she said, "Yes," her voice full of defiance and certainty.

"I think you're both a little ungrateful, is what I think," their grandfather said. "Here, gimme that," and he took the Leghorn out of Vinny's hands, and within seconds, the hen's neck was dislocated. "Now stand there like your sister, and hold her upside down so the blood drains properly. After that, we can start the plucking."

Vinny and Angela had to sit outside, spending their Easter afternoon plucking the beautiful hens who'd just given up their last eggs for them that morning.

"He's horrible," Angela said, when the two were left alone, a cloud of feathers swirling around them, "I hate him."

"You don't hate Grandpa," Vinny said.

"Today I do."

"He was just trying to teach us how to get our own food. We'll have to, one day, you know." Vinny realized he was trying to convince himself as much as Angela that their grandfather had been well intentioned with this life lesson. But really, Vinny was sick to his stomach, especially since the feathers on the hen had tightened after death, and he was struggling to pluck them without tearing the skin.

"I can't do it," Angela said, setting down the Buckeye and wiping her eyes on her shoulder. She was wearing purple corduroy overalls and a white turtleneck shirt. For the rest of Vinny's life, he would see Angela only in those overalls and that turtleneck whenever he pictured her.

At dinner that night, Angela was true to her word, refusing to eat any meat from either chicken.

"Then I guess you don't want any of the candy that the Easter Bunny brought you," Grandpa Bruno said.

"I don't think the Easter Bunny even came. If he did, you would have killed him and made us skin him."

Their grandfather turned red. "Don't you talk like that to me, young lady!"

"If Angela isn't going to eat chicken, I'm not going to eat chicken," Vinny said, feeling a rush of adrenaline and solidarity. "Not now, not ever."

Both kids were threatened with no Easter candy for the rest of their lives, and then with no dinner at all, but finally the adults conceded defeat, and the kids negotiated corn, green beans, but only one white roll each.

"A damn waste," their grandfather said, and then he muttered something that sounded to Vinny a lot like "ungrateful fairy," but he wasn't sure and didn't know what fairies had to do with chickens.

That night, the two cried silently in the back of the car on the way home. When they got into bed, Vinny swore to Angela that he never wanted to eat chicken ever again in his entire life.

"Promise?" Angela asked.

"Absolutely."

In the dark, he could hear that his sister was still awake by the fact that she wasn't tossing and turning, and her breathing hadn't slowed. "Still thinking about the hens?" Vinny asked.

"Not just them. Vin, I don't think I'm ever going to eat any meat again. Wanna try with me?"

No meat? Forever? "But what about Mom's hamburgers? I think I still kind of want hamburgers, at least once in a while. And meatloaf."

Angela sighed. "Well, I'm going to do it. No meat ever again. I read in *Time* last month about Japanese soybean farmers and this whole tofu craze, and how you can even have tofu steaks that have no meat in them at all!"

"Steaks with no meat?"

"Yep."

Mrs. Bruno went along with it for a time, although Vinny couldn't resist her meatloaf, and he still loved his Hamburger Helper, and they had plenty of cans of clam chowder in the afternoon. Angela said that clams weren't really the same because they didn't have a face, so she guessed it was okay. Mr. Bruno complained that his kids were too skinny and scrawny, not building up their muscles with enough protein.

"It's a phase," Mrs. Bruno told him, though even she wasn't entirely sure that Angela hadn't made a lifelong commitment.

"Eh, I give her until the end of the year," Mr. Bruno said.

It turned out they were both right.

Mr. Bruno blamed Angela's death in November on her being a vegetarian, but it was actually acute lymphoblastic leukemia, which had been undiagnosed for two years. Her parents had been lax about doctor visits, and when she did go, they attributed her weight loss and lack of energy on the diet change. Then, she cut herself on the monkey bars at school where she and Vinny were playing, and she wound up with an infection that sent her to the hospital, where the blood test revealed she was dying.

"But you're Wonder Woman," Vinny told Angela, who was balding after the second run of chemotherapy. "You can fight this." Angela nodded in her hospital bed, tubes in her arm and up her nose. "I mean it. You will get better, and then you can come home. And if you're not strong right away, it's okay, I can carry you around until you're able to walk again."

"I'd like that, Vinny." She smiled, but not with her eyes. Vinny thought her eyes already looked like they were seeing somewhere else, some other room, and that she could see through Vinny as if she were the one with X-ray vision.

Even in the hospital, Mr. Bruno tried to force-feed her meat, and he took her refusal as a personal affront to him and to God. "You're not even trying to save yourself!" he railed, until the nurse came in and told him he had to calm down or leave.

When Angela was too weak to talk, the rest of the Bruno family stopped talking to each other as well. In the last two weeks, Vinny didn't go to school at all. His parents had tried to force him to go, telling him he'd get too far behind, but he didn't see the point in going. So he jumped out the bathroom window during recess one day and was caught by Mrs. Bruno coming into the hospital an hour later, having walked the whole way. "I guess I was being stupid for trying to keep you from her," she said, offering him a quick kiss on the head. But that embrace was empty of a lot of things, as Mrs. Bruno's love had become a distant, detached thing that occasionally rumbled between her and her family like a loose hubcap on a car.

Vinny brought comics to read to Angela, but he wasn't sure that she was really listening anymore, so instead, he spent hours holding her listless hand. That's how he was sitting when she departed the earth, taking a big portion of Vinny's heart with her.

There was no Thanksgiving dinner that year at the Bruno house, and Christmas came and went, although Mr. Bruno gifted Vinny a bike on December 27, when he realized he'd come up short that year and a coworker offered him his kid's two-year-old bike that had barely been used. It turned out that the bike was the perfect gift for Vinny and possibly the one good thing his dad had ever done for him. A black and gold Schwinn Tornado, BMX style. The bike meant escape. Vinny could ride it around the neighborhood for hours, whizzing past homes full of people who didn't have dead sisters. If he couldn't talk to Angela, why would he talk to anyone else? No one said anything as interesting as what Angela would have said. Even teachers were just reciting their tired lesson plans out of a book and didn't really care about what the subjects meant. Angela had cared. But without Angela getting Vinny to care, he stopped caring altogether.

Which made it all the worse when, on New Year's Day 1982, a neighborhood kid took that bike. He'd seen the kid around at school, an older kid of about thirteen, but Vinny always thought of him more as a heckler than a bully. He wasn't even going to stop riding when the kid called out to him while he was riding through the alley. Normally, Vinny would have been suspicious, but the kid was smoking, and an alley was the only place a thirteen-year-old could reasonably go to secretly have a smoke.

"Hey, you! Kid, come here, I want to ask you something."

Vinny was wary. He slowed his bike to a stop and then turned around, keeping his distance while staying on his bike.

"What kinda bike is that? It's neat." The kid puffed out a plume of smoke. The older kid did seem genuinely interested. Vinny turned his bike around and walked to the kid, who was still sitting against a fence.

"Cool, a Schwinn," he said. "Is it easy to ride?"

"I guess so."

The kid stood up. "Great. I like this better than my old bike. All right, I'll take it."

"What?" Vinny was more confused than scared. He had no clue what was about to happen.

The kid held the handlebars of Vinny's bike, and Vinny tried to back away. "Hey, now, stop," the kid told Vinny. "Why don't you just hop off that bike now."

Vinny couldn't get over how calm the kid's voice was. Was he for real, Vinny wondered. He was waiting for the kid to say he was only joking.

"Let me go," Vinny managed to say, and he tried to push the kid's hands off the handlebars. That's when the older kid took a swing. And then swung with the other hand.

When Vinny got home, his dad was watching the Rose Bowl in the living room. The Huskies were trouncing Iowa. At first, Mr. Bruno didn't look up at Vinny, but he grumbled from the couch, "Look who finally showed up."

"I was just...outside," Vinny said.

"Come sit here," Mr. Bruno said, pointing to the far side of the couch he was on. "I want you to see this."

Vinny didn't have any objections to football, in theory, and he was fine with watching some big games. But like everything else, he just didn't see the point.

"Vinny, I want you to watch number sixty-seven. Mark Jerue. He's a middle guard—a lineman. Look at what a real bruiser he is. Six-three, two hundred and forty pounds. You got a build like he does." As he said it, he turned to his son.

"What? What is that on your face?"

Vinny unconsciously touched his cheek.

"Did you get in a fight?" Mr. Bruno asked, and Vinny thought he detected the smallest bit of pride in his father. "What happened, who won?"

"I don't want to talk about it."

Mr. Bruno sneered. "You don't wanna talk about it. That means you lost. What the hell happened?"

"A kid took my bike from me. I couldn't stop him." He wanted to keep it short, and he didn't make eye contact, instead trying to track No. 67 on the television screen.

"You mean you lost your new bike to a kid?" Mr. Bruno's voice rose. "And what did you do to him, huh?"

"I was scared. He punched me."

"You were scared? At your size? You're the biggest kid in your class, why would you possibly be scared of some punk bully?"

"Dad, he's thirteen."

"What, so? That means nothing when you're built like you are."

Mrs. Bruno came in from the kitchen with a plate of sandwiches. "What's all this commotion? Is it an exciting game?"

Mr. Bruno turned around. "Your son just let some bully steal his bike and punch him in the face, and you know what he did in return? Absolutely nothing."

"Frank, I don't think—" Mrs. Bruno began.

"I don't care about what you think. Now listen, I've let a lot slide, but it's time we get a few things straight." He grabbed Vinny by the shoulder, forcing Vinny to face him. "You're gonna handle this right now. You're gonna get your bike back, and then you're gonna make sure that you make an example out of this bully, so everyone knows never to mess with you again."

Vinny hung his head.

"Look at me!"

Vinny looked up at his dad, willing the tears to stay in his eyes.

"If you don't take care of this, I'm gonna beat your ass far worse than some little thirteen-year-old punk ever could. You understand?"

"Frank...," Mrs. Bruno said, the closest to intervening Vinny had ever seen her attempt.

"Hey, why don't you go back into the kitchen and stay out of this, okay?"

Vinny looked at his mom, trying to get her to do something, to pull Vinny in the kitchen with her, to beg his dad to leave him alone. She heaved a sigh and gave Vinny a sympathetic look, but she dutifully turned back into the kitchen without another word. Vinny was alone.

His dad released his grip on Vinny and got off the couch. "Now, here," he said, walking toward his desk in the corner of the room. He reached in the top drawer and removed a miniature baseball bat, an 18-inch commemorative Red Sox bat. "Take this. You say this kid's bigger than you, right?"

Vinny stood up and took the bat. "Yeah."

"And you know where he lives?"

"A few streets over. He delivers papers. Not to us. I just don't see how I can get my bike—"

"Dammit, Vinny! I'm telling you how." Mr. Bruno's face was red. Vinny waited for an explosion, as if something had been kept walled off while Angela was alive but now threatened to burst through in her absence. "You walk up to this kid, acting like you just wanna talk. Then, when he gets close to you, you take that bat and swing it right across the bridge of his nose." Then Mr. Bruno leaned down so his nose was almost touching Vinny's. "Got it?"

Vinny couldn't look away. He had no escape. "Yes, sir."

"Good. Now get the hell out of here, and don't bother coming home again unless you have that bike."

Who was this man who was supposedly Vinny's father? There had to be decent fathers out there. Wasn't that the reason they made things like Father's Day cards? Because of the good ones? Vinny felt that his father was looking for an excuse to beat him, and now he finally had it. Well, fine. Vinny wasn't supposed to be soft. He wasn't supposed to mourn his sister, the only person in the stupid world he had truly loved. He slammed the door behind him and felt the weight and texture of the bat in his hand. All right. Vinny Bruno was gone. He was up in Heaven with Angela, and they were reading comics and *Time* and talking about the most interesting things in the universe. He let go of that Vinny. His dad wanted him to be a tough guy? Fine. He'd show everyone he didn't care. He'd show everyone, and one day even his old man, that they'd better not fuck with Vinny Bruno.

Chapter 2
The All-New Vinny Bruno

Vinny walked back, the miniature bat tucked into the back of his pants, and found the kid a couple blocks from the alley, sitting on the curb and drinking a soda.

"Well, I'll be," the kid said, sneering. "Nice shiner. Come back for more, is that it?"

"I just want to talk, okay?"

"Talk about what, how I beat your ass and took your bike?" He laughed.

Vinny took a step closer, and the bully stopped laughing and stood up. He was about half a foot taller than Vinny. "C'mon, can I please just have my bike back? It was a present for my birthday."

"Aww, poor baby. Kid, are you really dumb enough to think you could come back here and ask really nice and I'd just give you your bike back?"

"No," Vinny said. "Not really."

"I should beat your ass all over again." He leaned in and pushed Vinny in the chest. "Whatcha gonna do about it now, baby?"

"I'm gonna take my bike back," Vinny said, clenching his jaw.

The bully laughed, but then something in his face changed. Maybe it was from Vinny's resoluteness, the look of nothing left to lose.

Vinny didn't just hit back—he retaliated. He pulled the bat out of his pants in a flash and smashed that older kid right across his nose with it, took back his bike, and then he saw the kid's money pouch that had fallen on the ground. He started to walk away but then turned around, picked it up, and unzipped it and took all the cash from that kid's paper route from that month, just to prove to the kid—and to himself, and a little bit to his dad—that he could. The great tragedy was in that exact moment, Vinny discovered he loved doing it. The cracking of the bat across the face, the taking back what was his, the taking of what wasn't his—the psychological warfare of the victim becoming the aggressor—he thrilled at the power he had. The shock on that stupid kid's face. Vinny had been sure and steady with that damn bat, and he stunned the shit out of that kid. So that's what it's like, he thought to himself. To run through somebody. That football player his dad had been watching, running into players, tackling them down, his dad saying Vinny was built like that guy—Vinny had no pretenses with himself that he was going to be a football player. That wasn't for him. But a ten-year-old kid who could beat up an eighth-grader in the middle of puberty? Sure seemed like a goddamn God-given talent to Vinny.

∞

So what did it mean to be a tough guy in the schoolyard racket? Near Boston, there had been plenty examples in the news, between the Italian and Irish factions of North and South Boston. Names like Patriarca and Winter Hill Gang regularly filled the newspapers, and Vinny devoured any news he could find on their dealings. "Don't read that filth," Mrs. Bruno would say.

"Mom, it's just the paper. You should be glad I'm taking an interest in current events."

"That's nothing but corruption sensationalized in order to sell papers. Just remember that, Vinny."

But it wasn't the sensational takes by the news, or the tales of murders and bombings. He was fascinated to learn what the actual business of the rackets was. Illegal betting on horse racing? Who was this RICO guy that prosecutors were talking about? And then, of course, in October, *Time* of all magazines ran a story on the crackdown on organized crime. In the library, he found another edition from 1977, highlighting terms like "loan sharking" and "racketeering." What he was most intrigued to learn were the details of solid protection rackets. It was simple, really. People pay money for protection. Not just anybody could provide this service—you had to actually be able to protect the kids who were paying you, so you had to be the strongest guy out there in order to corner the market share.

Vinny had watched his mom doing plenty of Jane Fonda workout videos, so he had a general sense of calisthenics, and every morning, he started with fifty sit-ups, and then as many push-ups as he could, which started out at nine and a half. It was a noble start, and soon, he worked his way up to fifteen, and then twenty, and then fifty. He biked harder, pumping his legs over every incline in town, zooming around cars and through alleyways. Now, when he was riding, he had a purpose, not just an escape. Vinny liked having a goal.

And his next goal was to test his new strength on the sixth-grade bully, Matteo di Marco. There were plenty of young punks like Steve, the bully whose nose he'd smashed, running around and stealing kids' bikes or lunch money, and Matteo would be a good start. Matteo was a small guy with a chip on his shoulder, and so he kept a collection of cronies, flunkies, and apparatchiks (another word Vinny got from *Time*) around him who otherwise might have been his targets. Vinny would have used *soldato*, the Mob title for soldier, but he didn't want to elevate a simple schoolyard bully to the level of major crime syndicate. Matteo was notorious, not only as a lunch money shark, but he had a knack for targeting kids, especially during the Scholastic Book Fair, whose rich parents sent cash instead of checks. Rumor had it he had once taken home over fifty dollars in a day, which Vinny thought was an exaggeration. But no one wanted to touch Matteo, because supposedly his dad's second cousin was a made man in the mob, and that was enough to keep anyone from going after Matteo or his parents.

Vinny didn't really buy into it. Saying you had a relative who earned his bones was a pretty convenient cover in this area, but he'd seen Mr. di Marco at a back-to-school night, and Vinny immediately smelled a rat. He waited until the end of pizza day, the day most kids brought money for lunch, and he followed Matteo out of school and walked half a block behind. Matteo and his henchman-apparatchik Reggie, a lispy boy who got bad grades on purpose, turned down the alley behind the corner packie. Vinny had to laugh—the little bully had actually pulled out his wad of cash and was counting it right there in the open. Anyone could come by.

"Hey, guys," Vinny said, and he walked up quickly to Matteo and Reggie. He didn't hesitate. He popped Matteo in the nose as soon as he was in arm's reach, and then he turned and did the same to the hench-man. While they were grabbing for their noses, Vinny pulled his dad's 18-inch baseball bat out of his waistband and cracked each bully in the ribs. Then, Vinny grabbed Matteo's fist, the fist still gripping the wad of cash. "Wow, that is a lot of money. Christ, some people really have no shame, do they? Taking money from defenseless kids who just want a slice of pizza?"

"You broke my nose!" Matteo shouted.

"I did? Huh. Yeah, you just got your ass kicked by a third-grader. Wait until everyone at school hears about that!" Vinny pocketed the money and ran off, taking an indirect route home. Once in the safety of his room with the door closed, he pulled the dollar bills out of his pocket. Seventeen dollars. Practically a goldmine. And only at the cost of some sore knuckles. He figured those would toughen up in time.

He picked out the other bullies, working his way up the food chain just enough that a lot of the tough kids were starting to take note. Eventually, he got his first challenger, a puffy-eyed sixth-grader who was middle of the pack in terms of hierarchy in the schoolyard underworld.

"You think you're hot stuff?" the sixth-grader asked.

Vinny saw through the posturing. He was fidgety, and clearly worried about a kid who was just shy of his tenth birthday. Vinny may not have had the height yet, but he was sure he outweighed this kid, and Vinny had been working on his quickness and sneaking into the back of the Boys and Girls Club to use its punching bag. Strong knuckles, strong wrists, fast arms.

The sixth-grader, named Mickey, got nose to nose with Vinny. "Look, there are some people you make a point with, but don't even think you can try any of that shit with me."

Mickey hadn't finished his sentence when Vinny hit him with a left hook to the chin, then with a punch to the stomach. While the kid was doubled over, Vinny kneed him in the nose.

"Thanks for the tip," Vinny said before walking away, looking down at Mickey's limp body. Later that day, Vinny heard that Mickey beat up a fourth-grader who had laughed at his bloody nose. Vinny felt responsible—he had nothing against that fourth-grader, and he knew the only reason he got his ass handed to him was because Mickey was trying to save face.

At night, though, when he was alone in his room, the room he used to share with Angela, still with her stack of *Time* magazines now stashed under his bed the way other kids hoarded a secret *Playboy* collection, Vinny wondered what Angela would say if she saw what he was up to. He was pretty sure he knew what she'd say, and it broke his heart a tiny bit every night when he acknowledged to himself that he probably wouldn't be doing this racket if Angela were still alive. On top of that, here he was, still eating Hamburger Helpers and pepperoni pizzas and regular old burgers. But no chicken, no steak, none of his mom's best pork chops.

"Angela," Vinny said to the quiet darkness, "I don't know if you can hear me. I'd like to think you can. At least, most of the time. Maybe not all the time. And look, I know I can do better. But things are hard. So I'll make you a deal. I'll go after the bad guys, and I will protect the weaker kids. But in the meantime, I'll follow what you were doing. I'll go cold turkey, so to speak, and I'll stop eating all meat. I'll do that for you starting now, and the rest, well, I'll work on. Only, please don't judge me."

He didn't really want to steal from just any kids, but he figured if the kids were willing to give up their money to him, then no one could bust him for anything. He'd do something helpful, he'd run a protection scheme, get the kids who normally get bullied by anyone to pay him a nominal fee, and then they could keep the bulk of their lunch and book fair money.

The first person he approached was the fourth-grader who'd gotten beaten up for no good reason. "Hey," Vinny said, and at first the kid cowered. "Look, I don't wanna hurt you. It's totally unfair that Mickey went after you. So how about this? How about, he harasses you again, I protect you from him or anyone. You pay me two dollars a week, and then any time Mickey looks twice at you, you just let me know and I kick his ass?"

"Really?" the fourth-grader said, knowing Vinny's reputation for handling himself around the toughest kids in school. "You'd do that for me?"

"It's a win-win. You're safe, and it only costs you two dollars a week. Not a bad arrangement, right?" The kid agreed.

"All right, have the money for me tomorrow, and you can pay me every Monday. But I mean it—you gotta pay me every Monday, okay?"

Next up was little Don Wilder, a kid who didn't so much fear violence as theft. Vinny figured he could reduce his rate for theft. "So, wait," Don said, "I pay *you* so that *my* money doesn't get stolen? Aren't I losing money both ways?"

"That's the thing," Vinny said, "you'd be paying me one dollar a week. That's four dollars a month, paid up front for the month. How much money has Matteo extorted from you in this last month?"

"I dunno, ten bucks? And some change?"

"See? You can spend four dollars and keep six. It's an investment. You're paying for security. I make sure that Matteo doesn't steal from you, and you don't have to go through every day worried if he's going to come after you. Imagine that. Living in peace." He spread his hands out, almost like a cinematographer plotting the scene of a big movie, a future in muted tones with birds chirping and water slowly rushing and no Matteo di Marco in sight. Damn, he thought, he was good at this.

For the kids who were getting truly beaten up, Vinny's fees were a little steeper at eight or ten dollars a month protection, because, as he put it, he would likely have to pull out all the stops to make a point, which always meant more risk. "More risk, higher price. Instead of you getting beaten up," Vinny reasoned, "I'd be beating them up. It's sort of like getting revenge and protection, all wrapped up in one."

He closed out his third-grade year with a total of almost two hundred bucks in protection money, an easy two-fifty counting what he stole from the bullies. By the start of fourth grade, he had kids lining up at his locker to buy protection from him.

The inevitable school fights ensued when Vinny had to follow through on his promises to his clients. It occurred to him that in theory, he could get jumped by multiple kids at once, but then, he could also insist on a fair fight. Plus, he carried the trusty Red Sox commemorative baseball bat.

Right before Halloween, though, he received his first sucker punch when a fifth-grader cold-cocked Vinny while he was at his locker. Vinny dropped to the floor. He learned two lessons in this. The first was to put up a mirror on the inside of his locker door so that he could always see what was behind him. The second, and the one he put into play as he pulled himself up off the floor, was that if he was going to be in this business, he was going to be all in. There were no halves, and he was certainly not going to back out like a little bitch. He'd learn to live with the physical pain. Losing Angela had done more hurt than anything some punches and kicks could do; he was already dead inside. So he'd take that pain and use it to fight. He'd show them that even though he was eleven years old, he had grown another inch in the last month and was now five-foot-seven and weighed a hundred and fifty pounds, and that size meant that they couldn't push him around. Working out had only increased his girth as he added new muscle tone to his otherwise dense body mass. That density was his secret weapon: Vinny didn't really ever feel the hurts of the fights unless some damn punk tried to cold-cock him in the back of the head.

The fight landed him and the fifth-grader in the dean's office.

"Why are we here?" the dean asked.

Both boys shrugged.

"I want an answer."

"Vinny beat me up for no reason," the fifth-grader said.

"Is that so?" the dean asked.

"Not how I'd put it," Vinny said. "Besides, I'm just in fourth grade."

The dean narrowed his eyes, and Vinny felt his bulk and heft in full view. "Vinny, did you have a reason to beat up Louis?"

"I'm not a rat, unlike some people," he said, giving Louis a withering glare.

"A rat, now, indeed? Well, that's something." The dean sat back and folded his hands in his lap. "Another student said you got hit from the back, Vinny. Is this true? Did Louis punch you in the back of the head?"

"Well, sir, did I stutter when I said I was no rat? All I'm going to say is that I don't start no fights. So if you talked to some kid, why are you asking me? I think, though, it's important for some kids to know that if they start sh— stuff with me, there will be serious repercussions." The repercussions for the fifth-grader, a red-headed half-Irish kid that everyone called Big Louie, started with a surprise uppercut under the jaw that laid him flat on his back, and then two swift kicks to the ribs—hard enough to bruise but not break them. Then Vinny reached into Big Louie's pocket and took whatever money he had out of his Velcro wallet. Vinny got called out of his history class to have his reckoning with the dean.

"Oh, really, Mr. Bruno," the dean said, "and don't you think that's the responsibility of the school administration to handle?"

"Well," Vinny said, "if you're handling it, you're doing a terrible job, because there sure are a lot of kids getting beat up."

The quip landed him in afternoon detention, but he didn't mind. He was glad he'd given the dean a piece of his mind. If everything worked perfectly and was fair for everyone, there probably would be no crime, so really, it was the school's fault and the government's fault and society's fault. Whatever the problem.

He didn't mind the consequences, but then the consequences added up. A couple of kids let slip to their parents that they were paying

Vinny to protect them. The parents called the principal, who started asking around, and then the weak kids who needed the protection were getting the squeeze from the authorities, and Vinny couldn't blame them really, because these were exactly the kids who couldn't handle the pressures of elementary school on their own.

So when the principal called in Vinny from another class, this time sending a school police officer to escort him to the office where Mr. and Mrs. Bruno were already waiting, Vinny knew he had to come up with a quick plan. He'd been ratted out, accidentally or otherwise, so he couldn't flat-out deny everything. He just had to hope they didn't search his locker and find the bat.

Mr. Bruno's face turned red when he saw Vinny come in. "Why is there a police officer with my son?"

"Mr. Bruno, it's just standard procedure for a situation such as this. We don't want you to be alarmed or feel that we are being hostile in any way."

If Vinny had known the term passive-aggressive at that point, he would have used that term on the principal every single day.

"What's he done?" Mrs. Bruno asked.

"Mrs. Bruno, do you know what a racket is?"

She said that she thought it was a loud noise or commotion, and the principal said he meant the other racket, the kind that criminals do.

"Oh, that. I see it in the papers."

"And does Vinny also read the papers?"

"Oh, yes, he's very devoted to getting his news every day."

"Well you might have seen, and I think Vinny certainly has, that the local Mafia in the Boston area specializes in rackets, illegal doings used to make money. And Vinny's preferred racket is a protection scheme, where kids pay him money and he then beats up their harassers."

Vinny saw the tiniest smirk pass over his father's face. "Is that true?" he asked.

Vinny shrugged. "It's not what I would say, which is why I don't want to say anything without a lawyer present. I plead the Fifth."

"Kid, are you for real?" the police officer asked.

"A lawyer, the Fifth?" Mrs. Bruno asked. "Where on earth would you get an idea like that, Vinny?"

"Like I said, Mrs. Bruno, kids these days watch a little too much TV, let their imaginations run wild, and then they think they know all about life."

The principal's voice dripped with condescension and fake concern. Vinny couldn't believe what a phony he was in front of his parents. "Mr. Bruno, we have identified Vinny as predelinquent."

"Predelinquent," Mr. Bruno said. "What the hell is predelinquent?"

"It's something that schools have been increasingly turning to in order to help…*redirect* the wayward youth who might find themselves in worse trouble down the line."

Mr. Bruno pounded the desk. "I mean, this seems like a basic disciplinary thing, right? What, you give him detention and he promises to straighten out. That's your job, right, we send our kids to school so you can straighten them out, not label them as a future criminal. Hell, everyone's a future criminal. And, and, one more thing, since when are elementary school kids picked up by cops while they're in school?"

The principal sighed. "Mr. Bruno, the sad fact is that schools are very different from the time you and I were this age. There are many new threats, and if we aren't tough—"

"Don't you say anything about being tough," Mr. Bruno said. "Vinny has it tough because I made sure he had it tough. And you know what, it's made him tough enough to take whatever from anyone."

"As I was saying, Mr. Bruno, the federal government passed the Juvenile Justice and Delinquency Prevention Act a decade ago, and it gives us, well, law enforcement the authority to assess juveniles for likely future behavior and make determinations on how best to stem that future behavior."

"Future behavior? What kind of messed up thing you got going here? He's a kid. These are all kids. Maybe if you kept them busier during school, actually taught them something, rather than going around punishing them for stuff that ain't even happened yet, then we wouldn't be putting these labels on eleven-year-old kids."

Vinny was surprised to find himself on the same side as his dad for once, although he was sure that would last only until they got home. For now, he was going to enjoy someone else taking the punches from his dad, figurative though they may be. Everyone at school knew that the principal was not the arbiter of blind justice and did plenty of looking the other way at kids whose parents liked to dig deep into their pockets during PTA drives and whose dads all had relatives who drove Lincolns with very big trunks. Vinny hated the fact that he was getting busted for the sole reason that he wasn't from one of those deep-pocket families. He knew, too, that he wasn't the kind of student who would have any teachers championing his cause to the administration powers, so now, his only ally in the world was the very thing—his dad's bad temper and prideful indignation—that had led Vinny into this lifestyle at the tender age of ten.

The principal was not conceding defeat, though. "I'm afraid that just isn't a satisfactory answer, Mr. Bruno. What we would like to do is just have Vinny come down to the police station, record his fingerprints, and give him an official warning."

"Well, I don't like that one bit," Mr. Bruno said. "My kid, down at the station, and for what? A small thing. Hell, the government does the same thing with our taxes! You want to know where Vinny learned it, he learned it from school, from what the government does. He was getting paid to protect kids? Maybe you and your school weren't doing their jobs, and so maybe Vinny did step in—"

"Mr. Bruno, if it were just about the protection money—"

"I just don't see where you get off labeling a kid this young. Just because he looks a little big for his age—"

"He *is* very big for his age," the police officer butted in, and it made Vinny want to break his nose with the officer's own baton.

Mr. Bruno sat back with his hands folded in front of him on his lap and his legs spread. He wasn't a tall man, but you wouldn't know it by the way he carried himself, the way he sat straight up in his chair and filled up the space, often taking all the air out of the room around him.

"Vinny, why don't you sit outside the office while we discuss your fate with your well-intentioned principal here."

Vinny did as he was told, and the officer followed him out. "Kid," the officer said, "you are some deal." Vinny didn't know what that was supposed to mean, and he couldn't tell if it was 100% an insult. Everyone in school hated this rent-a-cop, though.

"Kid, how much did you end up making in total?"

Vinny was trying not to be baited. He learned about this from *The Godfather II*. If he lied and got caught in the lie, that would be worse. If he gave specific details, that would be an admission of guilt. If he didn't say anything, the officer could find some way to make Vinny's life hell for the next few months of the school year.

When the door opened, Mr. and Mrs. Bruno were heading out. "Vinny, we're going."

"Leaving?" Vinny asked.

"Now."

"What's happened?"

"Well," Mr. Bruno said, "we worked out an arrangement. I'll tell you in the car."

Mrs. Bruno was nearly in tears as they left the school. "Is this what all those crazy movies have been teaching you?"

Vinny shrugged, and his mom shook her head and tsk-tsked all the way to the car. Of course it wasn't TV, what did she think, that he never absorbed the volumes of information he was reading every day? Half the time, he wondered if he was actually invisible to his mother.

The deal worked out was that they would take Vinny down to the station, have him fingerprinted, then the police would issue a warning citation. "It'll go on your record until you're eighteen, and then it can be gone," Mrs. Bruno said. "But you have to leave the school. Now, it's not an expulsion—"

"They wanted to expel you," Mr. Bruno said.

"Talking to a police officer like that!" Mrs. Bruno shook her head and blew her nose into a tissue that she dumped back into her purse. "Where do you get off thinking you know more than a police officer?"

"Don't even get me started on that police officer—or that principal," Mr. Bruno said, the rage in his voice barely contained.

"So I'm not coming back to this school?" Vinny calculated the payments he was going to be missing out on, although considering the circumstances, there was no way he'd get money out of kids if they knew he was leaving. Still, he was surprised that he wasn't finishing out the semester.

Vinny hoped that was the end of the discussion, but as soon as they got into the car, Mr. Bruno was shouting. "How could you be so stupid? Racketeering? A protection scheme? Doing it enough to get caught? Who the hell do you think you are, one of those guys uptown whose got eighteen cousins in every branch of government and on every Teamsters board who can just do whatever you want? Don't try to use your brains, kid, you ain't got 'em. Stick with using your body for something good. Go to school, play football, and who knows? If that don't work out, then you'd make a great Teamster. But do not go pissing higher than your eyeballs, kid."

That was a rich lecture, coming from his dad, who lost his insurance job in the recession when Vinny was born and wound up in construction, building office towers. He had been good at neither of his jobs. His dad was sore that he wasn't a fullback for the Patriots, or at least that's what Angela had told him years ago. He couldn't help but see his dad as a sum of wild inconsistencies.

They were going to move houses. Fresh start. Mr. Bruno said he had a friend out in the suburbs, in Stoneham, who was going to open up an insurance office and needed someone with experience. Mrs. Bruno said that being at a new school and in a new house would be a good, clean slate for everyone, and though she didn't actually mention Angela by name, Vinny knew his parents were wanting to get away from her memory. They'd even started taking down pictures of Angela, until Vinny protested. She was this vague idea that hung over everything, and it sure seemed to Vinny that his parents were trying to erase all the painful memories of their life with Angela, and Angela along with them.

Vinny knew, though, that he was not about to get arrested and that he had totally called that cop's bluff. Clearly, the stuff he was learning from the "negative influence of the media" was actually working to Vinny's benefit. Gently asked to leave school was a whole lot better than having an expulsion on your record, though he'd have to do research on whatever that predelinquent law was all about. He would need to stay at least two steps ahead of whatever that law said, or he was sure to get pinched.

Those poor suburb kids had no idea what was about to hit them.

Chapter 3
And Vinny Bruno Gets His Second Ally
Stoneham, 1984

When Vinny left the school, he walked out of there five hundred dollars richer for all the protection schemes and bully-thieving he'd done. His parents never found the money, which he'd stashed in different parts of his room, but Vinny also figured his parents didn't want to look too hard or too closely at what he'd done. Kids paying a couple of quarters here and there? Chump change. His parents probably thought he'd spent it all on candy or at the arcade. But that wasn't Vinny's style. All of this needed to be a job, an investment, and he might need that money at some point.

There were a few things Vinny knew for sure, and at the top of that list, he did not want to be like his father in any way. Laboring away at a job he hated, wondering what could have been, resenting his family and his kids, being a bully in his own house. Vinny may be a tough street kid now, but if he had a family of his own, he'd treat his wife like a queen, that was for damn sure, and his kids would be the treasures of his heart.

Another thing Vinny knew was that he'd have to set up a whole new system in a new neighborhood and figure out the lay of the land. He managed to transfer to his new school right in the middle of the school year and would be starting the first week of April. The Brunos managed to sell their house and find a new one in the suburbs, so they packed everything in boxes and drove it in a big truck up to Stoneham, where they could unpack everything at their own pace. Vinny couldn't believe how the whole first eleven years of his life could be dismantled so quickly.

His house wasn't the only thing Vinny was leaving behind. Vinny learned the first day of his new school that there wouldn't be any money in the protection racket. The suburbs might have a few tough kids, but it wasn't going to be anything like the old neighborhood in the city. No one was going to pay protection money, because no kid needed much protection from other kids. In Stoneham, kids had full faith, if not in their fellow students, then in parents, teachers, and cops having their backs.

The suburbs were altogether a new world for the Brunos. Angela would have loved Stoneham and probably would have had a lot more friends in her class, doing bookish things and being admired for it. This pissed off Vinny more than anything—he was getting what was tantamount to a second chance, though he had no intention of going straight, but no one had given Angela a second chance.

As Vinny watched his mom unpack knickknacks from a moving box and arrange them on their perfect suburban mantel. Vinny handed a framed school picture of Angela for his mom to place up there.

"Oh, well," Mrs. Bruno said, "maybe we can put that in another place. Would you like that maybe in your room, dear?"

Vinny set the picture on the mantel himself. "No, Angela's going here."

Mrs. Bruno stammered, and Vinny waited for the counter-argument, but Mrs. Bruno didn't make one, and the picture stayed in place. Mr. Bruno didn't seem to notice, half-snoozing to Dan Rather delivering the evening news when the doorbell rang.

"Oh, Vinny dear, would you get that while I just finish this up?"

"Sure thing, Mom."

It was their neighbors, whom Vinny had seen in passing but hadn't yet spoken with. The son, Tommy, was in Vinny's class, but they hadn't officially met.

"Hello! We're the Harris family!" Mrs. Harris said. "We wanted to welcome you to the neighborhood. We're sorry we didn't make it over sooner!"

Mrs. Harris held a basket with a kitchen towel draped over it, and Mr. Harris carried a bottle of red wine. Boy, the suburbs, Vinny thought. Tommy smiled at Vinny. "You're in my class," Tommy said.

"Yeah, I'm Vinny."

"Yeah, I know. Nice to finally meet you. I'm Tommy."

Vinny's mother was at the door to welcome the Harrises, saying, "Vinny, don't be so rude, invite them in! Please, come in, come in."

Mr. Bruno got up from the couch and turned down the volume, but he didn't turn off the television, and Vinny could tell he was annoyed for the interruption.

Mrs. Harris handed the basket over to Mrs. Bruno, detailing the homemade bread and muffins she'd packed up. "I thought we could open a bottle of Chianti," Mr. Harris said, "have something to drink and get to know you folks."

"Well, isn't that so nice?" Mrs. Bruno said. "Dear, didn't I say how life would be different in the suburbs? We never really got to know our neighbors." Vinny rolled his eyes at his mother's big fat lie as Mrs. Bruno led Mrs. Harris into the kitchen to sort out the baked goods and get the wine glasses. The truth was, she hated the neighbors, or rather, the neighbors hated Vinny's father for piling up old construction debris lifted from his work sites against the back fence. Planks of wood or metal always stood high above the fence, even leaning into the neighbor's yard. They had called it an eyesore, and Mr. Bruno had asked what the hell business was it of theirs what he did in his own goddamn yard, without bothering to tell them it was only temporary. Because they complained, he was going to leave it up for good.

"Hey, boys," Mr. Harris said, "why don't you two go outside. Tommy, give your new friend a tour of the neighborhood and let us adults talk some, all right?"

"Sure, Pop. Would that be all right with you, Mr. Bruno?" Slick manners, goody-two-shoes. Vinny would devour him in five minutes.

"Sounds good to me," Mr. Bruno said. "Just don't get into any trouble, Vinny."

Tommy and Mr. Harris laughed, as if Mr. Bruno was making a joke. "Not much trouble to get into around here," Mr. Harris said.

"Just be back before *Magnum, P.I.*," Mr. Bruno said. "I don't want to miss any of it," he added to the Harrises. Vinny waited to see if they would pick up on the hint.

"Oh, we'll be out of your way by then. Tommy loves the show, but he can only stay up for half of it. So hard on a school night."

Tommy looked down. What a wimp, Vinny thought. He couldn't even stay up to watch the second half of his favorite show? "So you never get to see how the cases end?" Vinny asked, but Tommy only shrugged.

"I mostly just watch it because I like the car, anyway."

Vinny couldn't believe his father was saddling him with this squeaky-clean Beaver Cleaver for the next hour and fifteen minutes. It wasn't long enough to fully ditch the kid, who'd probably go back to Vinny's house alone, which would inevitably get Vinny into trouble.

"Although there's no school tomorrow, so maybe tonight is your lucky night," Mr. Harris said. Good Friday. Good grief, Vinny thought. "Okay, now boys, go have fun," Mr. Harris said.

"All right. Thanks, Pop. Goodbye, Mr. Bruno, it was nice meeting you!"

What an absolute apple-polisher, Vinny thought. He followed Tommy reluctantly out the door and down the street, walking along the sidewalk of wide-laned roads. Vinny looked at Tommy, baseball player, always with his Red Sox hat—he was a blond-haired, blue-eyed nightmare, as far as Vinny was concerned.

"At least we don't have school next week," Tommy said. It was Easter week, though Vinny didn't have many plans other than riding his bike and watching television.

"Yeah."

"So where'd you move from?"

"East Boston."

"Whoa, you're from Eastie? What's it like there?"

"Look," Vinny said, "let's get one thing straight. I ain't here trying to make no friends, so you can quit trying to act all friendly. The only reason we moved out of the city was 'cause I got kicked out of school and taken to the police station. And," Vinny leaned close to Tommy, "as soon as I figure out how things work in this little neighborhood of yours, I'm going to be running things."

Vinny was not expecting Tommy to roll his eyes. "Come on, Vinny," he said. "Drop the tough guy act. It ain't gonna work on me."

"I once beat a kid to death for asking too many questions."

"Of course you did, that's why they sent you here and not to juvie. Listen, Vinny," Tommy said, his voice perfectly calm, but his face suddenly losing all appearance of the naïve little angel that it bore inside the house and at school. "You may be tough and all—and I'm sure you can hold your own in a fight, by the size of you—but like you said, you don't know how things work here yet. You're lucky you met me. You gotta know how to play the game, which most of the kids around here do." He held up his left hand, flattened like a lid. "Here's the radar," Tommy said, then swung his right hand below it, "and here's us. And that's where you gotta be."

"So what do you know about it anyway?"

Tommy shrugged. "That's only if I can trust you."

Vinny sized up Tommy again, really looking at him this time. His blue eyes were sharp, like he was picking up everything that was in Vinny's head, or at least he was picking up a lot. Vinny would have to be on his guard, even if they did become allies.

"Look," Tommy said, "my parents want to be friends with your parents, which would put us into a lot of constant contact. You're the new kid with a rep, and mine is spotless. You need cover, and I can be that. I also would rather work with a pro who knows what it's like to get pinched and doesn't want that to happen again. As long as you're not a rat—"

"I ain't no rat, and don't ever go saying that, *capisce*?"

Tommy smiled. "Excellent. Plus," he added, "you're a big motherfucker, and I want you on my side."

Vinny liked that Tommy didn't mince words. So few people were direct.

"So what did you get pinched for?"

"Taking money from kids to protect them against the bullies. Then I'd beat up the bullies and take their money."

"A protection racket, huh? Not bad. You're smarter than you look," Tommy said, and Vinny smiled. "But still, it's quiet out here. Doing that kind of stuff is just going to get you into trouble again."

"That much I'd already figured out, Sherlock. What do you actually got that I can't figure out on my own?"

"Oh, just the easy entry points for most houses in the area, plus a lifelong knowledge of the layouts of most of them, including the locations of stashed or otherwise valuable commodities, including hidden nest eggs."

"Shit, you're a cat burglar?"

"I prefer 'crafty opportunist,'" Tommy said. "You, too, if you're in."

Vinny nodded while he thought. He'd give this kid a chance. Certainly better to have an early ally than an outright enemy.

"Say, you wanna come over Sunday? My mom's making a ham for Easter. She'd love it if you stopped by, with or without your parents."

"Thanks, but—" Vinny didn't know what his parents had planned and would rather not spend Easter at the house. "I don't eat meat."

"What? No meat? Why?"

"I'm a vegetarian."

"What's that?"

"Someone who doesn't eat meat, hence, *veg*-etarian."

"Your parents, too?"

"No, they eat meat. My sister got me started on it."

"You got a sister? I didn't see her at the house, does she live somewhere else?"

"No, she—she died. Thanksgiving, two-and-a-half years ago. Leukemia." Vinny wasn't sure why he even talked about Angela. Normally, he wouldn't tell anyone about her. But he was mad that his parents, of all people, had stopped talking about her and didn't want her picture around, and that meant that Vinny had no one else to remember her with. "Our grandpa made us kill a chicken, and from then on, she said that was it, we weren't going to kill animals, and she stuck to it. Now, I'm sticking to it." He simultaneously wanted to keep talking about Angela and hated that he'd said anything about her at all.

"Oh, shit, man. I'm real sorry. I think it's wicked cool that you don't eat meat because of her. It's like, you're keeping her with you, you know?"

Just like that, Vinny had made a team. Tommy was the only person since Angela that he trusted, and trusted with his whole heart. Vinny was ready for Tommy to teach him how to take houses, but Tommy said they couldn't just start right away, or Vinny was liable to be pegged for anything bad that happened in the neighborhood, whether he was guilty or not. "You gotta alter your rep," Tommy said.

"I don't want to act like some angel. That's not for me."

"You don't have to do that, and I think your past will be of help. It'll keep other kids from sniffing too close at you."

"Nobody better come sniffing."

"Exactly, Vinny."

"I don't want to pretend to be people's friend."

"You don't have to, that's not what I'm saying. Strong silent type, keeping your head down, working hard, making it look like you want to leave your past behind you but that you don't quite fit in—it's a perfect cover. Unknowable man of mystery."

Tommy had a knack for understanding perceptions, and Vinny absorbed whatever he could. Tommy also had a knack for the best ways of casing joints to jack. He was naturally smarter than Vinny (though not as well read), though Vinny could keep up by doing his research and had a greater sense of self-motivation. Tommy pushed Vinny to be better, and Vinny did the same for Tommy.

The plan would be to scout the papers for robbery reports in the city, then copy one element of that robbery. Then, they'd bust into a house, always when the owners were on vacation or out for a game at Fenway. The cops would assume it was a robbery ring from the city or another homeless break-in, never once suspecting two fourth-graders from down the block.

At the end of each month, they'd take old silver and occasional VCRs downtown to a few different pawnshops, saying it was their grandparents' stuff they were trying to sell off. Nobody cared about stuff they didn't know anything about, and it was quick cash for Vinny and Tommy, on top of the cash they lifted from shoeboxes in closets and envelopes under mattresses.

Within six months, they'd each scored a thousand bucks, and Vinny couldn't imagine why in the world anyone would live life as a working stiff. As far as he was concerned, this life was perfect. And it was, for another three years.

Chapter 4

In Which Vinny Bruno Learns He's Not Invincible
1987

"You're sure everyone's away for the week?" Vinny asked. He and Tommy crouched under the rear wall of a house in the opposite end of the neighborhood. The house was a two-story colonial revival, with a fancy brick front, on an acre of property. The yard behind them was large, with a dense tree line fifty yards behind the house. It wasn't the nicest house in Stoneham, but it was close.

Tommy adjusted the black beanie over his eyes. "Positive," he whispered. "I heard Jerry himself say they were going to visit their grandparents this weekend." Jerry was a kid in their gym class, the kind of kid who would end up going to Harvard and then make a career out of stealing people's retirement pensions through shady investment schemes and bundling junk bonds to leverage for corporate takeovers.

The assurance was good enough for Vinny, who had trusted Tommy's instincts and knowledge for the last three, nearly four years, enabling each of them to rake in close to forty thousand dollars. Tommy slid a putty knife under the double-hung window and jimmied it open enough to slip his hands under and push it all the way up. Vinny hoisted Tommy through the window and then jumped up, pushing himself inside.

"Good?" Tommy said.

"Ready for action." They already had their plans set. Tommy would head upstairs, hit the master bedroom first, then the den, and Vinny would get anything valuable from downstairs. The trick, they decided, was to not go for everything valuable. Vinny loved taking the valuables that had been hidden—the stuff, he told Tommy, that probably doesn't get checked on every day. If the homeowner doesn't know something's been stolen right away, he figured, they wouldn't always be able to pinpoint when it went missing. Envelopes of cash under mattresses were his favorite, but he also learned that older people hid money in their freezer. That had been the goldmine, so to speak, of their endeavors. Snatch most of it, but not all, and then with cash, there's no dealing with pawn shops or middlemen. Middlemen were trouble.

The biggest lesson that Vinny learned from Tommy was not to buy anything big or lavish, probably ever, because what kid could afford that—certainly not in their part of the neighborhood—but absolutely never spend money right after a robbery. Tommy knew of a kid who'd planned everything out, from casing the house to getting in with the daughter, enough to see the lay of the land, and, after pinching the portable safe, getting some shady-ass mofo to open it and split the twenty thousand bucks inside. The dweeb rolls up in a brand-new red Firebird the next week, one that everybody knew he couldn't afford. Poor bastard's parents had actually turned him in. Now, those were two dirty snitches, Vinny thought at the time, the most ungrateful parents he could imagine. He didn't think his own would ever stoop that low.

But things were changing, and Vinny felt on the cusp, finally, of the big time. Two months earlier, one of their pawn shop connections, an ancient Dubliner named Murphey, of all things, handed them a folded piece of paper when they came in with dangling earrings that had eight carats' worth of diamonds. "I can't take these," Murphey said, "but this guy will help you."

"This guy" was Nicky Wrists, a fairly successful fence who occasionally moved goods for certain Bostonian families. Nicky Wrists was old-school Italian, in his early sixties, whose identifying characteristic was to rotate both hands at the wrists, palms open, like he was some kind of cultish healer, while he was making his negotiations. He had a warehouse on Fid Kennedy Avenue down at the docks and had plenty of cohorts in the Teamsters without managing to step on anybody's toes. "Boys," he said when they met, "the key is to know when you've outgrown the kiddie pool but to not jump in the big ocean before your time, you get what I'm saying?" Vinny and Tommy had nodded.

"That's good. You boys got some potential, from what I hear. And I see." He held up the dangling earrings, letting them catch the light of his desk lamp. "So look, I take a bigger cut than your mom-and-pop pawn dealers, but I also can give you your floaties for the ocean. It's up to you if you're going to be in the Coast Guard or lifeguard at the Elks Lodge."

Vinny was pretty sure he knew what Nicky Wrists meant, but either way, it was going to be big time. The plan was to go for bigger items, based on Nicky Wrists' current requirements, and then he'd drop them some information on the bigger fish to fry, once they'd proven they could do more than swipe from Nana and Pop-Pop's jewelry cases.

Their plan was to get some of the big-ticket items but get whatever they could of the smaller stuff, at least for now, so they wouldn't be entirely beholden to Nicky Wrists. Rolex watches, the more high-tech cameras, the mink furs—that would be Nicky's domain.

Vinny figured tonight would be the last of the small-time house burglaries. If they were going to be big enough to get their own fence, at fifteen years old, no less, that meant they were doing something right. Something exceptional. Vinny laughed, thinking of his dad, who was so sure Vinny was destined for greatness. Sure—he just didn't need pads and a helmet to get there.

Vinny was stooping now, unhooking a Nintendo game console from the television and stuffing it and the two remote controls into his backpack, when the flash of headlights filled the living room windows.

From the floor above, Tommy's footsteps stopped, and then Vinny could hear, "Fuck." Tommy rushed down the stairs, then the engines stopped and doors opened.

"No one's gonna be here, huh?" Vinny said.

"Shit, quick, zip up the bag," Tommy said.

"We're taking this stuff?"

"It's your backpack. Just put it on, we'll jump out the window and make for the tree line out back." Tommy peeked through the blinds, then immediately hit the decks. "Shit, it's cops!"

Vinny could just make out the shape of the lights on top of the car, the extra spotlight, all turned off, and the crackle of the radio. "Get up," Vinny whispered in the harshest whisper possible, and both boys ran for the open window out back. Tommy slipped through and hit the ground running as fast as he could. Vinny followed, but as soon as he landed, his ankle twisted, and he understood what the snapping sensation meant. At once, he was on the ground, and Tommy turned around, motioning for Vinny to come on, hurry up. Vinny clutched his ankle and shook his head, trying to wave Tommy to go ahead. Tommy ran back. "No, go, go," Vinny whispered, then stood up, hopped a few steps toward Tommy, and tossed him the backpack. "Take this and get the hell out of here!"

"But Vinny—"

Vinny knew it would be worse if they both got caught.

"Man," Tommy said before turning, "you know I love ya like a brother."

"Then get the fuck out of here, brother."

He watched Tommy turn and disappear into the trees just as the flashlight beams landed on Vinny, hunched by a hydrangea. Almost as soon as the lights were on him, Vinny was hit by an officer's body from behind, and he landed on his face, his wrists yanked behind his back. Then, there was the cold metal, and the click. There was no point in resisting, although when the cops pulled him up by the shoulders, he let out a cry from the pain in his ankle, then hated himself for showing the weakness. He hopped on one leg into the car, then heaved his six-foot, hundred and eighty-pound body into the back of the squad car.

"I don't suppose you got I.D., a license," one of the cops asked him.

"I'm fifteen," Vinny said, and both officers turned around to look at his face.

"Bullshit."

It occurred to Vinny they might go easy on him if they believed he was younger than he looked.

At the station, they gave him an ice pack for his ankle and let him prop his foot on a chair.

"Who else is working with you?"

"No one."

"You know, I'm sure they'd go a lot easier on you if you gave up your partner. If you're the fall guy, then I'm sure the judge would rather have the bigger fish that got away."

Vinny didn't say anything.

"Look, there are a lot of burglaries around this area. Perhaps we've been looking in the wrong place all this time. Perhaps it wasn't master criminals from the city or vagrants coming through. Maybe it was some high school kids."

Vinny shook his head. He wasn't going to give up Tommy, but he also didn't want the cops to act so smug. Like fifteen-year-old kids couldn't be master criminals. "I didn't rob anything and I got nothing more to say."

"Sure you didn't, although it doesn't matter so much what I think as what my boss thinks. And he's friends with the prosecutor, who's going to hang everything on your head, whether you did it all or not. Which I'm starting to think maybe you did."

Now Vinny knew way better than to say much of anything else. It turned out, though, that it didn't matter. The cops dug up his old record of schoolyard racketeering and fights, and all of a sudden, Vinny was hearing a new word, "superpredator."

"You're a juvenile delinquent of the first order," the bad-cop detective said in the fourth hour of his lockup. Juvenile delinquents, it seemed, were getting worse all the time, and the president even feared a whole generation of vicious criminals rising up to tear down the very fabric of the country, and that just could not stand. Superpredators had to be dealt with and made an example of, and these cops would make an example out of Vinny.

He eventually got his phone call, though his parents had already heard about Vinny's situation, because the police visited their house to check out his room for stolen property. Unfortunately, there was a Sony Diskman and a bunch of CDs that he'd lifted from a house a few months back, and though Vinny maintained they were his and he'd bought them and there was no proof to the contrary, he hadn't noticed that the previous owner of the CDs had written her last name on the back of the jewel case for "License to Ill."

They brought the Sony Diskman and the CDs to the station. "O'Brien, huh?" the cop said, holding up the scarlet-lettered Beastie Boys CD.

"A friend lent me that."

"Sure. Funny, because we have a report of a break-in, which included a stolen portable CD player and some CDs, made out by a young lady with that last name."

Vinny shrugged. What were a few CDs? They couldn't prove he broke into the house, he could have bought them from someone. They were grasping at straws here.

"It all adds up, Vinny. One thing here, another thing here—that's how superpredators are made."

His parents eventually showed up at the station, which wasn't the best of all situations, as his mother wouldn't stop crying and his father wouldn't stop yelling, both at Vinny and at the cops. His dad refused to post bail, which was high for a juvenile on account of the whole "superpredator" moniker, but the public defender assigned to Vinny got him home anyway, maintaining that a fifteen-year-old kid from the suburbs was hardly a flight risk. His parents said nothing to him in the car when they drove him home, but when he went into his room, his dad followed him.

"Was it Tommy who was with you? You can tell me."

Vinny looked long and hard at his father. He couldn't read him at all. "There was no one."

His dad shook his head, then slammed Vinny's bedroom door on his way out. That was the last moment Vinny's father spoke to him directly, ever again. He spoke through Mrs. Bruno, the "Tell Vinny his lawyer is going to meet with him tomorrow at noon," or "Tell Vinny he better make sure his suit isn't wrinkled," or "Tell Vinny he can get his noodles and oil as soon as I've gone up to bed" type of dialogue. That was the sum of the Brunos' perfect suburban life.

But age and suburbs meant nothing when Vinny was brought before the judge, who was too old for his job, too crotchety to be loved by anyone more liberal than the Spanish Inquisition, and seemed to personally resent Vinny's size, face, and sheer existence.

"I do believe in the power of incarceration as a form of punishment. Vincent Bruno, I think you show an absolute lack of remorse, a complete unwillingness to cooperate in refusing to name your accomplice, whom we know exists, in conjunction with your history of criminal activity and violence. I also believe that incarceration can be a form of deterrence, especially to your cohorts who remain at large, but I promise you that won't be for long. Mr. Bruno, I hereby sentence you to be held in a juvenile detention center until the day you turn eighteen." As the gavel banged on Vinny's fate, Mrs. Bruno cried out in the courtroom. When Vinny turned around, his father refused to make eye contact with him. What did his dad even feel for Vinny, he wondered. What had his dad ever wanted from him? To not be soft. That was all Vinny knew. Would his dad have minded so much if Vinny played football? Vinny imagined it would have hurt his dad worse if he had played football like his dad had wanted, then got pinched and was unable to play.

These weren't quite the coherent thoughts Vinny had while he was being led away, but more flashes of feelings. Later on, though not much later on, he would have plenty of time to think about his dad, the stupidity of his dad, what a complete asshole his father was, and what a waste it all would be if they found his stash of thousands of dollars—well into the five figures—in various denominations that Vinny had buried in an old foot locker he'd found at one of the pawn shops. He'd saved nearly all of it, except for a bunch of small things, some VHS tapes, a couple of bicycles, and his own Nintendo system.

He always told his parents he'd got the money from mowing neighbors' lawns, which only revealed his parents' stupidity or willful ignorance of the current rate of services versus goods, seeing as he only mowed a couple of lawns a month for five bucks a piece. As long as his parents didn't move in the meantime, Vinny would turn eighteen and saunter out to a substantial little nest egg. For one thing, he could immediately get an apartment of his own, maybe even get himself a decent house with the modest down payment, and finally be free of his parents. Better than most eighteen-year-olds had it.

No, what his main thought was—as he changed into his orange jumpsuit, careful of his ankle cast, and his clothes were put in a bag to give to his parents as he boarded the bus—was that he was glad Angela couldn't see what he'd become, couldn't have her heart broken by watching her brother shipped upstate to the big house.

Three years didn't seem like a long time away until the bus rolled him into the high-security juvenile correction center. While Massachusetts had formed the nation's most progressive youth detention and rehabilitation program, more young people sent to therapy or in daytime detention, there were still a few—especially the kids tagged with the superpredator label—who were sent to places like this, high walls and lots of barbed wire. Oh, Angela, Vinny thought. He squeezed his eyes shut and tried to remember what she smelled like. Tried to put himself back in their room together, reading comics and *Time*.

Vinny was informed by the admitting guards that the facility had a twenty-hour lockdown. All of Massachusetts' perceived-as-dangerous teens were stashed here, or at least the ones who'd been caught. It smelled of Pine Sol, urine, and fear. Vinny couldn't bring Angela into this world. No, he would need to keep her far, far away from this. He wouldn't think about her for one minute while he was here.

So the only love that Vinny ever felt was casked, encased in concrete, and sent deep inside Vinny Bruno's heart, which was shrinking by the day. The Vinny Bruno who remained wasn't going to let anything touch him here. He wasn't going to let anyone know him or get inside him. Places like this pretended to care about troubled youth, but really, they just wanted to send the problem away and hope that some miracle happened to bring them around. If any of the old Vinny were to survive, Vinny had to keep all the misery of the place from seeping into him. He wouldn't talk to anyone unless the guards forced him to talk. He would speak in as few words as possible. And he would spend all his time reading whatever books or newspapers he could. No fights, Vinny, he repeated to himself like a prayer and a warning.

Some guards treated fifteen-year-old punks and petty thieves like they were fifty-year-old hitmen. Vinny watched the bigger kids get hit with clubs across the back, and one guard in particular kept giving Vinny they eye, turning his club over in his hands, licking his chops. Vinny was not going to give that creep the luxury. Their mouths watered over kids who had been taught to be tough by parents with the same values imparted by these prison guards. Parents had turned their kids into criminals who were then sent to prison to be given more of the same by the guards. Vinny imagined Angela writing impassioned essays on the state of the juvenile criminal justice system—then reminded himself that he wasn't allowed to think about Angela. He watched some kids crying at night, in their bunks that looked more like an Army barracks than a prison cell, getting beaten up by other kids (who had previously had their asses handed to them for crying), all in a cycle of knocking out of the boys any emotion that wasn't rage or resentment. Without the thought of Angela, and not wanting to become one of those guys who grows up to be the husband and father who beats up his family because they dropped a piece of broccoli on the floor, the boy who had been Angela's brother went nearly as deep as the memories of Angela. The six-foot, almost-two hundred pound fifteen-year-old in an adult extra-large jumpsuit was all anyone saw of Vinny Bruno. That and the thing for vegetables.

A couple of bolder wannabe tough guys, the kind Vinny used to eat for lunch when he was prepubescent, sat next to him one day early on at lunch. Vinny never said anything he didn't have to and certainly wasn't going to be baited by these two bozos.

"So what, little boy doesn't like his meat?" the bonier of the two kids said. He had a skinhead haircut, and Vinny was pretty sure the kid was an actual skinhead. The partner wasn't a skinhead, just dumb, like Private Pyle in *Full Metal Jacket*, which Vinny and Tommy had snuck into the theater to see a month before Vinny got pinched. Private Pyle was almost as big as Vinny, but it was because he ate everything, which meant he didn't move quickly. He always had the sluggish expression of a giant baby who'd just drunk too much milk. So it was beyond ironic that the skinhead said, "Big boy like you doesn't wanna grow big and strong?" as if that was supposed to impress him. Vinny spooned in another bite of reheated vegetable medley. Unfortunately for the skinhead, Vinny had just finished a book from the library about Buddhist monks who were vegetarian and could meditate for hours and hours each day without eating or drinking. He was full to the brim with meditative inspiration and was not interested in performative fighting. He was going to save up his fighting for a time when it really counted.

The skinhead pulled at Vinny's plate, and for a second Vinny thought the skinhead was going to spit in it. Vinny pulled the plate back, not looking at the skinhead or his friend. "I been watching you and seen that you don't eat your meat, and that you tell them to stop putting it on your plate. You afraid of killing little baby animals?" Vinny imagined that this kid had gotten beaten up a lot, either by a bully or by his father, didn't matter which. He probably started off as a henchman under the local Hitler youth branch at their junior high, and now he thought he ran the joint and had no hesitation picking on the fresh meat, even if that meat outweighed him by a bill.

"Look at me," the skinhead said, "I'll stab you until my arm gets tired."

Vinny gave the skinhead the side-eye, then looked at his scrawny arms beneath the loose-fitting jumpsuit, and then at the trashcan at the end of the row, trying to let the skinhead know that he could very easily fold him into that trashcan, and he saw the skinhead stiffen his jaw. Then, Vinny leaned forward to look up at Private Pyle, with his slack-jawed stare, and, sensing they were only trying to look tough for whoever the hell was watching, which was probably everyone at that point, Vinny said to the kids in a low voice with no expression, "If you keep fucking with me, I promise you that you will both be Medflighted out of here." Then he went back to his tray, eating his vegetables and rice like the most disciplined Tibetan yogi. He realized then, though it was an observation that he'd noted off and on over the years, that most people didn't know what to do with silences or when people responded only in a calm manner. Outside, the skinhead might be able to challenge Vinny, use his Private Pyle muscle as his torpedo doing the dirty work, but in here? And Vinny being Vinny? He liked his odds. Besides, he knew he could take the pain if the skinhead brought in his own crew. Turned out the skinhead didn't have much of a crew, and the only guys who could match Vinny for size were completely disinterested in proving a point—they were all doing work programs to become cooks or carpenters. The skinhead and his Pyle shifted, looked at each other for a minute, and then the skinhead said, "I'll be watching you," before storming off. Vinny gave a half-laugh to himself and went back to his tray.

It was a lonely year, but Vinny's strategy worked. The system took note of his good behavior, and they sent him off to a minimum-security facility. A place where they at least try to treat kids like humans again. "You know, Vinny," the discharging officer told him they day he got his transfer approved, "I think the caseworker and I can even get you off the superpredator list."

The old Vinny would have been elated. But the one-year-in-prison Vinny nodded and said, "Thank you, sir."

"Man of few words, as usual."

Vinny nodded.

Chapter 5
A Whisper from the Future
Northern Massachusetts, 1988

The Keystone Juvenile Rehabilitation Center of Northern Massachusetts was the boarding school for young delinquents. There were no fences, minimum security. There were more classes, which suited Vinny fine, and on his file was included a list of all the books Vinny had checked out at the library of his previous residence—all two hundred forty-seven of them. It looked like a reading list for a Harvard sophomore, which the admitting staff told him. The names of the buildings were taken from Ivy League colleges, which Vinny thought was a riot. Clearly, they were projecting a certain image that said, No recidivism here!

Instead of a communal cell, Vinny was going to be put in a two-person dorm room with "another kid who doesn't say much," the admitting staff told him. Vinny exchanged his orange jumpsuit for a drab tan uniform that might have passed for a school uniform in an Eastern Bloc country. There were some motivational posters tacked up to the cinderblock walls, painted in a pasty yellow, and Vinny took in his new home for the next two years. He could live with it. What other choice did he have?

The man taking him around looked more like a Christian youth pastor than a guard, and that might have been what he was, though Vinny didn't ask. "Now, your new roommate, I think you'll find that he keeps to himself, though I'm sure once you break the ice, you can get along. This isn't like the prison—you might take some time to adjust, but you'll be happy to know we have an excellent library."

Vinny was led to a door at the end of a long hall, near the emergency exit, and then the youth pastor gave a quick knock on the door and opened it without waiting for an answer. A skinny Black teen with a gray knit cap was hunched on his bed, his back against the wall, reading the newspaper. He looked up when Vinny and the youth pastor came in, and nodded. "Mr. Jackson, this is Mr. Bruno. He's moving in with you."

Vinny nodded, then went to his bed. He didn't say anything to his roommate or the youth pastor, and only nodded when the youth pastor said, "Dinner at five. Just follow where everyone's headed."

No one said anything to each other—Vinny hadn't spoken to anyone that day. What he had noted when he rolled up in the bus to his new prep school campus was how open everything was. That "no walls" business was especially intriguing. He didn't know exactly how, but he was not going to spend the next two years as he'd spent the last one, in monastic restraint and immobility. He just needed to come up with some kind of plan and then find the right opportunity.

He was glad Mr. Jackson over on his bed with his paper was quiet—it would give Vinny plenty of time to think. An avid reader was also a plus. He'd get a better lay of the land when he went to dinner and could see the place more fully, see what kind of people he was dealing with. When the hallway bells buzzed—just like in school—his roommate got up, opened the door without looking at Vinny, and then turned down the hall, Vinny following after him. Vinny tried to do a head count—over two hundred, definitely not five hundred, all standing in line with their trays to get food. The meal was TV-dinner style slices of turkey with a gravy blob, which Vinny wouldn't touch, but the creamed corn was all right, and the black-eyed peas would give him plenty of protein.

The Spanish-speaking kids all hung out together, speaking in Spanish, better than most other prison code, at least for most of

Massachusetts. Vinny thought his roommate might go sit with the group of Black teens at the table against the wall, but instead, he sat by himself by the door, apart from everyone else. Vinny wasn't sure yet what to do, so he sat at his roommate's table but two seats away. They still hadn't spoken to each other. Some kids were giving him the side-eye, but otherwise, they weren't acting as tough here—they weren't *acting*. There were no points for top dogs, way less testosterone, and Vinny suspected it had to do with the guards who weren't merely criminals with badges like in the max. He stretched his legs out and felt the tiniest bit of tension leave his body.

He spent the meal trying to figure out the roommate, who kept his head low and ate slowly, methodically. Vinny finished, then walked over to the roommate and scooped his turkey onto the roommate's plate and walked out. He did a quick look back and saw him shoveling the extra meat into his mouth. It was free time, meaning the guys could go either to the rec center for television, hang out in the weight room, or go to the library. Vinny checked out the library and found it satisfactory. At nine p.m., everyone headed back to their rooms, kids cramming the halls like they were all headed to their next class. A few minutes after they were tucked back into their rooms, their door closed, and within an hour, the outer doors would lock. Vinny rolled on his side, facing his roommate, wondering what was up with this guy. The roommate lay in the dark, face up, and Vinny thought he might be watching the blinking dots on the digital clock count off the seconds. Well, if that was the kid's hobby, maybe he would be more annoying than Vinny thought. Quiet was one thing, but weird creepy staring was worse than overly chatty.

There were a few sounds in the hall as guards and staff closed down, making their final checks for the night—a routine that was all too familiar to Vinny, despite the variances in the details. Then it was quiet. Still, Vinny didn't sleep, and his roommate remained in the same position. Vinny was pretty sure his eyes were open and watching the clock. Then, after another forty-five minutes went by, his roommate abruptly sat up on his bed and went to the door, listened for a few seconds, then walked out. Vinny sat up, then silently followed him out, finding him in front of the emergency exit door to the left of their room. The hallway was empty and dark, with only the dim safety lights illuminating the drab walls. The roommate bent over and took something small from his sock, then knelt before the panel next to the door. Vinny couldn't see what he was doing, but he heard the panel door open and the sound of metal twisting, like a screw, probably loosening wires. Within a few seconds, the emergency exit door clicked open, no loud buzz, no lock barring their way. Vinny tiptoed after him, catching the door just before it closed. When he got outside, his roommate was leaning against a wall, lighting a cigarette.

"What the fuck?" Vinny said. "No alarms? How'd you do that?"

"What the fuck you mean, how'd I do that?" The roommate's voice was a crackling, back-of-the-throat whisper, as if his vocal cords had been shredded the way a cat shreds drapes.

"What the hell's wrong with your voice? Bro, maybe you should quit smoking—it's gonna kill you."

His roommate let out a hissing laugh—it sounded to Vinny exactly like the dog Muttley from *Wacky Races*. He made a stabbing motion with his hand. "Knife fight," he whispered, although that turned out to be his actual speaking voice. Then, the roommate pulled down the collar of his uniform. There was a two-inch diagonal scar just below his Adam's apple.

"Damn. That's crazy he didn't kill you!"

"I'm hard to kill," the roommate said with a smirk.

Vinny was impressed. This guy was a definite badass—and very cool about it. Vinny thought that if he'd been the one to survive a knife fight like that, he might have turned into one of those loud braggarts who tells his story to anyone in earshot. That is, if he still had a voice to tell it. "You must've pissed the guy off pretty good for him to try that shot."

The roommate shrugged. "I was about to steal his car."

"Theft or carjacking?"

"Theft. Caught me at three in the morning. Motherfucker turned out to have an early morning shift that I clearly did not know about, or I would have done my slim-jimming two hours earlier."

Murdering a teenager over a car was pretty serious—Vinny wanted to ask what happened to the guy who knifed him, but he'd wait for another time. "Your first time jacking a car?"

"It was my last time. Before I got busted, anyway. Otherwise, it would've been my crystal anniversary."

"Huh?"

"My twentieth car. Pisses me off that I didn't get to twenty." He took a drag from his cigarette, then asked, "So what about you? When did you get pinched?"

"Assholes got me for a B&E, tried to pin a bunch more on me, most of which were mine, but they could only prove I broke into a house with a silent alarm. Rolled my fucking ankle jumping out the back window, and that's how they caught me."

The roommate laughed his Muttley laugh.

"Oh, that's fucking funny to you?" Vinny said, feeling the old grip of needing to prove himself, the way he did back in school.

"It's a little funny," his roommate said. "Hey, put it there," and he switched his cigarette to his left hand and put his right out to Vinny for a pound, "Tracy Jackson."

"Tracy? You serious? No one named Tracy lives through getting stabbed in the throat."

"That's why everyone usually calls me Whispers."

"Wicked pissa. Whispers, I'm Vinny Bruno." The night was warm and clear, and crickets chirped in the low hedges, and for the first time in a long time, Vinny felt a flicker of contentment. Maybe this place, this guy, would mark a turning point, he thought. "Hey, so how the hell did you do that with the doors?"

"I opened them."

"Yeah, I noticed, but no alarms, no guards, nothing."

Whisper nodded.

"What, is that your thing or something?"

Whisper nodded again.

"Damn. I sure could've used you the night I got pinched—wouldn't have gotten pinched, that's for sure. And if I was at your back, you certainly wouldn't have gotten knifed in the throat."

"Well, if my aunt had a dick, she'd be my Uncle Vinny." Whispers laughed.

"So," and Vinny's wheels spun, "you can do that with any kind of security system?"

Whispers nodded. "Pretty much. I been doing breaking and enterings since I was little—started out looking for places to sleep. Then it became a thing, and I was handy to have around. I drive, too."

Vinny was more than impressed. This kid for sure knew his way around the block and had fallen into a bad situation that could have been avoided. But if he could do all that—"Wait, why don't you just leave, then?"

"Why?" Whispers shrugged.

"Why not? Wouldn't you rather be at home?"

"What home?"

For the first time, Vinny understood what it must be like to be in a truly bad situation. He couldn't wait to be out of his parents' house, and despite being away for over a year, he still thought of it as home, aside from being the place where his money was hidden. Despite the fact that his parents lived there and Angela—the sudden memory of Angela startled him. It was the first time the thought of her had slipped out in almost a year. All of a sudden, he felt like he couldn't quite catch his breath—Angela rushing back in, the longing—he had to shut it down, and quick.

"Hey, man, you okay?" Whispers asked.

"Um, yeah, all good. Was just thinking. Why don't you at least get out, have some fun at night sometimes?"

"What, like the underage inmate who goes to a club? The arcade? I'm kind of an easy mark. Besides, no one in this place at least is going to knife me in the throat."

"You don't know what kind of guy I am in my sleep."

Whispers finished his cigarette and wet his two fingers to stop the end from smoking before putting the stub back in his front pocket.

"Look, I don't know what I'm doing when I get out, but right now, I'm in."

"But a guy like you, with your skills? You could pull off all kinds of shit." Vinny had spoken more in these eight-and-a-half minutes than he had in a year. And he noticed it, too. His voice was rusty, and after talking so much, with Whispers' cigarette smoke and the night air, he felt his own voice cracking. "Look, really, we could do anything—it would be better than being bored here all day. Planning shit keeps you fresh, keeps your brain sharp. I read all about it."

Whispers nodded, and Vinny noted he had one nod for everything, for agreement, for pondering, for acknowledging amusement. He didn't show too much. Already, Vinny had shown more to Whispers than he intended, but he couldn't help it. The fact that Whispers had trusted Vinny to demonstrate his little escape plan meant something.

"Hey, look. We could just boost a car and go get some food or something. Number twenty, although it goes back at the end of the night. But we live a little. And look, I promise you, no one's gonna fuck with the two of us—I ain't letting that happen."

Whispers rearranged the knit cap on his head and then spit into the hedge. "All right. Count me in. But remember, you fuck with me, and I know where to stab to make it count."

Vinny laughed. "Scout's honor. I got your back."

Two nights later, same routine, Whispers unlocked the doors and stopped the alarms, and they cruised out the emergency door, down the side wall with no security cameras, and through the tree line down to the road that led to the nearest neighborhood. "All right, take your pick for your crystal anniversary," Vinny told Whispers.

"If you're gonna do it, make it count. I been thinking about this a lot, because twenty is important. Do you go BMW or muscle car? And if we're going to go on a joyride, I'm thinking—" and he scanned the parking lot of a nearby apartment complex, "that Camaro."

"That one?" Vinny pointed to a silver Camaro under a tree at the far end.

"Do you see another Camaro in this lot? And bro, that ain't just that one. That is a 1970 Z/28, with the LT1 V8, 360 horsepower. That motherfucker's gonna fly. And it's an old car, so it'll be a cinch."

The night reminded Vinny of the scene in *Ferris Bueller's Day Off*, which he and Tommy had seen, when the two parking garage attendants joyride in Cameron's dad's Ferrari. While they didn't peel out of the parking lot with the zeal that nonincarcerated teens stealing a car couldn't afford to do, they hit on a back country road, sailing down a narrow lane, as Whispers explained to Vinny about positraction and the four gears and eight cylinders that made the Z/28 special. They busted open two payphones and put together almost fifteen bucks, enough to score two Big Gulp Slurpees from 7-Eleven, along with a slice of cheese pizza for Vinny, a corn dog for Whispers, and four six-packs of miniature doughnuts. Vinny palmed a bag of corn nuts for the road. The attendant didn't give a shit what they were up to, as he was more focused on the midnight movie on the television above the register. And Vinny being Vinny looked like a grown man in a work uniform—leaving nothing to suspect. They drove the car back to the apartment complex, the gas not too much changed unless the car's owner hawked the fuel gauge, and then they ran back up to Keystone, Whispers getting them back in and then returning the wires to their normal settings, locking them back in their room by 2:55 a.m. They'd even manage to squeak in a couple hours' sleep before the 5 a.m. call.

"Man, I needed that," Whispers said. "You all right, you know?"

"Meh, I'm kind of an asshole."

No matter what, they weren't going to be assholes during the day. They went to their classes, and Vinny even ventured to talk with the teacher at the end of class, asking various science questions out of interest but also to show he was the guy who cared about the material. Vinny was a good egg who just needed to get his life in order—that was the thought voiced among the staff and written on his file. He and Whispers were two angels. Until after lights out. Then, anything was possible. And Vinny was ready to explore it.

Chapter 6
Vinny Forms His Plan

"I mean, it's not like we don't have the wicked perfect fucking alibi, being locked up here," Vinny said.

"Sure," Whispers said, nodding, "so what's your fucking point?"

"My point is, asshole, that we should be stepping it up. Joyrides are fun, but then what, we spend all these years having fun, hitting up 7-Elevens and Dunkies every night, and in a couple years get out, and then what? We'd wished we would have done more while we had the chance, that's what. And don't give me that look like you're just humoring me. You know I'm right."

"Look, Bruno, saying stuff is one thing. We've been lucky so far, but how far we gonna push it? How far can a couple of sixteen-year-olds push it, while our whereabouts are strictly monitored? It's not like you're the first person ever thought about this. You tell me what makes your ideas different, better."

How many people were actually doing what he planned to do? Their position was ideal—protection with incarceration, but enough freedom to be able to get out. "The difference is that people underestimate us. They don't think we're smart enough to pull more than a few easy jacks. This—right here, now—this is our school. You know, it takes two minutes to learn how to make a license plate or fit a pipe, the bullshit kind of skills we've been taught."

"It's our educational imperative to make sure we can be productive members of criminal society when we get sprung."

"See, you're catching on."

Whispers lifted up the newspaper in front of him, hiding his face from Vinny, or rather, hiding Vinny's face from him was more likely. Vinny hated when he did that. It usually signaled that he was about to go back into silent mode. At least that meant he was thinking. Instead, Whispers started speaking from behind his paper. "All right, dear home reform school instructor, so I can open shit and you can beat people's shit, how do we then take our delinquent asses to the next level? What do you suggest?"

Vinny resented the implication that he was only useful for his size. Motherfuckers been underestimating him since he was ten years old. "Look, Robert C. Maynard, half of your black may be from all the newsprint you take in, but that don't make you a genius—"

"Never said I was—"

"Let me goddamn finish, will ya? While you're researching your current events presentation for kindergarten, I been researching. Shit, there was plenty I wanted to do at thirteen, but how far can a kid go? Now I finally got the leverage I need to compete, you know. Negotiate with the grownups."

"You wanna be your own mob boss someday? Get yourself made?" The Muttley laugh wheezed from behind the Opinions section.

"Hey," Vinny said, "I don't want no part of that. All those turf wars and all the politics? Too many people involved, people you can't trust. Too many people to keep paying off. Nah, anyone who's really smart, you have a small crew, low overhead, and do it just enough to be completely comfortable for the rest of your days. It's like, you know, independent contracting work."

"Goddamn, Bruno, you dreamed up this perfect little fantasy life for yourself."

"It's not a fantasy. It's happening. Only question is, are you in?"

Whispers put down his newspaper. "Look—"

"Or are you going to stay home and do my laundry?"

"Bitch, now, just a minute," though even Whispers let out a laugh. "You're not the only one with a vision of the future, know what I'm saying? Plenty of cats here do. Plenty of other cats just scared-ass punks who'll end up making license plates. Now nobody here currently in this room wants to do that. But what we need is some rock-solid, military-grade strategizing, and I don't mean the punk shit that got them fucked in Vietnam. What we do here, now? This is got to be long-run, CIA-style shit. Now you and I and a fucking wish alone ain't enough to get that done. Not at the level you're talking about."

Vinny nodded. "We need a fucking team."

"A fucking rock-solid team."

Vinny knew what to do. "You know my real specialty, Whispers? Research."

∞

The records office, the repository of all Keystone's current occupants, was locked, which of course was no real obstacle to Whispers' talents. But the records office held the key to other talents, specifically, who of their lot had the optimal talents to form a crew. Once Whispers got the door opened, the two slipped inside. They weren't sure how many nights it would take to go through the one thousand or so records in the place, which meant many nights confined inside and not out on the road, but it was a necessary investment of their time and captivity.

Vinny handed Whispers a pile of folders while he stood guard with his ear at the door. "What am I supposed to do with these?"

"Read through them, see what they're in for. If it's garbage, we can't use them. If there is raw talent, we set it aside for the short list."

"So what, we're just looking for 'evil genius strategizer' on the sheet?"

"Shut the fuck up and get to work." For a guy with practically no voice, Vinny thought, Whispers sure could use that voice a lot, and at the wrong times. "Anyway, cross off the youngest ones. They won't be ready and we can't use them." Vinny thought for a second, then added, "And take note of the ones who wouldn't cooperate with judges and prosecution."

"What for?"

"They won't squeal."

Vinny had been thinking a lot about Tommy over the last year or so. They hadn't communicated at all—how could they? He had no idea if the police were still interested in his accomplice or not, and when Vinny was going through his hearings, he found out that Tommy had taken a lot of heat with his parents, who had asked him how he couldn't have known that his friend was a criminal. Supposedly, Tommy had told them he never believed Vinny was guilty, that the crimes had gotten pinned on Vinny because the neighborhood wanted it solved quickly and everyone wanted to believe it was a local punk and not some scary gang from the city. When Vinny heard that, through his mom, who'd heard from Tommy's mom, Vinny felt a welling of pride. What he would have given to tell Tommy he was grateful. How could he even have told Tommy without sounding like a sap? What was Tommy doing now? Vinny imagined his friend in high school, playing varsity baseball, sitting in classes, rooms that were familiar but seemed like another lifetime ago. He'd never see those classrooms again, and though most of the time he thought his school could go fuck itself, he was also a little nostalgic for all the things that could have been, in a different life. That wasn't this life, though, and Vinny Bruno had learned the way he wanted to live his life once he got on the outside. Would Tommy even want to see him, or had he gone straight in the last year? What had all the suburban kids thought of Vinny—was he the cautionary tale or the scapegoat?

No one communicated with Vinny at all, except for the monthly letter from his mom, who was careful not to directly address Vinny's incarceration. His mom probably liked to imagine he was off at some boarding school somewhere—which, in a way, he was now—and apparently his mother had joined a bridge club. He used to write back and talk about the food, how he was supplementing his protein with a lot of beans, but then he just gave up after a while. His mother probably didn't really care.

He wished, though, that he could have talked with Tommy. Have some tie with the outside world, the real outside world that he cared about.

"Hey, over there, hello?" Whispers whispered. "Check this out. Kid from the projects, dad was ex-Marine, dishonorable discharge for stealing guns, and this kid was caught selling a gun behind a Dunkin' Donuts."

"Name?"

"Daniel Alvarez, goes by Blaze. You know him?"

Vinny shook his head. "You been here longer than I have."

"Don't know him either, which means he probably sticks to himself."

That was another good criteria. Vinny didn't want anybody already attached, anyone who might go bragging to his homies about this side gig he'd snagged.

"Definitely on the short list, then. Guns will be handy, and if he's done work with his pops, he knows some military shit."

After another half-hour, Whispers was trying to get Vinny to wrap it up so they could put all the files back in their right places, but Vinny felt like he just needed another five minutes. "I got a feeling, it's right here," he said. He didn't know why he had that feeling, but he couldn't wait another night. And two files later, there it was.

"Jose Ramos, computer whiz—whoa, FBI tried to recruit him after he hacked into their system. He told them to fuck off, so he wound up here."

"Dude hacked into the FBI?"

"Do you know him?" Vinny asked.

"Jose Ramos—I know of a guy called Mexican Joe, and I think I heard the job trainer call him Jose, so maybe...let me see the pic?" The mug shot was clipped to the file. "Fuck, bro looks like he's twelve!"

"Probably an old shot. But these two are our guys. I feel it. Blaze and Mexican Joe. We gotta find them tomorrow and feel them out."

They put the files back and snuck back into their room. Vinny's mind raced with possibilities. A crew of four. Five would be better. Five would be perfect. Five, especially a guy who Vinny knew would always have his back and side with him...that would make Vinny feel like he could do anything.

At lunch, as the mess hall filled with gray-uniformed not-quite-students, Vinny scanned the faces. He narrowed in on a table of Mexicans and Puerto Ricans, listening for familiar names, but no Blaze or Jose or Joe or Mexican Joe. He got a few glares back if he looked at someone for too long. The one problem with keeping to yourself was the difficulty of procuring information by asking around without drawing suspicion. He worried that he'd run out of time and have to wait another day—Vinny in theory knew he had plenty of time to set this up, but now that he had a plan, he felt all the urgency of needing to put this plan into play at once.

"Hey," Whispers said at Vinny's ear, appearing from the other side of the mess hall, his tray of mac and cheese and Jell-O in hand. "Off in the corner, tattoos. What do you think?"

A stocky Mexican kid was writing in a notebook with one hand and spooning mac and cheese into his mouth with his other. He had the Mexican flag tattooed on his neck and an eight-ball on the top of his writing hand and a 13 on the top of his spooning hand.

"He doesn't look twelve anymore," Whispers said.

"Nope." Although, if he shaved off the mustache and goatee and didn't have the tattoos and grew his hair out, he might actually look a lot younger. Still, according to his file, he was sixteen, a few months younger than Vinny and Whispers.

Vinny walked over and Whispers followed behind, both sitting down across from the stocky kid.

"What's going on, my man?" Vinny asked.

The kid looked up from his writing at Vinny, then Whispers, then went back to his writing.

"You Mexican Joe?" Vinny asked.

"Who's asking?" he said, still writing.

"Vinny Bruno. This here is Whispers." Whispers nodded to Mexican Joe.

"I been meaning to talk to you," Vinny said.

Mexican Joe looked up and set down his pencil, though he took another bite of his food. "About what?" he said while chewing.

Vinny nodded at Whispers. "About an opportunity. See, I've got—" he looked to Whispers, "we've got this plan, but we need your help. I read your file. You're a computer whiz and you told the FBI to fuck off."

"That's nice that you can read and apparently break into the file room."

"We are but mere humble entrepreneurs in need of computer whiz-zing skills such as yours," Vinny said. "Hoping you would be interested in contributing your services to a sort of partnership."

Whispers sat up and asked, "How'd you get to be a computer whiz, anyways?"

"Bro, what the fuck is up with your voice?" Mexican Joe asked.

"What's wrong with his voice?" Vinny said. "He talks just fine."

Mexican Joe rolled his eyes. "Fine. So Whispers-with-the-fine-voice, you're asking how a tatted-up Chicano kid ended up a computer whiz?"

"Yeah, I guess so."

"Also," Vinny added, "you're young, you know. What, were you like a rich boy with ten computers or something?"

"Or something," Mexican Joe said. "One's all you need, but two computers are even better. And I thought Black guys like you weren't supposed to be racist."

"Shut the fuck up," Whispers whispered.

"Not that I owe you two 'entrepreneurs' anything, but I have do-gooder middle-class white parents who adopted this Mexican orphan," Mexican Joe said, pointing both hands at his chest, "and my middle-class white father taught computers at MIT."

"Bro, tight," Whispers said. "That's like real-deal shit."

"The FBI was real-deal shit," Vinny said.

"You sure as shit better believe it was," Mexican Joe said, his smile betraying how pleased he was at the compliment. That was when Vinny realized they had him. Just had to reel him in gently.

"I'd sure love to hear the story sometime," Vinny said.

"I bet you would."

Vinny nodded. "I bet you'd love to get your hands on a computer again."

"Wow, you're a real psychic, you know that?"

"You know, Mexican Joe, it's clear that you don't think we have anything to offer you, the great expert who's only in here because you likely went a little too big, too fast. Most of us are in here for similar reasons. But that's the difference between a gang and a crew—selection. You get the right people for the right tasks, watch each other's backs, don't go ratting—"

"Who said anything about ratting?"

"I'm saying we carefully curate those we're sure won't rat," Vinny said. "Frankly, I'm glad to see that's important to you."

"Man, what you got in that notebook?" Whispers asked. Mexican Joe had taken it up again and was scribbling something down.

He flashed a page at Vinny and Whispers—it was filled with what looked to Vinny like gibberish, letters and numbers and weird symbols he saw on the board of the physics class that he didn't take.

"Just 'cause I do not currently have access to a computer doesn't mean I can't write code, my gracious entrepreneurs. This my rec."

"What's that program do?" Whispers asked.

"Just how to trick a computer into thinking it's running a test while I can sneak in some malware and spy through the backdoor."

"I have no idea what the fuck you just said," Vinny said.

"It's a way to break into a computer so it doesn't know you're there, and then steal its information."

"Do you know if it works?"

"I'd have to test it, jokers, but I don't have access, since computers are one thing that this place wants to keep me away from for now."

"And if we told you we could get you to a computer by tomorrow? Tonight, even, if we were so inclined?"

Their time was up, and the hall filled with the scrape of chair legs signaling them to head to their afternoon work-study classes. Vinny and Whispers stood up.

"Wait," Mexican Joe said. "Listen, when can we talk more about this?"

"Meet us after dinner, by the benches in the courtyard," Vinny said. As he and Whispers turned to leave, Whispers nudged Vinny with his elbow.

"Nice work."

∞

Next up was the Puerto Rican kid called Blaze. He was easier to find—a rowdy guy who talked tough but also backed it up, without ever taking it so far as to get more than a stern admonishment from the directors of the institution. To get back on their good side, he'd flash a smile punctuated by two of the prettiest-boy dimples, which were entirely contrary to the straight and protruding unibrow that covered his eyes and made him look otherwise perpetually angry. Blaze could play it up—Vinny had been watching him on the handball court just before dinner. He really did blaze back and forth across the court and up to the wall. He was about as big as Vinny, with a gut, but he never seemed to tire of plowing right through his opponent to get to his ball. He kept yelling when his opponent scored a point on him that he'd made an illegal hit—"It hit the ground before it hit the wall!"—and when his opponent shook a hard hit off his hand after the third complaint and got in Blaze's face, Blaze turned on those dimples, pulling the guy in for a mob hug—"It's all good, it's all good"—letting the hulk of his body show that he wasn't backing down and would absolutely wreck this guy if he did more than front, but who wanted that here and now anyway? Vinny liked his style. Just shy of bombastic but never over the line, and he never seemed like he was backing down even if he was deescalating. It's probably how he didn't get shot when he got pinched while in possession of a cache of firearms.

"Not bad," Vinny said as he walked up to Blaze, who was wiping his face, alone at the bleachers after the match he'd won.

Blaze looked at Vinny but continued to wipe himself down, using his undershirt as a towel.

"You're Blaze, right?"

"That's me. Who the hell are you, freshmeat?"

"Vinny Bruno. I like your work and came to ask you about something."

"Well, then, speak up. I ain't tryna stand around all day."

"I'm putting something together. Want you on my team."

Blaze laughed, though it was superficial, dismissive. "Look, I don't know what kinda game you're talking about, but in case you hadn't caught on, I don't do teams. I'm the only team I need."

"I'm not talking about games. What I'm putting together is very real. And I know you know more about—" Vinny looked around to make sure no one was within earshot, "a particular style of hardware necessary to certain pursuits."

"Look, you don't gotta use that fancy speech with me. You got your facts straight, though I don't know how. I don't know if you realized this, but me procuring said hardware is a little difficult, considering the present situation."

Vinny had to laugh at how Blaze called out Vinny's language and then completely matched it. Blaze certainly was no fool. He observed, read the room, and was whoever he needed to be to stay in control. Until now. Until the exact time a perfect partner came along.

Vinny pointed around to the room. "And this? The 'present situation' you mentioned? Can be rectified as soon as tonight, if I want."

"Hey, now, what, *coño*?"

"If you're interested, after dinner, the benches by the courtyard."

Off the court, Vinny met up with Whispers.

"Think he'll come?" Whispers asked.

"He's definitely interested."

"Okay, so we got the four of us, unless your intuitions are off. We all agree tonight, and then what's next?"

There was one more person Vinny had on his list. It would involve a final after-hours field trip with just the two of them.

∞

Vinny and Whispers sat opposite each other, while Blaze sat on top of the back of the bench, his feet next to Whispers, and Mexican Joe stood next to the trash basket, scribbling in his notebook, trying to act as if he wasn't a part of any group. That, or Vinny pegged him for wanting to make a quick exit if something he didn't like started to go down.

Four guys collected there, Vinny thought, who were used to being in control of their own domain.

"I just don't know why we should, A, trust you," Mexican Joe said into his notebook, "B, believe that you are even capable of doing what you think you can do, whatever it is, and C, make it worthwhile for everyone here to team up like the fucking Justice League."

"Except to steal shit and do the exact opposite of the Justice League," Vinny said.

"Well, yeah, okay," Mexican Joe said. "I know why you need me, but why him?" he said, pointing at Blaze.

"Hey, I don't know why anyone needs you," Blaze said.

"I'm a computer genius," Mexican Joe said. Blaze scoffed.

"Top-notch hacker," Vinny said. "And Blaze runs guns, just like his daddy."

"Okay, now how the fuck do you know all this?" Blaze asked. "I don't go around shooting off my mouth, because this is kind of my line of work for the foreseeable future, once I finish with this clubhouse."

"They got your file," Mexican Joe said, before Vinny had a chance to respond. "They got all our files."

"Where the fuck did you get my file?"

"I can get everybody's file," Vinny says. "With my friend's help, of course."

"At your service," Whispers said.

"Fuck, *pendejo*," Blaze said, "is that what your voice actually sounds like? I just thought you were a creepy quiet dude."

"Right?" Mexican Joe added.

"What happened, *coño*?"

Whispers pulled down the collar of his shirt. Both Blaze and Mexican Joe flinched. "Hoh, shit, *coño*," Blaze said. He leaned in closer to inspect the wound, and even Mexican Joe put down his notebook and took a closer look.

"Well, I guess we know we can count on you to be quiet," Blaze said to Whispers. "One tough motherfucker. So, okay, what else you got?"

Whispers put his collar back up and crossed his arms, then Vinny said, "He's an expert with locks and security systems. And also—he's the best damn driver I've ever seen."

"So he's the infil-exfil, then?" Blaze asked.

"Huh?" Vinny said.

"*Infil*tration and *exfil*tration? Military for 'break the fuck in and get the fuck away.'"

Vinny smiled. "Exactly."

"And what about you?" Blaze asked. "Big guy, likes to talk..."

"He don't talk *that* much," Whispers said. "Spent a year in high security and didn't say a goddamn word to anybody. Right here in his file." Whispers pulled Vinny's file out of his sweatshirt.

"Only fair," Vinny said, "I know all about you, so here, what do you want to know about me?"

Blaze flipped up the pages and Mexican Joe leaned over his shoulder. "Dude didn't snitch." He nodded with approval.

"How many partners did you have then?" Blaze asked. "Didn't seem to help you much."

"One, and he was a great goddamn partner. We just operated with limited resources at fifteen. Also, we had a pretty good fence we'd just started working with.

"And so what?" Blaze said. "You see yourself as our great leader?"

Vinny shook his head. "Look, what I'm talking here is full trust. It won't work without it. We'd be full partners. We discuss ideas and plans and agree on them as a crew. Like Mexican Joe, who's been working out all his little traps once he finally gets his hands back on a computer, I've spent the last thirteen months mapping out the kind of future I want and what it takes to get there."

"His knowledge of the crime syndicates in the tri-state area is encyclopedic," Whispers whispered.

"Well, that's great," Blaze said, with more than a hint of sarcasm in his voice. "Just follow the mobster plan, like it's fucking paint-by-numbers."

Vinny rolled his eyes. He knew Blaze had to test him and was going to push all of them at some point. "No, man. The trick is to carve out our own space. Don't compete with those guys and get caught up in a turf war. They got politicians and Teamster heads on their side. Instead, we always do enough to make just under a shit-ton of money while staying under the radar and not calling unwanted attention to ourselves."

"Basically, that's just like every other petty crook ever," Blaze said.

"Did I just say we were going to be ripping off little old ladies at the grocery store? Look, my small-time B&E days are done. It so happens that right now, we got the world's best cover. Think about it, we're under eighteen, and we're currently locked in this place. We get out at night, as my friend and I have been doing for the last few months, we get back in by morning count, all without leaving a trace. No one'll be marking us."

Blaze looked across the tables, then rubbed his face. "You can really get in and out of this place at night with no one noticing? What about the guards?"

"The man just said we've been doing it for months," Whispers said, an edge to the rasp in his voice. "Been clocking them. Night shift does their 10 o'clock walk-through, and the dickheads sit on their asses, sleeping or watching porn, until the morning shift comes in. They think we're locked in."

"And what have you been doing while you were out?" Mexican Joe asked. "Stealing stuff and bringing it back here?"

Whispers shook his head. "We got a secret stash. But it would be a hell of a lot more convenient if, say, we knew a computer dude who could open bank accounts under fake names and have them getting interest and shit, in ways that don't put our faces in front of an ATM camera."

Mexican Joe nodded. "That would be convenient," he said. He scribbled something down in his notebook. "Then what about G.I. hoodrat here?"

"God help me, *cabrón mamabicho*," Blaze said, "how many fingers do you need for the computer, because you're not leaving here with all of them." He stood up, towering over Mexican Joe, and Vinny stepped between them.

"Be cool, Blaze," Vinny said. "You got a problem, we handle it now or you're out." He looked at Mexican Joe. "Everybody cool?"

Blaze nodded a few times, until Joe said, "Yeah, we cool. Not the one with the problem."

"I got no problem," Blaze said and sat back down.

"So what I'm asking," Vinny said, "is do you think you guys can live comfortably on a few million a year, once we get going?"

"That's the end game?" Mexican Joe asked.

Vinny nodded. "It's a more honest living than half the careers they're training for at Harvard."

Blaze rubbed his gut, then the buzz cut of his head. Finally, the dimples appeared. "So when do we start?"

Chapter 7
And Five Make a Crew

A week later, it was dry-run time for the crew. Blaze's room was the farthest off, so he'd head out toward Vinny and Whispers' room at 10:15 p.m., then by 10:20, Mexican Joe would head over. Whispers opened the emergency exit for them, and like a Desert Storm troop, Blaze led them through the darkness to a side street half a mile down, predetermined by Vinny.

"Hold here," Vinny said, then walked into the street, near where a car was parked. The headlights flashed twice, then the door opened.

"What the fuck?" Mexican Joe said.

Vinny stepped forward. "Tommy."

"Jesus H. Christ, Vin, it's you!" Tommy got out of the car and hugged his friend. "You really did it!"

Blaze and Mexican Joe ran up to meet them, Whispers sauntering behind them. "Hey, now, who the fuck is this?" Blaze asked.

"I don't like not knowing stuff in advance," Mexican Joe said. "If we're going to be partners, you can't leave us out of the loop."

"Look, guys, I'm sorry. I didn't want you to think you were being set up. This is my best friend, Tommy. The only other person I trust."

Mexican Joe looked quizzical. "This dude was the partner who got away?" The others waited for an answer.

"I went back for him," Tommy said, the smile faltering. He looked down.

"No, man, it wasn't like that," Vinny said, to Tommy as much as to Joe and the rest of the crew. "They get Tommy and me both? More likely to find out how many houses we really hit, plus link us to our fence, which would make us personas non-gratas, or something like that."

"A'ight, I dig it," Blaze said. "War Games, is that all right with you?" he asked Mexican Joe.

"'S all right with me, G.I. Hoodrat."

"Okay, then. We're set, this is everyone. Tommy, this is Blaze, Mexican Joe, and Whispers." Blaze and Joe said hey, and Whispers waved. "We're full partners on this, split evenly five ways. We don't go behind each other's backs, and we voice our concerns to each other like we're the fucking U.N. If there's something we don't like about a plan, we discuss. We use all our connections, but we never let anyone else fully in, got that?"

They were all in.

"All right, two things we get started tonight. Blaze, you get us set up with your uncle, and Tommy, first thing tomorrow, you get a pager so I can reach you from the payphone inside, give you all the info you need. Also, you talk to Nicky Wrists at all this last year?"

Tommy shook his head. "Only stopped by with the backpack the week after, to tell him you got pinched. He was worried you'd rat, but I promised him you wouldn't. I think by now he knows you didn't."

"I think it's time you reached out to him again."

"Hey," Blaze said, "who's Nicky Wrists?"

"Our old fence. Has a warehouse at the docks, and moves shit for Teamsters and mobsters, at least on occasion."

"Shit, man," Blaze said. "You more legit than I gave you credit for."

"Also," Mexican Joe added, "once we get everything set up, I will be needing regular access to an actual computer, not the shit job in the records office. And probably a place to…keep it."

"My uncle's got your back, bro," Blaze said. "And you can put whatever hoo-doo shit you need to lock it down, but I swear to Christ and San Antonio de Padua," he crossed himself and kissed his fingers, "it will be safe there."

Joe nodded. "Sweet, bro, you all right."

"Still a G.I. hoodrat."

"Speaking of," Vinny broke in, "want to take us there to get set up with some hardware?"

The guns were for contingencies, but if Blaze was also able to acquire or intercept certain shipments of said hardware, then Vinny had a feeling that Nicky Wrists would be more than ready to let them set sail on the open seas.

Tommy drove them to meet Blaze's uncle, who went by Chencho, even though his full name, Vinny was amused to learn, was Inocencio. Blaze knocked on his uncle's door, while the others waited in the car in the driveway for the okay to come out.

"Surprise, Tío."

Chencho hugged Blaze, then stepped back again. "You out? Nah, you not out. What the fuck you doing here?"

"I want you to meet some people—can we come inside?"

"Yeah, yeah, get your ass in here."

Blaze waved in the others.

"*Coño*, the fuck?" Chencho said when he saw the crew in their matching tan, plus Tommy in his Red Sox hoodie. He closed the door behind them, then took them back to the kitchen. "Yo, your pops will be mad pissed at me if I'm responsible for you getting an extended sentence for sneaking out like you're in some kind of fucking after-school detention or some shit."

"But you ain't gonna tell him nothing."

"Oh, right, *mijo*, like I'm going to write to Leavenworth and tell your pops you sneaking out of your little group home for criminal boys? *Carajo*."

"You hear from him?" Blaze asked.

"A letter a month, with a few things for you. I'll show you later," he said, looking around the room. "So what, how's the chow there, you getting enough good food? You boys want something? I don't got much, but there's some leftover carnitas and tortillas."

"Oh my God, yes, please!" Mexican Joe said, beating Blaze to the punch. Whispers nodded.

"What are carnitas?" Vinny asked Joe.

"Only the best and most succulent pork cooked slow over hours."

"Nah, man, thanks though."

"What, you Jewish?" Blaze asked.

"No, I'm vegetarian. I don't eat meat."

"The fuck?" Blaze was already helping himself to a cold tortilla and folding it into his mouth.

"Why the fuck don't you eat meat?" Joe asked. "This whole time you haven't?"

"Nope. None." He waited for the inevitable ribbing or posturing. Here, in Blaze's uncle's house, were only tenuous allies and no long-term trust.

"Dude. And the food ain't even that good—how you been surviving?"

"I'd say better than the poor little pigs you're eating." Vinny smiled.

Blaze nodded, then Chencho said, "But hey, you hungry, right? 'Cause I got some beans and rice, be just as good."

Vinny took him up on the offer—something told him not to refuse his host's hospitality—and like that, they were all breaking bread in Chencho's house, talking about lean times running hardware after Blaze's father got put away, and then Blaze two years later.

"So you haven't been moving anything?" Vinny asked.

"Hey," Chencho said, "lean times does not mean fasting, *mijo*. I am not the primary procurer or distributor, though, which has led to certain lifestyle changes."

Vinny thought for a minute. "But say you had a guy, or a few guys, who in no possible way could be suspected, and they had a guy who could move just about anything?"

"And these few guys," Chencho said, "I'd have a vested interest in their well-being, and so would pass along certain info on jobs, see if they could get something from Point A to Point B under the radar and better than old Tío?"

"Tío, it ain't no disrespect," Blaze said. "We know our old contacts got busted, and you've been on the outs since Pops got taken in. Now I know you ain't in for the big scores, but I know you keep your toes dipped in, so do us this solid. A few times you pass some bread our way, you won't even have to get involved and can be back to working at your super legit Data General day job."

Mexican Joe perked up. "You work at Data General? Do they still run things on Fortran?"

"*Pendejo*, I work in receiving. I have no fucking idea what you just said."

"Okay, but like, do you maybe have access to any of the Data General Ones, maybe Model 2Ts, that are lying around and no one would notice if one or three went missing? And like however many floppy disks you can get your hands on?"

"Well, that sounds like it would be mighty convenient for you that I work at Data General, now, wouldn't it? *Esto en un mamey—lo puedo hacer.*"

Mexican Joe smiled. "¿Neta? Güey, muchas gracias. Oh, and if you know anybody who can get a Hayes V-Series SmartModem, the 2400s should be out."

"Bro, you gotta write this shit down now," Chencho said.

"Well," Vinny said, "Scarecrow's got his brain, and Tin Man's got a heart, what else you got for us, Chencho?"

"*Coño*, you just got your fucking *frijoles—cálmate*. Now you got a good place here—you can stash whatever shit you got for a bit, as long as it doesn't fucking pile up, ¿entienden? My boy Blaze here is my number-one priority, or his pops will bust my skull when he gets out, though I also am happy to help out with planning for my nephew's future. So if you can guarantee me that you won't fuck that up, then we cool."

"*Todos bien*," Vinny said.

"*Todos bien*," Chencho repeated, laughing. "*Jincho*, you are one big *hijo de la gran puta*, but you got *más cojones*. You all right, though, I like you. And you, quiet fucker, you ain't said one damn word all night," he added, looking at Whispers.

"Dude got stabbed in the fucking throat," Mexican Joe said, clearly still impressed. "Show him, Whispers."

"Want me to dance, too, *pendejo*?" Whispers said, but he pulled down his collar to show Chencho, who started as soon as Whispers finally spoke.

"*Carajo, güey*. That shit's fucked up."

"Well, now that everyone's suitably impressed," Whispers said, "what's the plan?"

"The plan is," Vinny said, "Tommy will call our old fence and see what he's got for us. However, Tommy, it is important that you do not mention my name, or any of us, *capisce*?" Tommy nodded. "Joe, once you get set up with your machinery, your job will be to get us into places that don't wanna be got into. The kind of places even Whispers can't get us into. Track deliveries, warehouse drop-offs, you name it. Blaze, once you get your connections, we can play some ball. You and I will be the enforcers, Tommy will do recon, Whispers, as you put it, infil-exfil, with Tommy's help, and we keep at it and we keep at it. We let them underestimate us, and then we'll laugh about it all the way to the fucking bank, where Joe will make sure we have safe accounts and a big fucking nest egg waiting for us on our eighteenth birthdays. Now, how the fuck does that sound to everybody?"

Blaze reached out a hand to shake Vinny's, and, as if exchanging rites of peace in a solemn mass, they each took turns shaking hands, including Chencho, who swore his house to be a safe one for all the teens.

At the end of the night, Tommy drove them back to their meetup point, with the plan to meet back there in four nights. "Hey," Tommy said to Vinny as he was getting out of the car, "you trust all these guys?"

"Yeah," Vinny said. "I really do."

"If they're your guys, then they're my guys," Tommy said. "You take care of yourself in there, okay?"

"You take care of yourself out there."

"Oh, one more thing," Tommy said, hugging Vinny. "Happy birthday tomorrow."

Vinny had almost forgotten—he couldn't believe Tommy had remembered. It had been a long time since Vinny cared about birthdays. Whispers whispered them all back into the emergency doors. Vinny didn't care that he didn't get a minute of sleep that night. His dream of the last few months—really, of his whole life after Angela died—was coming true for him, finally. A birthday wish. He had a crew of his own, and after that night, he felt in his gut that these guys would become his brothers.

∞

Two days later, Whispers snuck Joe into the records room so he could finally get his hands on a computer. The first order of business was for Joe to get himself and Blaze moved into the same room, right across the hall from Vinny and Whispers, to avoid any notice in all the comings and goings. The pairs stuck close to each other, careful not to interact too much during the day in front of the others, to avoid suspicion. On the fourth night, they snuck out once again to meet Tommy, who gave Vinny the number for his new pager and said that Nicky Wrists might have something for them.

"He was real smug, too," Tommy said, "when I drove up last night. First, he acted like he didn't know me, but he made a big show of remembering, then said he had something, but it was far too much for one guy to handle. So I told him, it ain't just one guy. He raised an eyebrow—he was interested. I said let me prove it, and he said to make sure no one gets caught by any silent alarms this time."

"Good job," Vinny said. "And you didn't mention my name, did you?"

"No, not a word."

"Okay, so what's the mark?"

It was a shipment of parts coming up on a box truck, but a lot of copper pipe and wire. Nicky Wrists supplied the delivery tracking number, and with that, Joe was able to trace the shipping company, the bills of lading, and the other shipping schedules, which would come in handy for future use. Blaze's contacts came through with two guns, for their personal use, with the promise of more, and those were stashed at Chencho's place with plenty of ammo. The truck would be coming to a warehouse on Thursday night. Whispers rolled by his old chop shop and "borrowed" a hot car with the VIN numbers rubbed off, and Tommy would be driving in his own, separately, to the site.

"What's the take, though?" Vinny asked.

"Twenty," Tommy said.

"Twenty thousand?" Joe said.

"I don't know," Vinny said, "that's good, but split five ways?"

"I know, but he said after the last time, I have to earn his trust back, prove I'm a sure thing, me and whoever is with me. So that was the offer. It's a good take, Vin. A good first run."

"Four apiece," Blaze said, "minus three hundred for the guns, and a little startup fee for Chencho—call it rent money."

"Seven hundred for Chencho, then," Vinny said, "three for the guns, then thirty-eight hundred is the take for each of us. Not a bad night's pay."

"It's a start," Tommy said. "Gets our foot in the door."

"Vin, this is good," Joe said. "I'm in. Blaze, you in? Whispers?"

They were in.

Thursday night, Whispers drove Vinny and Blaze to Chencho's house for the guns and a change of clothes, then to the warehouse, stopping fifty yards back, with the lights out. "K, boys, you set for this?" he whispered.

Vinny looked at Blaze. Blaze's brow was furrowed to a point, but his dimples sank in. He pulled the clip on his gun, then stashed it in his back waistband. "I follow your lead, lieutenant."

"There it is, boys," Whispers said, as the box truck pulled up to the front of the warehouse. The truck parked in front of a loading dock, and the driver got out and went inside, leaving the truck still running.

"That's it?" Vinny said. He and Blaze ran to the back of the truck, then Blaze rounded and checked the cab, climbing in from the passenger's side. Vinny pulled himself up to the driver's side.

"How did you know he'd leave the truck running?" Blaze asked.

"They usually are left running."

"But not always. Did you have a backup plan?"

"The backup is this," Vinny whispered, holding up his spanking-new Glock 19. "Besides, in the future, when we have more time to plan, we can track the shipments and get the trucks before they get to the warehouse."

He was confident in his plan, but it was back in the saddle for the first time in two years, and this was the biggest job he'd done. They'd jumped straight from small time into this, and Vinny knew he'd lose all credibility if he didn't pull this off perfectly.

"All right, this is it," Vinny said, putting the truck into gear. It rumbled and jumped—Vinny hadn't driven anything this big in his life, and had only driven in Tommy's car a few times, years ago. "Shit."

"What shit, we good to go or aren't we?" Blaze said, looking terrified for the first time since Vinny had known him.

"No, I got this, I got this." Vinny ground the gears a bit, but Whispers had told him to press harder than he did on Tommy's small car so he wouldn't stall the truck out. They were rolling, then Vinny picked up, made it to second, and then third. Whispers pulled out twenty seconds behind them.

Then, the cab radio crackled. "You motherfuckers!" the voice said, "I'll kill you motherfuckers, we're after you, you can't get away from us!"

"Oh, shit!" Blaze said, laughing. He moved to turn off the radio, but Vinny told him no, to leave it.

"If they have anything to say to us, we want to hear it."

They had mapped out a back way to Nicky Wrists' warehouse, and a block away, they saw Tommy's parked car. Vinny flashed the high beams, and Tommy got out and came up to the cab. Vinny jumped down, and Tommy climbed into the cab to take the truck in. He handed a dark baseball cap to Blaze and told him to put it down low. "Hide that brow of yours, and don't fucking smile," Tommy warned. "You gotta look like nobody."

"I know, I'm just too beautiful for this life, huh?" Blaze said.

They drove off, Whispers pulled up, and Vinny hopped inside. They crept toward the warehouse but stayed at a distance, waiting for Tommy and Blaze to come out.

"So why you not in there?" Whispers asked Vinny.

Vinny didn't really know. He'd wanted to keep his alibi rock-solid, though in theory he should trust Nicky Wrists. But he had to make sure Nicky needed them as much as they needed Nicky. "It's just for now, and then we'll see. I don't want anyone being able to point back to us, cover blown." But the other truth was that Vinny liked the idea of the element of surprise, and the possibility of a big reveal sometime down the line. It was theatrical, sure, but he'd also make sure it was strategic. Right now, Nicky Wrists might look at them as some punk kids. One day, Vinny and the rest of the crew would be running guys like Nicky Wrists. That was the goal.

"Hey, there they are," Whispers pointed, and there were Tommy and Blaze coming out of the warehouse, Tommy's hands stuffed in the pocket of his hoodie, and Blaze carrying a duffel bag across his back.

"Hot damn," Whispers whispered. Once Tommy and Blaze were in Tommy's car, Whispers followed them back to Chencho's place, where Joe was waiting for them.

They unzipped the duffel bag and counted all the cash together, then divvied it into piles. "Twenty thousand, all there," Tommy said.

Chencho took the three hundred for hardware and put it in an envelope and was gracious about the seven hundred for himself.

"Now you boys are going to have a feast coming to you," Chencho said. "And Vincente, for you, I will make *mi abuela*'s best *maduros y arroz con habichuelas negras*, and hey, what about seafood, do you eat seafood? I can dig up some *camarones*—some great little shrimpies. They don't have faces, right?"

Vinny didn't know about seafood and hadn't eaten any in years. He'd never had shrimp before, just clam, crab, and once, a lobster roll. "Maybe I would try one, but don't make it special for me. 'Cause really, I'm no meat."

But Chencho was ready to go gourmet for the guys, and so as long as the guys were happy, then Vinny would go along with it.

"And for the next surprise," Joe said, "if you will follow me to the back bedroom," and he led them to the back room and opened the sliding doors of the closet to reveal a computer that was really two minicomputers, folded up and open with the green lettering on a black screen, the modem blinking next to it. "Bank of Eastern Mass. has a password that's in its user manual, so getting in is about as easy as pushing a door open. I have opened two bank accounts—one in Chencho's actual name, and one in my dead birth-father's name, and I have the passwords for both, so nobody can get any funny ideas. You can ask me any time you want to see the money, and I will show you exactly where and how much it is. But until we can get our own accounts at eighteen, and we also want to protect our identities and account holdings, it'll take about a year to get an offshore account—and by then, we should have the baseline amount to get in there. I'm thinking Aruba, also Switzerland, Lichtenstein, and Malta. That's what we want to hit. But we'll want a hundred fifty grand for each account when we open them. So that will be the goal over the next while, yeah?"

"Amigo," Vinny said, "you had me at a hundred fifty grand. Looks like we got work to do."

Chapter 8
The Trucking Crew

Vinny checked the local papers over the next few days, saved for him by Chencho, but there were no reports of the heist in there. He was glad. Part of him had worried that maybe, just maybe, he was pushing all their luck. Or that Nicky Wrists was having a go with them. No police came to Keystone. And as far as Nicky Wrists knew, Tommy had a whole new set of acquaintances working with him, which wasn't entirely untrue.

But Nicky was a fence, not one they could rely on to throw them steady work. That's where Joe came in. Thanks to Joe's new computer and modem, he could, in just a handful of hours, canvas trucking shipments coming through for the crew to pick off. They meanwhile waited for another score thrown their way from Nicky, who made it clear to Tommy he was doing the kid a favor because he was a nice kid and had so far come through, albeit on small-time situations, though he nonetheless was going to "keep Tommy in his Rolodex." Vinny didn't like the minor condescension, but he filed it away as a grievance to be sorted later. Once he had greater power and leverage. That was everything. For now, it would be grunt work.

Joe hacked into a logistics and distribution center, running everything from live and frozen lobsters to electronics equipment to shoes and clothing to even household appliances. They were going to go for all of it.

"The best part," Joe said, "is that half the trucks are making multiple stops, and a quarter of those are scheduled to be overnight."

"Okay, so, convenient for us," Tommy said.

"But also," Joe continued, "that makes it easier to go in with some bolt cutters to the trailer and take out a load of whatever's in there while the truck is at the warehouse."

The third job, they'd gone for an unhitched trailer left inside a closed-up warehouse for an appliance company. The gate was away from the warehouse, and Whispers found and cut all the cameras in the yard. They cut through the chain-link fence, cut the lock off the back gate, and pulled out the first dozen boxes of electronics, taking them back to Chencho's for assessment.

"The first rule," Vinny said, "is that Chencho can't sell this stuff directly. Word gets out that he's working on the side, then someone sniffs around, and soon our whole operation is shot, and we all go back in, this time not as minors."

"I don't want no part of the grunt work," Chencho said. "I'm happy with you renting a little space on my property, procuring me the occasional new stereo and Nintendo system."

Joe looked up the going rates for all the equipment they had, and the MSRP of everything totaled just over two hundred fifty thousand dollars. "Holy shit," Joe said. "That's taking a big cut for the electronics company."

"That's what insurance is for," Vinny said. "Besides, they're not hurting. *We're* hurting."

"Not for long," Whispers said, and everyone laughed. "But look, MSRP and what we can get are two very different numbers."

"It's not my business," Chencho said, "but I wouldn't take less from Mr. Wrists than a hundred. That leaves him with a good take, and then if he sells for more—well, let's just say, there's the leverage you've been wanting. But that's just me."

Vinny reminded himself that he was only seventeen and needed everybody on this crew, and that Chencho thought of them all as nephews now, so he was going to speak his mind. He had to remind himself that Chencho was not his father.

The next night, they assembled at Chencho's, and then Tommy drove Blaze to Nicky's warehouse, while Whispers and Vinny followed behind them. Blaze's role was as visible enforcer and muscle, and though Nicky was slick and used to dealing with all kinds of tough guys, Tommy told Vinny that Blaze's presence had seemed to completely unnerve Nicky. So until Vinny announced himself to their fence, Blaze would be the only person other than Tommy to interact with Nicky. Blaze and his two Sig Sauer handguns. They walked out of there with eighty-two thousand that night. The five of the crew agreed to take fifteen apiece and gave Chencho seven thousand.

"It may not always be this good," Vinny said, "but you take care of us, and we'll take care of you, the best we can. I won't forget what you've been doing for us here."

"Hey, *hijos*, we family now," Chencho said. He made *tacos mariscos* for the guys but had grilled squash and yucca for Vinny. "You tell me what you like, and I'll get it for you," Chencho said.

Nicky Wrists sent on more jobs to the crew via Tommy, and most of the takes were between fifteen and thirty G's. Within six months, each of the guys had more money than they'd known in their lives, at least that they'd been able to get their hands on personally. Chencho deposited the money into several different banks using two separate ATM cards, one legit-only-on-paper ordered by Joe, and all Joe had to do was go into the bank records and move money around and then erase the paper trail. After enough money was saved up, the crew got Joe another computer with a bigger processor, which made his work even faster.

Blaze stockpiled his own small cache of various calibers at Chencho's, so the entire crew had a preferred piece at their disposal, depending on the job, though Joe said he wasn't really interested. "It's if you need it, not if you want it," Blaze said.

"I need to never want it, as my *culo* is staying with the computer."

On off nights, Whispers gave out driving lessons to the guys who'd hardly been behind the wheel in their lives, working on shifting, and then borrowing a semi-cab to learn shifting on a thirteen-gear rig. Blaze took them to the woods for target practice, and Tommy provided them with an endless supply of junk food and dirty magazines. What Vinny wanted, though, was access to books and newspapers. He'd read just about everything in the library that he could get his hands on, including war biographies from Vietnam and World War II, macroeconomics, which he partly understood, the complete collection of Mario Puzo books, old Westerns, Spanish-language books, Zen Buddhism, and veganism. He'd never heard the term before, but he liked the idea of not eating any animal products at all. Don't keep them in pens for milk or butter or cheese. No honey. Absolutely none of Chencho's *camarones*, though the two he'd tried were delicious. He'd see how long he could go, though it was hard to monitor the food at Keystone. Joe did help him find out that if he specifically said he was a vegetarian, he could have a special meal plan offered him, and it was actually better food than what was mass-produced for the general population. Soon, everyone but Blaze was listed as a vegetarian at Keystone, though the rest of the crew got their fill of meat at Chencho's or the White Castle drive-up. At nights, whether at Chencho's or with the four crowding a room at Keystone, they worked out targets and logistics.

"Hey," Joe said, "you know, if we target the third-party companies hiring non-union labor, they're less likely to report and have no leverage. Most of them pay their employees under the table."

"No, man," Blaze said, "absolutely not. I mean, if it can't be helped, sure, but we don't target them."

"Why?" Vinny asked. Joe's plan seemed sound.

"Because, who do you think are taking the jobs under the table? Huh?" Vinny and Whispers shrugged.

"Poor local guys?" Vinny said.

"Nah, bro," Blaze said, shaking his head, his brow in a low point. "Immigrants. People like Joe and me, like our *tíos y primos*. They become targets, they get fired, they get fucked. So no."

"All right," Vinny said. "I'll honor that."

"All's I'm saying is let's not fuck with the people who can't afford to be fucked with."

"Point taken," Vinny said. He was impressed—another sign that Blaze, for all his toughness and his shark-like monitoring of his surroundings, he did have a couple of soft targets.

Vinny kept his soft targets to himself. He still thought of Angela now and again, or at least, she was always the presence deep in the back of his mind, like white noise. But all this time with her gone, with Vinny pushing her back, it was as if a callus had formed over that part of his brain or his heart. He'd found a family in the guys, even when they were pains in his ass. Still, none of their friendship could come close to filling the trench left gouged out not only by Angela's death but by his parents' sociopathic burying of her memory. Vinny had read all about sociopaths in a psychology book. While his parents did not fit the textbook definition, he thought they had some of the habits down. His dad was definitely a narcissist.

Which was why he was stunned to get the news that his parents were coming up to Keystone to visit him. In the two-and-a-half years he'd been sent away, they hadn't once come to see him. Not birthdays, not holidays, though his mother sent her weekly letters.

"Dude, fuck them," Vinny said that afternoon while shooting hoops in the yard with Blaze, whose entire family would be coming up to see him, which they did every month. Every six months, they'd drive down to Leavenworth to visit Blaze's dad.

"Look, your folks will be happy to see you when they get here. It's always a little awkward. How long's it been?"

"Since I've seen them? Since they took me from court and loaded me on the bus."

Blaze stopped dribbling. "What, bro, they ain't been up to see you since you got sent up? For reals?"

"Straight up."

"Whoa. That's—I'll say it, that's fucked up."

"My mom wrote that she wants to see how I'm coming along, now that my release date is closing in. My fucking dad probably wants to test whether I'm a threat to society, at least in the way that will affect him. That motherfucker was the one who handed me a bat and told me to beat up other kids when I was ten."

"*Puñeta*, bro. Okay, look, be chill, and focus on your mom, right? Moms are softies."

"My mom might have been, if she weren't with him."

"Hey, not good to talk that way about your mom. She writes you all the time, though, right? She can't be that bad."

"She lets my dad walk all over her, just like he did the rest of us. Well, with me."

"Let's look at the logistics of this problem, like we do for our work. What is it you are worried about? Do you think they'll give you shit?"

Not his mom, though his dad would inevitably turn this visit into a cause to tear him down in some way. He had to laugh to himself. His dad hadn't seen him these last almost three years—he had no idea that Vinny had grown six inches and gained fifty pounds of man weight. In fact, now that he was thinking about it, he hoped his dad would start to give him shit. Those tables would be fucking turned, and finally.

"Look, if you're worried, you can bring them over to meet my family, maybe take the chill off. It's harder for families to give you shit if outsiders are watching. You know, they like to keep the business in-house."

"Thanks, I'll think about it."

"Hey, and there's decent food in the visiting room, too. Are your folks vegetarian?"

"No, that was just me, though my mom did try to play along."

"Hey, Vin, I been meaning to ask you though, about another thing. So we're about to get out, right? And have access to a shit-ton of money?"

Vinny knew where this was going. "How we explain our solvency, right?"

"Our what?"

"The fact that we actually have a shit-ton of money that we didn't have when we came in."

"Exactly."

As far as Vinny was concerned, his parents didn't need to know about his money. He could always bullshit that one of the coordinators at Keystone had set him up with a great job or some shit, and they'd never follow up. But for the others, ones who actually communicated with their parents and would likely be seeing them regularly afterwards, that was a different matter.

"So what are you planning on doing when you get out?" Vinny asked.

"I don't know, I just figured we'd be doing more of the same, right?"

"Right," Vinny said, nodding absently. "Look, they don't have to know anything before our little lunch next week, right? So we got some time to think things through."

Vinny hadn't gotten things sorted with the guys, though, not yet, anyway. As he got ready to see his parents, the program director gave him and Blaze and the other guys with visits collared shirts so they could appear extra spiffy. Blaze buttoned his collar tight, and then Joe came out with not only a collar but a sweater vest.

"What the fuck is that?" Blaze asked. Whispers almost fell off his bed, he whisper-laughed so hard.

"What, you fools don't know fashion."

"Dude, your parents are going to be there, too?" Vinny asked. He felt bad that Whispers was the only one not being visited that day—if anyone had it worse than Vinny in the home life department, it was Whispers.

Joe was cagey. "Okay, what's up?" Vinny asked.

"Well, they're not actually coming *in*," Joe said.

"Then why the fuck you dressed up, to wave at them from the window?" Blaze asked.

"It's just—I got a twelve-hour furlough to go with them. There's actually a great little place down the road."

"You don't mean the Scarsdale Country Club, do you?" Whispers asked. Joe hung his head. "Ho-ho, the fancy motherfucker!"

"Are you kidding me?" Vinny said.

"How the fuck did you swing that? MIT profs get special rules or shit?"

"Well—you do when you go to school with the governor."

The guys roared, laughing and groaning. "Is that a rub-off tattoo?" Vinny asked, taking the side of his hand to Joe's Mexican flag tattoo. "Because bougie people like you can't possibly have this kind of art."

Joe pushed him back. "It is a symbol of my heritage."

"What," Blaze said, wiping tears of laughter from his face, "that you got just before you came in here so that you wouldn't get your ass beat?"

"I'm leaving," Joe said, and he walked down the hall to whistles from the crew and then just about everybody else he passed.

"Oh, hey, Vin, just a heads up—Chencho's bringing my moms, so you gotta act like you ain't never seen him before in your life, got it?" Blaze said.

"Blaze, I know you're used to dumbass motherfuckers, but consider who you're talking to."

Blaze bowed to Vinny, then, when he was bent forward, made like he was going to punch Vinny in the nuts. Vinny flinched, and Blaze laughed. "I gotcha, bro," he said.

The levity, at least for Vinny, was short-lived. He got to the visiting room and found only his mother.

"Hey, Mom," he said, confused, as she came in for a tentative hug, kissing both cheeks. For the briefest of seconds, he found reassurance in the reunion.

"Hello, Vinny. You're looking—so well. So big! But well. That's nice. My big boy."

"You look nice today, Mom. Where's Dad?"

"Vinny, I'm sorry. Your father...he isn't here. I came alone."

"You drove out from Boston by yourself?"

She looked down. "Not exactly. He dropped me off and is waiting at the IHOP we passed while coming into town."

Vinny knew that IHOP. He decided in that second he would never set foot in that IHOP ever again. "So that's it, huh? He doesn't want to see his own son? What, is he worried about me coming out?"

"Vinny, about that—your dad doesn't think it would be a good idea if you came home to live with us when you get out."

It couldn't have been worse if his mother had kicked him in the nuts. Vinny hadn't really been planning on coming back to live in the house, but being told he couldn't was something else entirely.

"Oh, he doesn't, really?"

"Please, don't take that tone with me. Look, it's not me. You know—he is set in his ways."

"And he sent you up here to do your passive-aggressive dirty work." Passive-aggressive was another term he'd read about in the psychology book.

"Vinny, that's not—I don't—well, yes."

"So you're here as his errand girl? Well, do me a favor and tell him I'm all grown up now, and I said he didn't have the balls to come in here himself and tell me."

"No, please—Vinny, please, this is so hard for me to be here and to say to you. It's so much easier writing things down and then sending them off."

Yeah, no shit, Vinny thought. She'd completely compartmentalized her life so that if one compartment flooded with hurt, she'd just lock herself into another.

"I didn't come here to fight with you. I'd like to be able to see you back in Boston. You are coming back to Boston, right?"

"Well, up until two minutes ago, I'd pretty much assumed I was," Vinny said, deliberately to hurt her. It worked. She pulled out a tissue and held it to her nose. Then she cried into it.

"Nobody's looking at me, are they?" she asked Vinny. "I don't want to make a scene."

She wouldn't be the first mother to cry in the visiting area, but as Vinny scanned the room, he caught sight of Blaze with a crowd of smiling family members around him, including Chencho. They all looked like a military family (except for Chencho), all crisp edges, but otherwise a homey Puerto Rican family. And then, there was one face. A goddamn supermodel's face. She might have been a year or two older than Blaze and Vinny, but she looked like she was ready to take her place as queen of the world. Her black hair flowed down her shoulders and over a USMC sweatshirt, but then perfectly tailored pants that narrowed to her ankles and delicate slip-on shoes. Her nails were painted black. Vinny had to remind himself to breathe. It took a solid thirty seconds for Vinny to process that the young woman was Blaze's older sister. ¡Puñeta! he thought. He was indeed fucked.

"Sweetie, is everything all right?" Vinny's mom asked him.

"Uh, sure. I guess. Well, no, I'm upset, but I'll get over it."

"Well, dear, what are your plans for after? Do you have something lined up? Does this place help you find stuff like work?"

"Yeah, something like that."

"Well? You're not going to talk to me at all now?"

Vinny looked back from Blaze's sister. "Mom, we're talking right now. Sure, I got something lined up, thanks to a friend of mine in here, his dad has some connections, some dads care about their kids." Another zing. Vinny wanted to keep things as vague as possible, and he wasn't entirely sure of whose father he meant in that moment. But if a dad was helping, as far as Vinny's mom was concerned, that would be as good as gospel.

"Oh, you have a friend in here! I'm so glad. You know, we heard the reports from the last place that you didn't do much talking or fraternizing." The way his mother said "fraternizing" was stilted, clearly not a word that was her own.

He wasn't listening to his mother any longer. Instead, he was stealing glances over at Blaze's family. It was hard to take his eyes off the sister, but the whole dynamic at their table was a parallel universe from Vinny and his mother's table. Blaze had a family. He'd known that Blaze was close—even seeing him with Chencho had left a twinge in Vinny's gut and kindled the anger against his own parents, though he had thought, before this visit, that maybe things would mellow out with his dad. That maybe time and age would have changed him. But if losing Angela couldn't change him, then he was probably a lost cause of a soulless cocksucker. Fuck his dad. Maybe not his mom, she was caught in the middle.

Blaze's family, though—it was like they were celebrating Christmas morning, right there at Keystone's crappy lunch tables. As if Blaze wasn't incarcerated, following in his father's footsteps—or that, in their line of work, everyone ended up doing some time. Like a First

Communion or something. Blaze's mother sat right next to him, rubbing his back and kissing his cheek, and Chencho—he could hear the familiar laugh, and Vinny figured he was probably telling some joke. And the sister—the sister. She was looking at Blaze with a little more reserve but still with total love. There were two other women there, a grandmother and probably his mother's sister.

"Vinny, dear, did you hear me?"

"What, Mom, yeah. I just..."

He caught himself staring at Blaze's sister again, and then—she caught Vinny staring. He immediately looked back to his mother.

"So how the hell have you been doing, Mom? I'm sure things have been absolutely great for you and Dad."

"Vinny, please, don't do this. You're almost an adult now, and so we're all adults here."

Vinny bit his tongue. His mother was an adult in age only. She'd never once taken responsibility for anything in life, except a few chores that any teenager could do. He felt that anger swelling inside him and didn't know how to tamp it down.

"Hey, Vinny!" It was Blaze, calling him over from his table. "Vinny, come bring your mom over to say hi to the family!"

"This is my friend, Blaze."

"Oh? The friend whose dad is going to help you?"

"Uh, no. Not that friend."

Vinny's mom followed behind as Vinny walked up to Blaze's table, trying hard not to look directly at the sister or at Chencho. "So, this your family? Nice to meet you, everyone, I'm Vinny."

He reached his hand first toward Blaze's mom, then the grandma, who took both of Vinny's hands in hers and shook them gently. "*Que lindo, buen chico. Muy guapo. Si eres amigo de mi nieto, entonces eres bienvenido en nuestra casa.*"

"*Gracias, Señora,*" Vinny said, his accent less than perfect, but a noble attempt nonetheless.

"*Hermano, ¿desde cuándo tienes amigos tan guapos?*" Blaze's sister. The voice was deep and raspy, like whisky and cigarettes.

Vinny reached out for her hand. She smiled at Vinny as she shook it.

"*Oye,*" Blaze said to his sister, whose name was Reina. "*De ninguna manera, Reina, él no es para ti. Ni siquiera lo pienses.*" Everyone laughed.

"And though I'm not as good looking, I'm Chencho, Blaze's pop's brother," Chencho said, reaching out his hand to Vinny.

"Nice to meet you. Chencho?"

"Yes, Chen-cho." Vinny felt the grip tighten ever so slightly on his hand before Chencho let go.

"Vinny, dear, aren't you going to introduce me?" his mom asked.

"Ah, I'm sorry, yeah. Mom, this is Blaze and his family. Everyone, this is my mother."

"Tina," she said, shaking hands with everyone, though only using her fingertips to hold the others' hands. "Nice to meet you. Well, isn't this a fun crowd!"

Everything his mother said was rubbing Vinny the wrong way, but he didn't want to let it show in front of Blaze, and especially not in front of Reina.

Reina. He knew Reina meant "queen" in Spanish, damn she was one.

"Okay, well, we should be letting you all have your visit," Vinny said.

"You're welcome to join us," Chencho said, a gleam in his eye, and Vinny knew Chencho was making him uncomfortable on purpose.

"You know, maybe next time," Vinny said, and Reina laughed. "I mean, maybe when we're all in a nicer…place…with better food." Jesus H. Christ, Vinny thought, what was he saying? And fuck Blaze for not warning him about having a smoking-hot sister. You gotta prepare a bro for that shit.

It took all of Vinny's self-control to remain civil toward his mother for the rest of his lunch. He didn't hate her, although he was committed to his hatred of his father, but he'd lost all respect for her, despite her meager attempts to show affection. Vinny half-wondered if she was the type of person whose kindness was motivated by a self-interest in not wanting anyone to think she wasn't the proper, good housewife and mother. This was conjecture, but it did match his interpretation from the psychology book. Not that Vinny was an expert, but it didn't really take an expert to decode his fucked-up family.

His family. Maybe they really weren't his family. Maybe they were just people who had given him life. Angela was family. He looked over at Blaze's table. *That's* what a family was. And that's what he felt when he sat at Chencho's table, surrounded by Blaze and Joe and Whispers and Tommy. Maybe he had to let go of everything he'd felt and experienced in his life before this. Sometimes you had to choose your family. He took one last good look at Reina as she said goodbye. He caught her eye, and she turned and gave a final wave.

Blaze's warning be damned.

Chapter 9
Blood and Fire

Vinny's blood was on fire that night. The day had been a revelation of sorts. He hadn't intended to be back with his parents at all after leaving Keystone, but his father's absence and his mother's hesitation and inability to stand up for her one living kid were confirmation that he would never find a home with them.

He wasn't ready, however, to be without a family and wanted to float to the guys the idea of maybe getting a place together. Turned out, he wasn't the only one with this on his mind.

"So, man," Whispers whispered the next afternoon while they were sitting on their beds, reading. "You know, I'm out in a month. And I got a place I could crash at, but it's not ideal. Plus, you and Blaze got another two months-plus after that, and Joe in four. That's a long time but not that long."

Vinny nodded. "So what were you thinking?"

"I don't know, I mean, what are your plans? Don't seem like you're going back to anything. And we got a pretty good thing going that we have no plans to stop. So what, where are we all going at the end of this?"

"You tell me, Whispers—are we living together? Because that sounds like a fucking plan if you're asking."

Whispers smiled, and Vinny saw him sit back, as if a tremendous tension had suddenly been unfastened inside of him. "All right, then."

"Yeah. All right."

"Should we call in the others and ask them, too?"

"I think it's past time," Vinny said.

Both Joe and Blaze took some minor convincing. "I mean," Joe said, "is it going to be a house? Are we going to keep it nice and shit, because I don't want to live in some animal flop house, you know? I'm going to need my own room for all my equipment and we will need to keep things clean around it.

"Dude," Vinny said, realizing that Joe had been counting on moving back into his really nice tenured-professor-at-MIT-style house, with people probably doing a lot of the household work for him. "Think of the money we have saved up—you know, if we each took half of what we have, pooled it, and put it toward a down payment, what kind of kickass house we could have? A house that no other eighteen-year-olds have any right to have. But we're gonna do it. And I don't know about you, but the rest of us are used to cleaning up our own shit, so the question is, are you gonna keep your shit clean?"

"You both are definitely living together?" Blaze asked Vinny and Whispers. "And if you go, Tommy will go, right? I mean, I was going to kick it at my moms's place, but like, that was mostly just because she'll want to spend time with me once I'm out. Since it's been a few years."

"But then," Vinny said, "you weren't going to stay with her forever, were you?"

"Oh, shit, no, 'course not."

"And I'd imagine it'd be hard to run some jobs, especially at night, if she's going to be around, waiting up for you." Vinny knew he had to be careful not to paint it too much that Blaze was a mama's boy, but it was clear he could easily stay with her for the foreseeable years to come.

"*Coño*, I know that. You know, my pops being gone, that's the concern, but she's got her sister—"

"And your sister," Vinny ventured.

"Nah, my sister's in New York. School and shit. She's gotta do her thing."

Vinny looked at Whispers, who shook his head. "Man," Whispers said to the other two, "you boys like being taken care of, don't you?"

Vinny burst out laughing. They were quite the motley crew, indeed. Joe with his adopted privilege, maintaining his ties to his heritage as best he could, but mostly doing it for street cred. Blaze being more rough and tumble, but still from a solid family unit—enough to send a sister to New York for college. Then Whispers, who was almost killed at fourteen and had been living by his wits since then, with half a voicebox. Then there was Vinny, whose primary influence was a dead sister and a father who wanted him to stop reading and be an ass-kicking football star, except he turned Vinny into an ass-kicking thinking-man's blue collar criminal. He should put that on some business cards, Vinny thought ironically.

"Okay," Blaze said, "I'm in. Just give me like a month to be with my moms and my tía, and then I'll go wherever we're going."

"Sweet," Vinny said, then turned to Joe. "You're the last one. You really want to work out of your parents' mansion and wear sweater vests all day long?"

The guys all burst out laughing, except for Joe, who had a round of ¡Vete a la chingadas! for each of them. "Besides," he said, "you *cabrónes* would be fucking lost without my little codes that are going to hide your money and keep you out of prison."

"Yeah, how are we going to explain all our money to our families or, like, our social workers?" Blaze asked, and it was the question that Vinny hadn't fully settled on.

"First off," Joe said, "we can't let on how much we actually have."

"True," Vinny agreed. "And all of us can't magically have rich, long-lost uncles who pass away and leave us inheritances."

Joe nodded and then looked down.

"Joe?" Vinny asked. "Joe, I was speaking hypothetically. Do you have something you want to tell us?"

"It wasn't a long-lost uncle. It was my *abuelo*."

"Dude, you're fucking loaded and you're stuck in here?" Whispers said. "Even if you fucked with the FBI?"

"Would have been a longer sentence, I guess," Joe said. "Look, so no one's going to question the kind of house I live in, and if I live with a few guys. My folks will be making sure your asses aren't taking advantage of me, but they'll be less worried if you all have fucking day jobs."

"Not a problem," Vinny said. "We go legit, do our other work on the side, work both angles, and you move our money around and make it all look like clean investments."

"So, uh, then I should tell you I already got a job. I'm technically not allowed to own a modem until I'm twenty-one, but I can work in computers, and I got a job programming for this IT company in the city. I'm supposed to start in eight months."

"What's it like to be born rich?" Whispers asked. "Do things just happen for you, or do you have to, like, try to get things?"

"Like you can talk," Joe said, "you might not have been born rich, but *pendejo*, you rich as fuck now."

It was likely the first time this had really dawned on Whispers that he had money, Vinny thought. It struck Vinny, too, that once they were out, which was soon, their money was no longer this hypothetical sum that was being stowed away. They'd have access to it. It was real money that could build them a life. That was a strange prospect. So much of Vinny's existence, all their existences, had been about the plan, the score, the future. The calendar was turning over.

"All right," Whispers said, "so we all go legit. Our rich friend here has got his setup. How do we all roll convincingly so we don't track on anyone's radar? And I'm talking real-world radar, not just online."

"What is it we want to do?" Vinny asked. "Do we stay with our specialties, do we try to work our asses off by starting up our own business? Do we each do our own thing and make like we're pitching in with the meager take-homes?"

"If it was me," Whispers said, "I think it would be fucking hilarious to set up a security company. Who knows break-ins better than we do? All we'd need is to get a logo and get some signs in people's front lawns. Is that something we could actually do?"

Vinny loved the sound of it but wasn't sure a bunch of eighteen-year-old juvenile felons could quite pull it off. At least, not yet. "Plenty of ex-cops do that kind of shit," Vinny said. "It'd be a lot of work, though."

"But, like, we could get licenses to carry and shit," Blaze said. "I mean, there are probably ways to get this done, then hire a couple guys to run the everyday stuff once we get up and running."

"So is this what we're going with?" Joe asked. "I mean, not that I'm going with it, because I have my own job, but I'm sure you'll need my help and I can be, like, an investor or something."

"It would give us a logical reason to all be in regular contact," Vinny said. "People might think we're idiots for trying, but they don't know us. We know better. We know better than all of them what we're capable of doing." It was true. They'd managed to do more than most meatheads did in their entire lives. And they'd keep doing it, too. One day, they'd show all the doubters that they weren't just some punk kids. Running their own heists and setting up a security company—no one had to know about their real money. But no one was ever going to look down on Vinny Bruno again.

∞

The new job that Tommy arranged with Nicky Wrists was going to be their trickiest heist yet—and their last big take before Whispers was out. Another truck carrying a ten-foot cube container up from Biloxi, though Nicky hadn't been forthcoming about the contents of said container.

Joe looked through all the manifests in the shipping company's directory, and though there was a registry for the truck's trip, the cargo was marked as "misc. personal items" for a private client, set for a small warehouse north of Boston.

"So, when does it arrive?" Blaze asked. Nicky only had the figure of when the truck was leaving Biloxi and the estimated arrival time in Boston, which would take thirty to forty hours to arrive.

"This isn't good," Joe said, looking at his computer at Chencho's house. The rest of the crew huddled around, waiting for Joe to make sense of the data climbing down the screen while Chencho finished up his *mofongo with guisado*, plus a small veggie version for Vinny. "There's no real place to snatch the truck along the way."

"So we get it at the warehouse," Vinny said. "Not a big deal, we've done it before."

"Yeah, but at this warehouse, the trucks all load inside a big complex, and there is no good place to get in and out quickly."

"It doesn't make sense," Whispers said. "These kinds of containers are mostly used for, like, when people move. Hardly anything can fit in there."

"We got a delivery window of twelve hours," Joe said. "We don't even know if we'll be able to get out of here to pick up the truck."

"This is a shit job," Whispers whispered, and everyone looked at Tommy. "I don't like it. I think we should tell Nicky we're off this one."

"What," Tommy said, Vinny recognizing the defensiveness in his tone, "and lose the next three jobs?"

Blaze crossed his arms and sat back. "Maybe we don't need Nicky's little bones thrown our way anymore. We got our own scores."

"But we still need Nicky to fence for us," Tommy said. "We start saying no to him, he starts saying no to us, and then where are we?"

"Maybe we need a new fence, then, or do our own selling."

"That's really fucking hard to do when I'm the only one out here, doing all the work for you," Tommy said. "I'm not some fucking errand boy who—"

"Hey, hey, Tommy, we know, we get it," Vinny said, trying to pump the breaks on what he saw was going to head off the rails. "Look, guys, I don't love this situation. What this means, though, is that we can't be fucking lazy about this. Special ops style, got me?" Vinny said to Blaze. He could tell Blaze was reluctant, but he shrugged, half-dismissive, half-acquiescing. "Look, we're about to be big boys out on our own. At some point, we'll likely have to face an impossible job. Well, right now, we got an impossible job. But we also got, at least for now, the best cover. We go in stealth and don't get caught, take extra precautions, and if things get hairy, then we act like we're the fucking Marines."

"Like the fucking Marines," Blaze said, "except with no tactical training, *coño*. Ops like this, they take weeks to plan, and if they don't, it's because you've had years of experience to pull off and a massive fucking team. We got five on it, and we're all eighteen years old and have not gone through special ops training."

Blaze was right, but Vinny didn't want to give up, especially not for Tommy, who'd come through so many times for them, being the liaison for Nicky. Tommy had mostly kept quiet, not fully confiding in the other guys, not speaking up or speaking out—until now. Vinny had been his biggest champion—and he still worried that all the guys saw was the one who didn't get pinched with Vinny and wasn't a homie, hadn't done the time. That was clearly on their radar any time there was a plan Tommy proposed that had some kind of hitch. They didn't trust that Tommy's clean-cut suburban-boy persona was a cover. It was true that Tommy complained more than the others and thought the guys were taking advantage of him being on the outside, making him do more work than anybody else. That wasn't the case. Once they were all out, things would be cool. Vinny didn't want to lose any of the crew in the meantime, though.

They broke for dinner and stuffed their faces while Chencho warned them about biting off more than they could chew. "You're all just so close to being out," he said, then quickly added, "but I know it's not my call. I'm not your crew—I'm just here for moral support and the occasional guidance."

Vinny was thinking, half-doodling on a pocket spiral notebook he kept locked in Joe's computer cabinet. He wanted to let the guys eat in peace, but he had to find a way out of this, a solution, and talking through things out loud always helped him. "Look, the biggest issues will be point of entry. Can Whispers drive us up to the back of the truck, which will be shipped on a twenty-foot flatbed, and we get on while it's moving? Maybe. Or we trail the guy for a while, Joe calculates how often he stops for gas, then figures out where the last stop is going to be, and we intercept him before he makes the stop, following him to the station."

"That's a lot of maybes," Whispers said. "So what, we steal the truck? Hijack it? That's the most likely. It risks the driver fucking us up. We can't outrun somebody long-distance in a stolen truck. And we are not getting that container off the truck. That's just insane."

It did sound insane when it was all outside Vinny's head. But what if? "It's a ten-foot container, right? Unless it's the fucking *David* of Michelangelo, then we can probably take whatever's in there out of the container while it's still moving. And the driver would never know."

"Who's David Michelangelo?" Blaze asked.

"Brother, you need to open a fucking book," Vinny said. "If we get this score, I'll fucking take you to see the real thing someday."

Blaze punched Vinny in the arm, then shook his head. "Um, excuse me, Mr. Houdini, but how do we take what's inside the container without taking the container, while it's on the back of a moving vehicle?"

"We get inside the container while it's on the moving vehicle," Vinny said. Actually, that wasn't just mouthing off. They could do it. "Look, it's even better this way—we can take it on our time. We just have to meet it on the road."

"This ain't some spy movie, Vin," Joe said.

"Wait a minute," Chencho said, "I don't mean to sound like the killjoy dad calling curfew, but you really need to think this through. Jumping from one moving vehicle to another moving vehicle on a highway, at night? Come on, now."

"It'll be going slow," Whispers said, "and we can make sure the truck stays below fifty."

"It's still dangerous—reckless!" Chencho said.

"*Oye*, Chench," Blaze said, "if we don't like the looks of it, we'll bow out. How 'bout I promise you that?"

That seemed to satisfy Chencho, but Vinny thought he looked uneasy.

"Actually, that plan's less insane," Blaze said. "You, me, we jump on, scout it out, Whispers has a truck and we pass the stuff off to Tommy or something, then jump back onto the truck. Whispers just has to drive so that it's not obvious to the driver we're there. And we have to be quick and do it when other people aren't driving right next to us."

"Presumably, it will be locked, yeah?" Joe asked. "So you'll need to also be able to open the container with bolt cutters, on a moving vehicle, oh, and without the door swinging out, shifting the load, and signaling to the driver that something's up and he pulls off the road."

"He pulls off the road, and we pop him," Blaze said, and Chencho almost choked on his rice.

"*Oye, mijo, no. Absolutamente no matar.*"

Blaze looked down.

"Your pops does not want you going down that road. You want killing, you join the fucking Corps."

"Fine."

"¿Oiste?"

"*Sí, tío.*" Then he muttered, "I don't know what you think the guns were for that you've been keeping for us, but whatever."

"For your protection!" It was the first time any of the guys had ever heard Chencho raise his voice. "You don't take these matters lightly. You don't just kill like it ain't no thing. And I already don't like this job. A personal container that Nicky Wrists wants you to take, but there's no easy in or out? It's bad. Sounds bad. You fools are good, but you don't got the training or the experience. You're still kids! No, not little boys, you're all grown, but you're kids. You're tough as hell, but that ain't *todos*. Besides that, don't you see that I'm technically responsible for you *pendejos*? All of you are my responsibility. It's on me if anything happens to you while I'm taking you into my home. You can't just bring that into my home, got that?"

The guys were somber, especially Blaze, but Vinny knew that Chencho was feeling more paternal than necessary. Chench and his fucking points he had to keep making. Chencho gripped Blaze's shoulder, and then Blaze gripped Chencho's shoulders, and they leaned close to each other, touching their foreheads.

"Anyway, we could still move the cargo from the container while it's on the road," Vinny said. "It's safer for everyone, and if something goes wrong, then we all jump onto the truck and we can beat it the fuck out of there." He eyed Blaze, who was now looking deep into his *guisado*.

They hadn't settled on anything when they went back to Keystone an hour before dawn. Vinny heard Blaze say once, from the backseat,

"Gotta grow up sometime," but otherwise he was quiet. If Vinny didn't come up with a better plan, this job would be over. If that happened, the crew might lose faith in him—they'd more than likely lose faith in Tommy. And then what, they're all too busy the next few months, spending time with families, and put off moving in until they're all just a bunch of strangers who have to hassle Joe to get their money unlocked from offshore accounts? No, Vinny thought, he was just letting his mind wander. That didn't mean he couldn't let this job pass. It was true what Chencho warned about Nicky Wrists. It might be time, if they finished this job, to finally have words with Nicky.

The next night, they were back in Chencho's home, the mood restrained but not bad. It was Joe who startled them when he called out from his computer.

"Whoa, whoa," Joe said. "They've put a beacon on it. Look, it's flashing! I don't know where this beacon is actually going—like, who's receiving it. But there is no taking of this truck without somebody knowing exactly where it is."

Vinny wasn't going to be deterred. Now that the challenge had grown, it was like a drug, like the weights he and Blaze benched. He wanted to go harder. He wanted to prove to everyone that he knew what he was doing.

"Hey, this beacon isn't necessarily a bad thing," Vinny said. "It's actually letting us know exactly where it's going to be. And if it's going to arrive in Lowell sometime after ten, three nights from now, then this will turn out to be good for us."

Whispers shook his head. "How? If someone is following it, we know for sure there's no taking the truck, no matter what, or we'll lead them right to us. Or to Nicky, and do you think that guy's going to take the fall and let us go?" He looked at Tommy.

"It's clear, then," Vinny said, knowing they had the only option. "All that matters is what's in the container, not the container, not the truck." He took out a sheet of paper and made diagrams all over it. "We have the bolt cutters—all we need is to put a strap through the handles so one of us can strap it across our body. Less likely to clang against anything, and we don't have to fish around in a bag once we get on the truck. We should be able to get into the lock in under a minute."

"What if the lock isn't facing forward?" Whispers asked. "You know, like what if the door is facing the truck? Even if you could get back there, the driver's gonna see you at that point, and then the whole job is fucked."

"Then the job is fucked." That would be their out. "But how likely is it really to load a container backwards?"

"True," Blaze said. "Let's take our chances. Only one way to find out."

"What we'll need, then," Whispers said, "is a sound distraction for the bolt cutters."

"Any thoughts on what? Joe probably can't program the radio to play loud or anything like that." Although Vinny wasn't sure—maybe he could?

"Ah, if only," Joe said. "But that kind of tech is probably twenty years out."

"We don't need a radio," Whispers said. "We get a chopper."

"And where the fuck are we going to get a helicopter?" Tommy asked, and Whispers and Blaze laughed.

"Not a helicopter," Whispers said. "A chopper. A wicked loud fucking motorcycle. Which I can get."

The impossible plan was a little less impossible. All that night and all day, the guys could barely stay inside their skins. There was the mystery of the cargo, the excitement of escalation, coupled with the fact that things had worked out so far, but this was the hardest job they'd ever done, and the stakes—and risks—all were higher.

They could barely eat at dinner, though Vinny told them they needed something in their systems—but nothing heavy, no dairy or meat or anything that would make them sluggish. "Veggies and starch," he said, though he told Blaze to eat a couple of hardboiled eggs so he wouldn't get cranky. Joe had followed the truck's beacon until the last minute he had to leave his computer, figuring it could take one of three routes from Montgomery, Alabama: the eastern route, through Atlanta, Greensboro, Richmond, DC, and Philly; or head up to Birmingham, where there were two options: the northern route, through Louisville, Columbus, coming across all of Pennsylvania; or the central route, heading northeast to Chattanooga, Knoxville, and Roanoke. Eastern and central met up in Hackensack, so the only difference would be in the time it took to cross into Massachusetts. Joe calculated that the most likely place the driver would make the last stop would be at the truck stop in Wellington, Connecticut, just outside the border of southeastern Massachusetts. It would take less than an hour to drive out there.

It was also the first all-hands-on-deck operation, since they would need the road to look like a traffic cluster, have a reason for a chopper to be cruising alongside—"drafting" the truck without looking suspicious. Whispers gave Tommy a crash course in chopper driving, though he'd ridden a Honda a couple of times. All he had to do was be loud and steady. Whispers would have done it, but since Vinny and Blaze were hopping from the truck bed to the flatbed, Whispers trusted only himself to get them there and back safely. They needed one more car, though, as a sort of pace car on the road to keep the truck driver focused in front of himself and not behind and also to help set up that buffer—they couldn't all be close to the truck, but they could take turns looking like a regular traffic flow. They'd have walkie-talkies to communicate between the two vehicles, and Tommy would have to sight when Joe and Whispers pulled away, keep following for another ten minutes, then rendezvous back at Nicky's warehouse.

∞

Everything felt hotter that night, seemed more difficult. Whispers was irritable, kept talking about all the moving parts, and he questioned whether Tommy was ready to handle the chopper so many times that Vinny was worried that Tommy was going to resort to blows. It was a sticky heat that seemed to ooze out of the trees. Their dark sweatshirts clung to them. Blaze was the least bothered, saying Puerto Rico had come to Massachusetts that night, and besides, in a special op, you did your duty, no matter if the sun was hot enough to cremate you.

There was no sun anymore, just the humid night that choked out the stars. Tommy's car was waiting for them, and they swung to the chop shop to get the pickup truck, an old hulk of a Dodge repurposed by the shop, and the chopper. As soon as they got there, Joe climbed into a sedan to head out south—it was his job to clock the truck at the projected gas station, and he wanted to be nearby, waiting, and radio them when the truck came through. Then, he'd be the de facto pace car, staying just ahead of the truck until the rest of the crew met up.

"You sure you got this?" Whispers asked Tommy.

Tommy squeezed the clutch and pushed in the choke.

"Just remember," Whispers whispered, though he had to shout-whisper over the engine, "You're completely on your own out there. We can't communicate, so if you get in trouble, you gotta sort that shit out and make your way back here."

Tommy nodded and walked the bike forward as Whispers, Vinny, and Blaze climbed in the truck, and they all set off for the highway. The truck was quiet. Behind them, Vinny heard the rumbling of Tommy on the chopper, sometimes closer, sometimes pulled back. He had to stay with them to know when to turn off to intercept the truck. For now, though, silence as they waited for the crackle of the walkie-talkie with Joe telling them he and the truck were on their way. It was 12:48 when they got the signal.

"Take the next exit, head back north, and hold at about fifty-two miles per hour," Joe instructed. "We'll catch up to you in under ten minutes—then match speed."

Whispers pulled off the highway and Tommy followed, then they circled to the on ramp and headed north. Just before one a.m., they saw the distant headlights behind them. "I mark you," Joe said. "Hold speed, then slowly increase. The good news is I think our trucker is getting tired—he drives like he's zoning out."

"That's good for us," Whispers said. Vinny and Blaze ducked down into the back of the cab. "All right, here we go," Whispers said. "I'm letting him pass us."

Joe maneuvered around them as if to get out ahead of all the cars, but then the truck sped up a little, playing a game or coming back to life after having "zoned out" again, as Joe had put it. There was the truck, no longer hypothetical, a flatbed for a twenty-foot container, and the ten-foot container lashed close to the cab. Ten feet of clearance on the bed behind the container, for Vinny and Blaze's jump. The two soon-to-be daredevils slipped out the back window of their cab and into the bed of the pickup to set up for the jump. Vinny put on the backpack with the bolt cutters and then leaned back through the window to tell Whispers they were ready.

Whispers clicked on the walkie-talkie and told Joe to keep the driver's attention onto the left side of the truck.

"Copy," Joe said, and he surged ahead, in and out of the driver's blind spot, preplanned to frustrate him, before surging ahead and getting in front of the truck. Whispers let the truck go all the way ahead, and then crept forward toward the bed. Vinny took one last look behind them at Tommy and gave a salute, which Tommy returned, briefly, before returning both hands to the grips.

"All right, Evel Knieval," Blaze said, strapping on a pair of safety goggles while Vinny did the same. "Let's do this."

It would all happen in seconds. Vinny eyed his landing spot, where he would drop to his stomach as Blaze instructed, and then crawl up to the container. He had to do it without thinking—just react, he told himself, but as the thought flashed in his head, he was already jumping. He hit the hard metal of the bed and felt his momentum want to carry him to the other side, so he sprawled onto his stomach and grabbed for the ridges in the bed. He tucked in his knees and crawled up to the container, careful not to make too much noise. Already Whispers was driving the truck back up to tease in and out of the trucker's right blind spot. Then, there was a flash of panic—where was Blaze? Whispers was up there in only two seconds, or what Vinny figured had to be. Vinny turned and there was nothing behind him, and then he turned left, and there was Blaze, smiling away.

"Dude, the fuck?"

Blaze leaned in close to Vinny's ear to avoid shouting. "This ain't my first salsa, *coño*."

Vinny couldn't believe how quick and stealthy Blaze had been—he must have jumped nearly at the same time, without waiting for Vinny to clear. Risky, but he'd done it. They were on. His blood pumped with all the adrenaline and invincibility that only an eighteen-year-old could have.

Blaze turned back toward Tommy and waved, and the chopper crept up closer to the truck bed. The front of the container was indeed facing the cab of the truck, and even though there was clearance between them, there was a small window in the back of the cab, which meant the driver would see the door opening. Vinny was relieved for their Plan B. As long as Joe and Whispers did their little dance and lulled the driver into a comfortable rhythm, though, they should have enough time to get in and out with the goods.

Vinny grabbed the bolt cutters out of his backpack, held them tightly to the locking pin, and squeezed. A loud click, partially drowned out by Tommy's chopper, and Blaze was able to pull open the door while Vinny replaced the cutters in the backpack. Vinny squeezed himself into the container, Blaze following and closing the door tight behind them.

"Shit, bro, buy me dinner first—talk about a funky roll," Vinny said laughing, feeling Blaze's entire weight press on his back. He clicked the walkie-talkie to Whispers. "We're in."

There were large bubble-wrapped packages on pallets with almost no clearance around them. "Do we both need to be in here for this?" Vinny asked.

"I'm not waiting on the back of a truck bed for you to party on your own."

"Well, then, let me see if I can climb up on top of this so we can inspect what the fuck is so important to Nicky." Vinny used a small flashlight from his pocket to look over the layout. "I can get up there," he said, putting the flashlight in his mouth and climbing up to the top of the cargo, where he had about two feet of clearance. It was hot as hell on the top of the container.

"Dude," Blaze said, pulling at the bubble wrap in front of his face, "What...the fuck?" Vinny pulled open the wrapping on top and at first flinched, but then calmed himself. The container was filled with alligators. Stuffed alligators. Was this all to make some fancy shoes and jackets? Those weren't going to fit into Blaze's duffel bag, big as it was. He reached around for a nose, though the teeth bit into his thick gloves when Vinny tried to pull up. It was a heavy fucker.

"Are you fucking kidding me?" Blaze said. "I mean, I guess we could call Whispers and have him get close, then throw these bad boys into the back of his truck one at a time, right? Might take a little while, but not impossible."

"Wait," Vinny said, reaching into the alligator's mouth and feeling around. At the back of the throat was some stitching. He pulled the switchblade out of his boot and sliced the stitching, feeling a thick plastic bag. He gripped it and pulled it out.

"Holy fuck," Blaze said.

Holy fuck was right. It was brick-shaped, like a loaf, in brown wrapping, then plastic wrapping, then bagged and taped. Only one thing was bagged like that and hidden inside other shit. "You don't just lift a full container of this shit," Vinny said. "Not without making a shit-ton of enemies."

"No wonder it had a fucking beacon on it. I knew Nicky was fucking with us!" Blaze said, and Vinny was worried he'd blaze right through Nicky Wrists the first chance he got. They had to make it off this truck bed first.

Vinny didn't like it. He didn't think it was a setup, but Nicky was sure throwing them out to the winds to see where they scattered and what came back. Drugs were one thing Vinny wanted to stay out of. Drugs were what the big sharks went after, what started turf wars. Vinny was all about owning the streets, but in secret. An anonymous kind of ownership, lurking in the shadows and living a good, long life in comfort. With drugs, you either had to have a family with the power of the Kennedys backing you, or you had to have a death wish.

"Quick, gimme your duffel bag," Vinny said. "We're not taking all this shit. We'll open three of these alligators, and Nicky will be fucking grateful for it."

The animals were heavy to pull up by the snout, and then Vinny had to slit the back of the throat and pull out the bricks, while Blaze did the same with the lower ones within reach. He wasn't sure if it was cocaine or heroin, but they'd have to figure it out before they got to Nicky's warehouse. There must have been close to a dozen alligators in the container, and they seemed to range in size—some might be close to twelve feet, if the tails had been stretched out. But they were all fat, stuffed to the gullet. Vinny emptied the first one of fifteen bricks, which had been expertly arranged into every spare crevice by what had to be the world's greatest Tetris master. They emptied three of the gators of about forty-five bricks, filling Blaze's body-sized duffel. Forty-five kilos of whatever it was. He thought for a few seconds about trying to cram in a few more into his backpack and even his sweatshirt, but they were now far across the border into Massachusetts and heading east, so they would take what they could get and make their escape. Vinny had no idea what the going cost was, but there were likely tens of millions of dollars total in that container, and they'd managed to lift a not-insubstantial portion of it.

"Do you think we can get one full gator, just to show Nicky? Maybe it's the skins Nicky wanted?"

"Are you serious? You know how heavy those are, and to pull it all the way out?"

"I can do it," Blaze said.

"And then we're just going to toss this motherfucker into the bed of our truck?"

"Why not? How about the little guy up there that's already empty?"

Why the fuck not, indeed. "All right, sir, after you. I'll radio Whispers."

Blaze went to open the door. "Huh."

"What, *huh*?"

Blaze pushed at the door, then put his shoulder into it. "Vin, flash your light over here, too." They both pointed their flashlights to the door. There wasn't a handle, just a vertical lip along each door where they joined. "Why isn't it opening?"

"Did you let it click behind you?"

"Containers aren't supposed to lock without the locking pin, which you cut."

"Is there another lock, then?"

"That's what I'm fucking trying to see right now."

"Here, I'll come down," Vinny said.

"No, stay the fuck up there," Blaze said. "You think there's room for me to see shit with these lizards, the duffel, *and* you?"

Vinny wasn't sure what a heart attack felt like, but he wondered if he might be having one. Sweat streamed down the backs of Vinny's legs and seemed to pool on his entire front side, pressed against the alligators and bubble wrap. He called in to Whispers.

"So, uh, Whispers—what do you know about containers that lock behind you?"

There was silence on the other line, and for a second, Vinny thought Whispers hadn't heard. Then, his voice came through. "I don't fucking believe this."

"Yeah. Door's locked on us."

"Lemme ask Joe," Whispers said.

"What, so Joe's going to be able to hack the locks or some shit while he's driving the pace car?" Blaze asked.

"How do I know what Joe's gonna do? What you need to do is find something to cut. Here, take my backpack—the cutters are inside." Vinny reached behind him, next to his knees, and passed down the backpack. Blaze continued to feel all around the door hinges for some connection.

"Hey, Vin?" Whispers crackled through. "Joe says the only reason the doors should lock behind you is if someone wants the doors to lock behind you."

"Is this a setup?" Vinny asked, feeling like they may actually for real be fucked.

"Not necessarily. He says drug dealers get paranoid and have been known to install them as an extra precaution. Remember, Nicky didn't know how we were going to take this."

"You're right. Over." It wasn't much comfort, considering the present situation, but at least he didn't have to worry about a double-cross on top of everything else.

"So what if I can't find nothing, do we pound through?" Blaze asked. "Poke a hole with the bolt cutters?"

"Wait a minute. Can you cut the lip of the door, and maybe keep cutting across so we can see where the fucking locking mechanism is?"

"Uh, bro, I'll try."

Vinny held up the flashlight toward the bottom, where Blaze began his series of slow, painfully slow, cuts to the metal door. "Aw, man, my hands keep slipping in my gloves."

"Want me to get down there and try?"

"Not yet. I need the space to get leverage. I just got to see."

Vinny could feel the truck slow, and then Whispers hit them up again. "Yeah, uh, your truck is exiting the highway."

This was not how it was supposed to go. He didn't know what was going on with everyone else, whether Joe was still out front, though he hoped not, since that would be too obvious if the whole pack got off the road at the same time. The chopper whizzed up the left side of the truck to pass them, so Vinny figured Tommy was improvising. And with the fucking beacon on this thing. And their fucking five a.m. curfew.

"Fuck, man, I don't know. My hands are cramping up."

Vinny hopped down, this time the space even tighter with the duffel bag propped against the wall behind Blaze's legs. Vinny took over the cutters and continued the cuts. "Try putting your shoulder against the door—maybe if we get some air, we can get a good view."

Blaze leaned in, grimacing in the strain, barely making a dent.

"Come on, just a little more. We can't be in here."

Blaze pushed again, and Whispers came on with a new update. "We're at the wrong warehouse in twenty minutes."

Vinny didn't respond, and Blaze kept pushing, and then—there was a little light coming in from the headlights behind them, and Vinny got a glimpse of one vertical bar locking the door to the floor.

"I got it, I got it," he said. "Keep pushing, but don't fall forward in case the door swings open." He squeezed in the bolt cutters and snipped. The door briefly jerked open, and Blaze fell forward, until Vinny caught him and brought him and the door swinging back—and this time, the door didn't lock on them.

Blaze pulled his walkie-talkie from the backpack and called in, "We got a funky drummer," the signal taken from a line of Blaze's favorite song of the last year, one he hadn't stopped rapping months later. "We all clear to come out?"

"Roger that, Chuck D," Whispers said, "Joe's right behind you and no one else."

"All right, let's get the fuck offa here," Blaze said, holding an alligator. "What are we waiting for?"

They opened the door to see Joe, who waved from behind his windshield. They were on a narrow industrial road, passing locked-up warehouse yards and shuttered factories.

Whispers then slowed back down into the trucker's blind spot and then a little farther back, lining up the bed of his truck with Vinny and Blaze.

That was supposed to be the cue for Tommy to accelerate and start a slow pass on the trucker's left, while Vinny and Blaze got ready to move back to Whispers' truck, so instead, Joe had to do the work while making sure not to actually pass the truck, revealing the familiar back end of his car to the trucker. Whispers got so close, Vinny could have stepped right into the truck, but he and Blaze had to throw in the alligator and then the duffel bag. Blaze tossed the alligator into the bed, then followed after. He turned back to Vinny, who was ready to throw the giant duffel over. It weighed a shit-ton, but Vinny couldn't stop to think about it, he needed to get a good shot and have it clear the bed. Blaze nodded, arms out, and Vinny tossed the duffel just to Blaze's right side, where he helped it land in the back next to the gator.

Just as Vinny made the jump, Whispers slowly pulled away from the flatbed. The second Vinny was flat on his back in the bed, he felt the full soreness of his arms, and all the tension he'd been holding with the drill. His shoulders and forearms were on fire, and he couldn't make a fist.

"You okay?" Vinny asked.

"I'm sore as fuck."

"That makes two of us."

Blaze smiled, then helped push Vinny in through the back window of the pickup. As soon as they were both in, Blaze hooted, "Fight the motherfucking power!" and launched into the full Public Enemy rap that would be stuck again in Vinny's head for days.

"We out," Whispers said into the walkie-talkie. "See you on the other side." He made the first right turn away from the truck. "You know how motherfucking close we're cutting this?"

"Where's Tommy?"

"He radioed me fifteen minutes ago that he'd wait for Joe at the White Castle parking lot." Per the original plan, Tommy would jump off the bike and hit the payphone to Whisper's friend's chop shop, leaving only the address of the White Castle, then leave the key in the wheel well and hop into the sedan with Joe. From there, they'd rendezvous with the others at Nicky's warehouse, which now meant backtracking for Joe. It also meant Grand Prix-level driving from Whispers to get back to Nicky's warehouse on schedule.

Vinny took off his sweatshirt and wiped his head with a towel from Chencho's.

"So?" Whispers said, once they rerouted and everyone had a second to calm down. "What happened? What the fuck was in there?"

"Fuck, man," Blaze said, "I'd say about several million."

"Dollars? There was cash in there?"

"Brick-cash," Blaze said. "My guess is about two hundred kilos total."

"Cocaine?" Whispers more than whispered. He was quiet for a minute. "Fuck, man."

"Fuck yeah, maybe cocaine," Vinny said.

"Let's find out for sure," Blaze said. He pulled a brick out of his sweatshirt and cut it open with his switchblade. "*Coño*."

"*Coño*, what *coño*?" Vinny said.

"*Coño*, it's brown. That's some Mexican mud."

"What," Whispers said, "heroin? It's heroin? Like, pure heroin?"

"Shit, I don't know my heroin by percentages, man, but this—this is a fuck-ton of *dinero* right here. My guess is that we got three-and-a-quarter million of it in our duffel bag. Plus whatever our little friend's worth."

"What friend?"

Blaze laughed. "Oh, just a seven-foot-long alligator. No biggie."

"The fuck?"

Whispers' reactions had all been the same as Vinny's, except now that the adrenaline was slowing down—though only by about half—Vinny could appreciate the humor in the sheer bizarreness of it.

"Is that really the going rate for heroin?" Vinny asked Blaze.

"*Sí, hermano*. When you know the going rates of guns, you also end up knowing more than a lot about the other big-ticket cargo. I don't know if it's been cut, but let's assume not yet. So that's the wholesale price, not the market price, so don't let the Wrists lowball the total below thirteen million. Whoever is selling is about to make a killing. And we should be making a lot more than a hundred grand for our troubles, get me?"

"Yeah. More like that should be the minimum rate for each of us."

"Think we could get a mill?" Blaze asked. "Two hundred G's a pop, that's a pretty fucking wicked-sweet Keystone going-away present."

Whispers laughed, and then after a moment, he shook his head. "The person on the receiving end of that shipment is about to go off the rails."

"Goddammit," Blaze said all of a sudden, "that trucker is a dead man."

Vinny knew he was probably right. "He got in the wrong business, then," Vinny said. "We all know what we're getting into."

"What if he didn't know?" Blaze said.

"We didn't know either," Vinny said. "And that's what makes me very, very angry. We never do another job without knowing the score."

"Abso-fucking-lutely," Whispers said. "Tell that to your buddy Tommy."

"He knows," Vinny said. Tommy had better know, he thought. He reflected with sadness on being a new kid in the suburbs and Tommy showing him the ropes. Another lifetime ago, Vinny thought. They were two different people now.

∞

It was nearing 3 a.m. when Whispers pulled into Nicky's warehouse yard, though everything looked closed up for the night. Whispers hung back while Vinny and Blaze put on baseball caps and pulled their hoodies over, careful to keep their faces out of any streetlights and far away from cameras, which they regularly scouted. Whispers leaned over the back seat and looked into the bed of the cab for the alligator.

"For real, though," he said.

"These are some crazy fuckers," Vinny said.

"Serious fuckers," Whispers replied. "You sure you're ready to go in there?"

Vinny sighed. If the Keystone portion of the crew was already feeling like Tommy was lightweight, he could only imagine what Nicky Wrists thought of Tommy, even with Blaze standing next to him. Blaze adjusted his gun in his waistband. He'd strapped another two to his back before they'd gotten to the warehouse. Vinny felt the cold metal warm in his own waistband.

He wasn't one to be afraid, but right now, at the start of his new life, he didn't have a death wish. He was going to make it clear to Nicky that they weren't disposable.

Tommy radioed that they were five minutes out, so Blaze and Vinny waited for him to arrive before heading in. Blaze and Tommy would go in as usual, but Vinny would hang back with the smack in the duffel bag.

"You mean I gotta carry the fucking gator?" Blaze said.

"It's like a really big football," Vinny said.

"*Fútbol Americano es estúpido. El fútbol es un deporte puro.*"

"Soccer's stupid," Vinny said back.

The sedan pulled up near Whispers' truck. As soon as Tommy got out, Joe drove away, heading a few blocks over to wait for the signal to head back to Chencho's or come in for backup.

Vinny looked at his watch. They were going to be pushing it for time. If they weren't all tucked in by five, they'd all be fucked.

Blaze banged on the side door, and Vinny worried that they were about to be fucked anyway. He hadn't been inside the warehouse since that first time, when he was fifteen. On the other side of the door, a lock unlatched and the door opened. A cinnamon-roll-faced man sweating in a polo shirt sneered at Tommy and Blaze, then gave Vinny a once-over before letting the three of them inside.

"So Nicky," Tommy said, "we got your order from McDonald's. You're in luck, they extended the shamrock shake season."

Nicky Wrists looked exactly the way Vinny remembered, suited up like a dandy, though he was trying to look old school. He looked more like Sinatra's bank teller. Nicky Wrists had seemed like such a big, important, all-knowing man when Vinny was fifteen. Now? There was something worm-like about him.

"I see you brought a friend," Nicky said.

"So did I," Blaze said, holding up the alligator.

"What is that shit—I asked for the container," Nicky said, waving his hands at the wrists. "This is a duffel bag and a stuffed alley-gator."

"You knew full well that no one could get that container off the truck and back here," Tommy said.

"No one?" Nicky said, shrugging. "That's a bold statement."

"If you thought anyone else could have lifted a container of two hundred kilos of heroin, then you wouldn't have asked an eighteen-year-old to do it," Vinny said between his teeth. He took a couple of steps toward Nicky.

"Who the fuck are you?"

"You remember my partner, Vinny," Tommy said. "Got sent up? Turns out, he found a way that sent up doesn't mean locked away."

"Whoa, hey, Tommy's friend—you're an even bigger fucker than you were a few years ago."

Vinny stood straighter and stepped next to Blaze, hoping to screen in Nicky and form an imposing, immovable force. "Yeah," Vinny said, "and I went away for you and said nothing."

"And that, my boy, is an incredibly admirable trait. But remember, you didn't go away *for* me. That wasn't one of my jobs—I was a mere fence for that job. I'm pleased to see you kids are doing so well now."

"That's the thing," Vinny said. "We're not kids anymore.

"Well, sure, but you didn't do the job I asked."

"Well," Vinny said, "We did the job you needed. The container was being monitored. It had a beacon on it—would have led right back to you."

Nicky's eyes widened, and that's when Vinny knew he had him. Nicky could play at holding the upper hand, but now it was clear he didn't have all the pieces of intel, either.

"Ah, I see you didn't know that part. Well, it's a good fucking thing you had the right crew at work. See, we aren't sloppy. You get a sloppy crew, and the drool marks easily lead right back to you."

"All right," Nicky said, "point taken."

"I don't like what you done," Vinny said. "It was a lousy job that could have gotten us all killed or permanently locked away. Sounds an awful lot like you took a shot at a big job that you didn't think you could pull off and were okay with letting us be your fucking guinea pigs. Do we look like guinea pigs to you?"

"Come on, Vin, it's not like that," Nicky Wrists said. "And look, you pulled it off like total pros. You *are* total pros."

"Also," Vinny continued, "now you know we know what was inside that container. Couldn't take it all—no one could have taken it all, not without marking yourself out to some pretty powerful enemies. But you have about three and a half million, between this bag and this alligator." Vinny rounded up. "That's more than nothing, and it's better than getting your hands on all of it for about ten minutes before the Feds rolled up. Tommy, what was Nicky's quote on the job?"

"A hundred."

"A hundred. Well, it seems to me our take is worth well more than a hundred. I'd argue about ten times that." He didn't dare break eye contact with Nicky, but he felt Blaze stand up straighter next to him.

"Don't start with me, Vinny. You could walk out of here with nothing or with a bullet in your back. But I'm a nice guy. I wouldn't want to do that."

"I wouldn't be too sure that plan would go according to your best interests," Blaze said, pulling a Glock out of his waistband. Then, the dimples flashed. "But I'm sure we don't need to go down that road at all, right, Vin?"

Vinny nodded. "I would argue it would be unwise to underestimate a crew of far more than you see here, who are highly equipped with instruments to ensure our ongoing well-being, and we may just have a pipeline to the governor. Crazy, I know. Who'd of thought a bunch of amateur punks like us. Unless…" and Vinny took another very small step closer to Nicky, "we aren't just a bunch of amateur punks."

"You're smart, boys. I see it, you're smart. You got a chip on your shoulder, but that isn't my concern. Look, I think we got off on the wrong foot," he waved his hands at the wrists, "so let's take a step back and have a reasonable, relaxed discussion."

"That sounds perfect to me, Nicky. How about you, Tommy? Blaze? See, Nicky, sounds good to us."

"All right, then. So you have what for me."

"Forty-five kilos of Mexican heroin," Vinny said. "Almost a quarter of what was inside. A quarter is not a bad take."

"A quarter is not the whole thing," Nicky said.

"A quarter is a quarter more than you'd get from anyone else. A quarter is going to make you an even richer man, and it'll go a long way to sponsoring some fine young men not bound for the college trade. You have about what, three and a half—Blaze?"

"Three and a half," Blaze said.

"Three and a half million there," Vinny said. For a quarter of the total, you only have to part with, say, one quarter of the take. You ensure our well-being, and we can ensure continued success on your end."

Nicky sat for a moment, then looked at the man with a cinnamon roll for a face, wrapped with more folds than a pug. After about three minutes, Nicky said to the breakfast-shaped guy, "Bring down what Mr. Bruno has asked for." He looked back at Vinny, Blaze, and then Tommy.

"Eight seventy-five," Vinny said to the cinnamon roll.

"This is a thank-you. Don't get too big for your britches, though. You don't want to make any enemies on the outside, just when you're taking flight. It would be a shame to deny the world such talents."

"I always appreciate your words of wisdom, Mr. Wrists," Vinny said.

"Nicky," Tommy said, as the bag of money came down the steps with Nicky's right-hand Danish, "always a pleasure doing business with you."

"Just do me a favor and don't spend it all in one place," Nicky said. "I don't trust people who go through that much money like it's spaghetti. They have a tendency to get desperate. Desperate guys make enemies. Desperate guys get sloppy. Remember that."

"Again," Vinny said, "excellent advice." He turned and walked out, while Blaze set down the alligator, patting its head, and Tommy followed the two of them back outside. Vinny felt his chest relax and realized then that he'd been breathing shallow. He made eye contact with Whispers and nodded. Whispers held the walkie-talkie to his mouth, calling to Joe, and then Blaze got in Whispers' truck.

"I'm going to ride with Tommy," Vinny said, though it hadn't been the plan.

"Wait, what? Nah, I don't like it," Blaze said.

"What do you think, we're going to skip town with this? And go where without passports? You can follow us, I just want to have a little chat."

"Man, they cool," Whispers said.

"So Tommy doesn't have to be alone," Vinny said. "That's it. Gonna chat."

Blaze nodded—Vinny had assured them he'd keep Tommy in line, and they knew that was what Vinny was landing on.

They got in their cars and drove back to the highway, taking back routes but not doubling back as much as they might normally do, considering the time frame to get back into Keystone. They weren't going to have much time for celebrating.

"Whew!" Tommy whistled. "Eight hundred seventy-five thousand fucking dollars! Man, Vinny, that was a hell of a job. You and me, we're unstoppable."

"Tommy," Vinny said, his mood darkening. "It's not just you and me. It's the crew. You gotta remember that."

"Yeah, but, come on, it's always been the two of us."

"It was. And Tommy, you're still my bro. There's nobody closer. But these guys too, they're also my bros. And they're your bros."

"Nah. They don't like me," Tommy said.

"They don't fully trust you—but that's only the inside-outside hesitating. Come on, you know us guys inside get paranoid. But look, this was, and I have to tell you, a bad job. It was risky. And that wasn't all on you, but you also gotta know you're taking heat for that."

"I couldn't turn it down," Tommy said.

"Maybe. But we definitely couldn't turn it back over to him once you'd accepted it on our behalf. You know, you taught me plenty back when, but now, you know, and I know you're smart, but we can't just be smart with what we're doing. We gotta outsmart everyone else."

Tommy's jaw was clenched, and Vinny could tell Tommy was holding something back.

"Look, I'm not here to chew you out. We're cool, we're all cool. They trust you because I trust you, but we all have to be blood brothers on this one. And we can only do this because of the five of us. I know you didn't get a pick of the crew, but you joined the crew. And we couldn't have done none of this without you, that's the straight-up truth."

Tommy shifted in his seat. Vinny put his hand on Tommy's shoulder. "You my bro," he said. "That's forever."

Tommy looked at Vinny and smiled. "It might have been a shit job, but it was a shit job that made us fucking immortal."

"Immortal," Vinny said, smiling. "Fucking infinite."

"Nobody else could have pulled it off with the same circumstances."

"Hell, no."

They both let out their own wolf howl into the darkness of the car, all while Vinny clutched almost a million dollars in cash on his lap. The road to Chencho's felt smoother that night, as if the road was pulling them on, taking away any other obstacles for them.

There are pivotal moments in in life that clearly mark a "before" and an "after," moments that transform a person so clearly that they can no longer call themselves the same person afterward. Vinny had already had five of those moments in his life so far: his grandfather making him kill the hen, Angela's death, his dad handing him that eighteen-inch commemorative baseball bat, getting pinched, then that first night with his new crew—and friends—at Chencho's house. This night, though, would mark a sixth and pivotal change in the person who was Vinny Bruno. He had pushed himself harder than he'd ever been pushed in planning around an impossible—and probably stupid—job. Still, he made it. He'd confronted the only person who'd ever intimidated him—because Vinny assumed his power was infinite. But those had been the fears and assumptions of a boy. Vinny was beyond being afraid. He'd been tested and had passed the test. He was damn near a demigod, ready to overthrow Titans with his bare hands. Tommy was right. Demigods were immortal. Vinny Bruno was determined to live forever.

Chapter 10
The Big House
1990

Whispers had been the one to pick up Vinny at Keystone two and a half months later. Up until then, he'd been crashing with a couple of friends from the chop shop. They'd stopped off for lunch at Chencho's, savoring the freedom of daylight. Chencho told them both that they were more than welcome to stay at his place for a couple of days, but Vinny was ready to start on the rest of his life. They'd be back when it was time to get Blaze out, and then they'd drive Blaze to his mother's place.

Vinny and Whispers set up shop temporarily in a three-bedroom apartment in Medford, Mass., while they made plans for a more permanent future. Tommy came over every evening, and, though Whispers wasn't overly chatty, he seemed, at least to Vinny, easier in Tommy's company.

Tommy was still living with his parents and working at his father's boxing company. He'd worked part-time through his graduation, and since the summer, he'd been working full-time and saving his money in an account. "It's backup," he said, "so my folks'll think I'm living off that money." It took Tommy a few weeks to confide that his parents didn't want him hanging around Vinny and, in fact, didn't know that they were still in contact. "You know how it is—they came down hard on me back then. But in a few months, I'll move out and in with you, and they won't be able to say a thing about it."

Ever straddling the divide between schoolboy and criminal, Vinny thought. He feared it would always be Tommy's dilemma. His weakness.

Tommy's level of experience eclipsed Vinny's in other ways, most importantly, in that he'd had a girlfriend for the past seven months.

"I can't believe you didn't tell me, bro," Vinny said.

"I didn't want you to feel bad, you know, that I was dating someone while you were stuck in sausage buffet. But Carla's great—you'll really like her."

"Carla," Vinny thought, "was she in our science class?" He remembered a tiny brunette, feisty as hell.

"That's the one," Tommy said.

"Well, congratulations, I guess," Vinny said, not entirely sure what was protocol for learning your best friend had a secret girlfriend. Well, secret from Vinny. She'd cheered him on all through the baseball playoffs, and then they went to the prom together, so everyone else in Tommy's universe knew about him and Carla.

"So, Whispers, I gotta ask you," Vinny said, one night when the two of them were alone, playing *Altered Beast* on their Sega Genesis on their 42-inch television. "You ever been with a girl?"

Whispers smiled. "A few times, when I was fourteen. Right before I got this," and he pointed to his scar. "Been a long time."

Vinny nodded, continuing kicking one of Neff's minions with his werewolf. Then he said, "But, it's like getting back up on a horse again, even after it's been a while."

"No, you don't forget how."

"Mm-hmm." Vinny's werewolf got to Athena. "And say, for instance, your first time, that's automatic."

Whispers smiled again, and, to Vinny's relief, all he said was, "Yeah, except lasting."

The next day, Vinny found a VHS porn film set out on the TV stand. He'd seen sex in regular movies, and he and Tommy had looked at their share of girlie magazines, but the detail and angling of the VHS was like learning a whole new set of anatomy. It also reinforced how much he needed to get a girl.

He thought again of Blaze's sister Reina, of how beautiful she was and how sophisticated she seemed. Though he was mostly focused on working out the next phase of his career with the guys, there was plenty of room to think about Reina. He thought about whether she'd been with someone before, and what kind of guy she'd go with. She had to have experience, though Vinny was not about to ask Blaze about her. Maybe not right now, but one day, there was going to be a time when he would see her again, and he would win her over—and Blaze would come to accept it. In the meantime, he would do like he'd done his whole life: educate himself and acquire as much experience and knowledge as possible in preparation for the future.

Vinny wasn't going to waste a minute of his time in this new life. This was the first time he didn't have to answer to anybody. He and Whispers both had to check in with a continuing education counselor, making sure they had jobs and housing and weren't sliding back into old habits. They played their roles as perfectly as choirboys. The Keystone counselors helped Vinny get a job sorting mail for a banking firm, and Whispers was set up in a mechanic's shop. They went through the motions of returning to civil society, though Whispers was set on their security company, rewarding the clients who bought their services and helping the general public along the way decide their services were necessary. Vinny had to admit it was a good idea, but they needed everybody on board, especially Joe, despite the fancy computer job waiting for him. The conversation would need to be had in a couple of months. What Vinny really needed was the security of his friends, the guys who had become his only family over the last two years. Living with Whispers was great, especially with Tommy coming around. He liked showering without having to wear flip-flops and having to take everything with him. He liked wasting toothpaste. He liked buying whatever food he felt like eating on a given day, and he bought so much food to experiment on new ways to cook. He had no idea what he was doing, but he didn't care. Sometimes, he'd drive alone to Vincenzo's in Chelmsford, or take the guys out to Florence's in the North End and chat up Florence, the proprietor. Still, the nights felt too quiet. The two of them sometimes stopped where they were and stared at each other, waiting for someone else to come in to make something happen.

"It's weird, right?" Vinny said.

"Yeah, a little."

"Man, I could use a beer, though."

Because of Vinny's size, he quickly learned he could show up to at least three different packies and pick up a case of Heineken without getting carded, which was a good thing, since he didn't have his ID yet. He and Whispers both had to go through the process of getting driver's licenses, returning to society, and setting up their primary bank accounts—completely separate from the ones Joe arranged for them. The thought of that money burned against Vinny's insides like a nuclear rod in a reactor, but he was determined not to touch it yet.

Vinny spent time driving the city by daylight. There was so much he had missed when he was fifteen, and the last two years, he'd only seen it in the dark. He spent a lot of his free time reconnoitering Nicky Wrists' warehouse, watching the comings and goings, making note of license plates and names on trucks, and then following them to other warehouses or rail yards. A few cars even went straight from Nicky's to a big colonial in Newton. Vinny kept his distance, making sure he didn't look like competition or the Feds, and it only took three trips before he recognized a face from the newspapers. He was a well-known member of one of the two top crime families in Boston. Vinny kicked himself for not posting Tommy on duty to see where the heroin and alligators were going, but that was at the height of the tension with Tommy believing he was stuck doing all the grunt work.

There certainly were increasing tensions between the two main crime families the last month, and the carnage made daily headlines. This was exactly the kind of interaction Vinny was determined to avoid. This sort of life, always looking over his shoulder, not knowing who could be trusted, sounded like his worst nightmare. Trust and security—everything that Vinny had been deprived of in his young life—were what he wanted now. That, and a shitload of money, too.

There was no reason he couldn't have a house like this one, maybe not that style, but certainly with five, six, seven bedrooms. A big yard, big pool, anything he ever wanted. That was all within reach.

One thing that he was figuring out, though, was that if there were two families engaged in a war against each other, they'd be too busy with each other to notice a smaller outfit setting up shop, even snagging some business while they weren't paying attention. He'd keep a close eye on Nicky's place, see if things ramped up or slowed down.

By the time Blaze was released, Vinny was restless, itching to get back into the swing of real work, real plans, not making eight dollars an hour sorting and filing paperwork and delivering mail. He and Whispers and Tommy drove back to Keystone and waved to Joe as Blaze came out. They'd all spoken by phone a few times, always using the future tense. Blaze hugged everybody, and Vinny felt almost a shred of nostalgia as they walked across the lawn they'd sprinted across hundreds of times under the cloak of darkness. Chencho had a tray of food waiting at the house, which they immediately tore into, even though they would all be driving to Blaze's mom's house for a party that evening.

As they got closer to Blaze's house, Vinny's heart beat faster. Blaze mentioned Reina's name in passing a couple of times, and it was clear that she was going to be at the party. He barely registered what anyone was saying at this point. And he was even more intimidated when they pulled up to a house full of people, so many that they were spilling out of the doors, out of the open garage, the open gates of the backyard, and onto the driveway.

"Are all those people your family?" Vinny asked.

"Nah, not all. Some are neighbors, and some are friends we've known for, like, my whole life. All the parents came from the Island together and worked their way out of the projects."

You'd never be lonely in a family like that, Vinny thought. Somewhere, in all of that crowd, there would be Reina.

Vinny would have to wait, or rather, to first wade through the introductions of everyone outside. Finally, his mother made her way to the door, crying that her son was finally home, saying he was even more handsome than the last time she'd seen him but that he looked too thin. Behind her was Reina, her hair down, dressed in a black collared shirt and fitted black pants. Her face was pale, but her eyes were lined like a cat's. Her lips were blood red. If she asked, Vinny would let her eat his heart right out of his chest.

"Vinny, Tommy, Whispers, you remember my family—Mama, Luisa, and my sister Reina."

"Reina, hi."

"Vinny—I remember you." Reina gave Blaze a quick look.

"So how is life? How are you keeping yourself busy in New York? You're still in New York, right?"

"Still in New York," Reina said. "You have a good memory. "I'm at my last year at The New School and intern at an art gallery in Manhattan."

"Oh, like for famous artists? Alive or dead? Basquiat? Warhol?" He threw out the only names that came to him, and he hoped it would impress her.

"No, none that big. All contemporary artists, though some are up and coming. Maybe a future Basquiat."

"Ha," Vinny said, though he wished he had said something better. More dashing or sophisticated. "When do you go back to New York?"

"Tomorrow morning. I have work."

"Ah, right."

Her dark eyes sparkled. They hadn't been talking long, but it was long enough for Blaze and Whispers and Tommy to have been pulled into the crowd. Tommy was being served a plate of food.

"Maybe we should get you something to eat," Reina said.

"Oh, that's okay. Chencho already made me some fried rice."

"We have lots more than that."

"Yeah, but I'm a vegetarian."

Reina paused. "And Chencho knows you're a vegetarian?"

Shit, Vinny thought. "Blaze told him. He knew what I hard time I'd been having with the food, so he asked your uncle to make some for me."

"Oh," she said, letting the vowel trail on a little too long. Vinny was ready to kick himself. He couldn't get sloppy, though damn, Reina caught him off his guard. No one had ever done that to Vinny.

"Well, Vinny, if you get hungry, I'm sure there is something here without meat in it. There may not be a lot, but you'll find something. Talk to you later." She turned to head to the kitchen, and Vinny called her back, unsure of what he wanted to say, but he didn't want to leave their conversation off at such a bland ending.

"What's the name of your gallery?"

"Why, you going to come up and visit me sometime?"

"Maybe."

"You an art fan?"

"Me? I love art. I'm a fan of anything."

"You know a lot about art?"

"I love learning about art. You could teach me."

Reina smiled. "Rex Wurther Gallery. See you there sometime, Vinny."

With that, she disappeared into the crowd. Vinny was bumped on all sides by people, and he instinctively balled up his fist, but there were three women Blaze's mother's age all shuffling around with plates of food and bottles of beer. Everyone was in a great mood, and another man in his sixties came and handed Vinny a beer. "*Bebida,*" he commanded. Someone was playing guitar and a group sang along. It was the first party-party Vinny Bruno had attended in his life. And it was a blast.

∞

Joe's parents drove him home when his turn was up, and Vinny was worried when they didn't hear from him for a couple of days, but then he called, saying his mother had been hovering over his every move until then. He wasn't going to be ready to move out for a few months, he said, because he was going to try to build up his parents' trust and spend quality time with them. After a couple of weeks, Joe invited everyone over to his house near MIT for a barbecue to meet his family and to reconnect. Tommy picked up everyone, and, as soon as they pulled up to the address Joe had given, Vinny immediately saw why he was in no rush to leave, especially after a few years at Keystone.

"Jesus, this is quite the pad," Whispers whispered.

"You ain't kidding," Vinny said.

It was the kind of house Vinny and Tommy wouldn't have bothered to rob because of its size and state-of-the-art security system. It was almost as big as the mobster's house that Vinny had staked out, though it had a much more modern style, and Vinny found he preferred these clean lines to the colonial home.

Joe was wearing a turtleneck, of all things, and Blaze couldn't hold it in anymore. "Bro, *coño*, come *on*." He pulled down the neck of the sweater to reveal the Mexican flag tattoo. "*A tu mamá no le gusta?*"

"Guys, come on."

"You bougie as shit."

"I will fuck you up," Joe said, but they all knew he didn't mean it. "Anyway, my mom said to bring you into the backyard for refreshments as soon as you got here."

Refreshments. Like they were all MIT students here for a jolly evening with the dean. Vinny was ready to piss himself for all the laughter he had to stifle.

"Boys, young men, come here, come here," Joe's mother said, a small and dark woman with a green Ralph Lauren sweater. Boston Celtics green. "How nice to see all of you, finally!" She took turns shaking each of their hands, gripping their right hand with both of hers. "Call me Teresa."

Teresa, it turned out, was a psychologist and used to have a private practice catering to corporate clients. She now taught at Harvard. "This is surreal," Vinny whispered to Whispers.

It took all of ten minutes for Vinny to figure out that Joe sure as shit wasn't adopted. He hadn't gotten a good look at the parents on visiting day, but no, he was one hundred percent Mexican, raised by Mexican parents who were from straight up Mexico City elite. Joe's dad was grilling chicken and *nopales*, as everything they had in their house was a hybrid of Mexican culture and Boston country club. "Vincent, please," Joe's father said, "call me Carlos. I have cactus for everyone, but we also have a whole tray of roasted vegetables and corn for you. What do you normally eat?"

"Honestly, Carlos, I'm still trying to figure that out. I'm used to beans and pasta, and I'm just now discovering all the things I can do with veggies. I spent six months eating cottage cheese twice a day."

"I'll bet. Listen, one of my colleagues is also vegetarian, and she leads meetings at the Boston Vegetarian Society. A lot of good ideas for any budget, but if you're looking for people who understand what it's like to try to find good food around town, I'd be happy to give you her contact information, but only if you really want it. You'll have to ask for it. I'm not one of those people who placates and gives unwanted advice."

"Sir. Yes, sir, please, I'd like that very much," Vinny said. Joe's hesitation over moving out was making even more sense—it was hard to say no to his parents.

"Great. I'll give that to you before you leave. Now you will call her, yes? Because I will tell her to expect your call. It's very important for you to follow through with obligations, Vincent."

"Absolutely, sir."

He had to hand it to the guy, framing an interrogation in a way that seemed harmless, but checking to make sure if Vinny was accountable. It was a test, but a well-meaning one.

"You check in with Teresa. We have some wonderful *aguas frescas* that are homemade, and you won't find any better."

Vinny did as he was told and picked out a cucumber-kiwi drink. It was indeed *fresca* and one of the best drinks he'd had in a long time. He imagined it would go great with rum.

Teresa the psychologist was in the middle of a friendly chat with all the other guys, although Joe looked like he was ready to turtle up into that turtleneck, and everyone, including Blaze, looked like they were sitting at Saint Peter's gates, waiting for a final decision. "Oh, Vincent, just in time," Teresa said. She looked ready to dole out cookies to small children. "I was just finding out a little bit about your friends."

Blaze looked at Vinny as if he'd washed overboard in a typhoon. He'd only been talking to Carlos for maybe five minutes—what had been going on? Had they all walked into some kind of trap?

"Blaze, I appreciate your honesty. It's not easy when you look up to a man who can be really good but who also enjoys the thrill of danger. Remember, we are not fated to become those who begot us."

"Yes, ma'am," Blaze said.

"*Que es* ma'am? *Llamame* Teresa."

"*Sí, señora.*"

Damn, Blaze couldn't even bust out the dimples with this woman.

"Tell me, Vincent, you're a big guy who probably gets seen as the tough guy. When was the first time you felt lost?"

"Geez, I don't know," he said. Who was this lady? But Teresa had a stare that could light your soul on fire. "Probably when my sister died?" It flew out of his mouth.

"Shit, Vin—*lo siento, señora, pero* Vinny, I didn't know you had a sister who died."

Three years and innumerable group counseling sessions at Keystone, and he'd avoided the topic so successfully that he'd only talked about Angela with Whispers one time.

"She died when I was a kid."

"Were you close?"

If she wanted directness, he was going to take control of this and lay it all out. "Teresa, she was the only goddamn person I had been close to as a kid, up until I met these guys here."

"Ah, and your father probably couldn't handle it." Teresa nodded, her hands folded on her lap. "Tommy, your glass is low, go get a refill and bring the pitcher back for Tracy."

Whispers shook his head. "*Teresa, por favor, llamame* Whispers."

"Good point," Teresa said. "Tracy is a good name, though, and what happened to you doesn't have to be who you are, not if you don't want it to be."

"With all due respect, Teresa," Whispers said, trying to speak as clearly as Vinny ever heard him, "this—" he pointed to the scar on his throat—"is a part of me and is exactly who I am. I'm not ashamed. I certainly can't hide this voice."

Teresa smiled, not missing a beat. "Then I like 'Whispers,'" she said, definitively. Vinny was almost hoping he'd gotten off the hook with the digression, but Teresa was a pro. "Now Vincent—or Vinny? Vinny, your father. You don't think much of him, do you?"

"His only goal was to get me to become a starter for the Patriots so he could live vicariously through me. Half the time, he didn't notice he had a daughter, and he didn't give a shit that we cared more about books and comics or that we were vegetarian."

"Ah," Teresa said, leaning forward, "your sister was the vegetarian?"

"She got me to stop eating meat, yes. It was a pact."

She reached out her hand for Vinny's. It was an odd intimacy that from anyone else would have felt artificial or cloying. "Vinny—the way you talk, whatever you've kept in, one thing I know for sure is a devoted and protective sibling. That's who you are and what you have. And I promise you, you still have love to give to people."

What the fuck. He was expecting her to say some bullshit like he didn't need to be a criminal or whatever. This wasn't patronizing. She was looking into each of them, and sure, telling them their lives, which none of them wanted, and yet, here they were, as if cleansed, somehow. She didn't really have that kind of power, though. Did she?

He recognized that this was an ample situation for the other guys to start teasing the shit out of him, but everyone was sober as a funeral. There would be no teasing in this house. Whatever humor Joe had, it sprung from his own personality and was not fostered by Carlos and Teresa.

After asking Tommy about being without his best friend for so long, Teresa told him that he would have to learn not to be the perfect one all the time, or he would start carrying resentment. Suddenly, Vinny was taking notes and was sorry he'd missed what she'd said to Blaze.

"Oh, but look, Carlos is ready with the dinner. Shall we eat out here where it's still so nice?"

As Teresa stood up, every single one of the guys stood and asked if there was anything they could do to help.

"Such good young men! You are guests in this house tonight, so we will take care of everything for you. And for José. It's good for him to be around his friends again."

Vinny looked at Joe. José?

Vinny loved the dinner, though he and the others were more in silent reflection mode after Teresa did her number on them all. He loved the house, the outside area, the smell of the barbecue, and he was already fantasizing about the kind of house he wanted.

As soon as Teresa cleared the plates, Carlos came in for his blitz. "So José tells me that you have a business proposition."

"We do?" Tommy asked. He looked at Vinny, but Vinny shrugged. Tommy wasn't left out of the loop any more than the rest of them were.

"You all seem like focused guys who maybe didn't get the best deal. Look, we aren't always like this—"

"You kind of are," Joe said, though he kept his voice low.

"My son says you're interested in opening a business together. Now, I imagine you lack the connections and the capital necessary, and perhaps a group of eighteen-year-olds leading a security company will come across to many people as suspect. I think I may be of assistance, if you are interested. José trusts you all, and we're encouraging him to take on adult responsibilities. If he vouches for you all, and, after meeting you, Teresa and I will vouch for you as well, the proposition is this: Our community association has a security company, but it is mostly retired cops who are too old to do much but fall asleep in their cars. I'm on the board of the community association. If you gentlemen don't mind paying some dues and working your way up, taking on a gig such as this could be a stepping stone in the direction of a future business. One that I would be happy to help you invest in."

"Carlos, that's very thoughtful of you," Vinny said, immediately thinking of how inconvenient it would be to have a new or possibly overnight schedule.

"Before you say 'but,' this can be open to any or all of you. You'd have training and certification and could learn about how the company is run. There's a need that we have, and it would make us happy if it helped you."

Realistically, Vinny couldn't hope for a better setup. He technically had to have a job for now, and he was always up for an opportunity to learn more about the trade. "I can't speak for anyone else—I know Tommy works for his dad, but—"

"I'm in," Tommy said.

"Really?"

"I'm ready to be out from under my folks," he said.

Blaze shrugged. "Works for me."

"Okay, but Whispers? You wanted this the most, but you also have a good mechanic job."

"Hey, I can sleep when I'm dead," Whispers said. "I can swing a couple shifts at the garage on the off hours."

"So what, do we answer to some company here or to you?"

Carlos explained that the community had its own local security force, so the board could hire them directly. "Great. Well, why don't you all discuss? José, you can take them up to your room for a bit, then let us know when you're ready for dessert. We made cheesecake. Fruit for Vinny."

Joe didn't say anything until they got to his room, which was more like his own wing of the house. Though he wasn't allowed to have a modem until he turned twenty-one, he said that technically, the ones in his room were owned by his father. "I pretty much have all the tech I want here. Everything we can use."

"So, do you have, like, a curfew?" Tommy asked him.

"Dude, come on, no."

They sat on futons and beanbags scattered near the computers. "I used to have gaming parties here," Joe said, offering an explanation for all the seating.

"What the hell went down these last few days?" Blaze asked.

"Look, you saw how they are."

Whispers started laughing. "Man, you are like the poster boy for code switching. That, or you got that multiple personality thing."

"Shut the fuck up," but Joe was laughing a little. "It's actually a good opportunity. Look, I was considering joining you guys instead of doing the IT job, and my dad started asking all these pointed questions. He said that though I could get plenty handed to me on a plate because of him, not everyone was going to just hand out prime businesses to guys our age without degrees and who'd finished high school remotely. And he's right."

"Yeah," Vinny said. "He is."

"And we have to make it look like we're earning money," Blaze said. "No way my moms is going to trust me if she doesn't see me with a nine-to-five."

"But what about, you know, the other stuff?" Tommy asked.

"Still on the table," Vinny said. "I've been following leads all this time. We get a couple good scores a month, there's no reason we can't do other stuff in the meantime."

"But like, we don't need to work that hard," Blaze said. "All our *money*."

Vinny rubbed his face. He was torn between being ready to be semi-retired and not wanting to get slow or sloppy. "We're going to be smart about it. What, we won't be the sole security guards, will we?"

"No," Joe said. "But it will look better if you can work full-time."

"And we get a couple nights off a month, all together, to run our jobs?"

"I'm sure we can."

"So, José," Blaze said, "you're going to be a Mr. Security Guard, too?"

"Sort of. I'm going to work the monitors. A few nights a week. I'm still starting the job at the tech company."

"Well, who knew not going straight would be so square?" Whispers whispered.

"That doesn't mean we don't have a little fun," Vinny said. "We have to actually live. And use a little bit of all that money."

∞

Within the month, Tommy moved in with Vinny and Whispers, especially since his father was ready to kick him out of the house when he said he was leaving the company to work as a security guard. Blaze and Joe were both going to stay home for six months, though they'd crash at the Medford apartment a couple nights a week, and sometimes they'd all spend the night at Joe's, either on his pull-out couch bed or in one of the guest rooms.

It occurred to Vinny that there could be other people in the community who had dealings with Nicky Wrists, or people like him, and sitting in front of their houses in a parked security car would give him license to snoop all he wanted. He was more than happy to say goodbye to the mailroom, and his Keystone continuation counselors signed off on the switch. Carlos probably called them and told them this was what was going to happen, and they couldn't refuse him.

Life as a security guard in a high-income community was far less consuming than he imagined it would be. It turned out that big guys in patrol cars were a solid deterrent to…guys like Vinny. All they had to do was drive around in a couple of cars in five-hour shifts, occasionally parking along streets for an hour at a time. If residents were gone, they'd put in a request for extra patrol. Most people who were sneaking around the neighborhood were just looking for a place to have sex in their car or smoke pot. They'd drive off when they saw Vinny, but otherwise, he wasn't going to harass kids who needed a dark, private spot to themselves. Not unless there were calls from watchful residents who could "smell something funny going on."

In all, it was a great time for Vinny. He tried to put the bank account out of his mind, but every time he deposited a paycheck into his "public" account, he thought of the secret one. Joe reminded them, too, giving updates on interest rates. "Guys," he said one day, "this last week, we made a thousand bucks just on interest."

All right, Vinny was patient, but he wasn't going to just hang out forever. There were bigger plans in store.

Chapter 11
Boys of (Late) Summer

Her name was Michelle. She was friends with Carla, Tommy's girlfriend, and she'd come to the party at Blaze's mother's house. Vinny had hoped that Reina would be there, but when he'd asked Blaze casually if all his family would be there, he said that Chencho was coming over, so Vinny had to wait for Reina's name to come up in conversation. Finally, Blaze said, "We gotta hit up New York, have my sis show us around," he said.

Vinny perked up. "Is she going to be at the party? Maybe we can ask her then."

"Nah, she's got some test or study group or some whatever."

Vinny tried to hide his disappointment. "Sucks for her—but better her than us, right?"

"Better her than us what?" Blaze asked.

"Having tests and shit."

"Ha, right on, bro."

So Vinny's expectations were low when Tommy and Carla picked him up, until Vinny saw Michelle in the backseat. She was cute. Tall, almost six feet, more the sporty type, and she was getting ready to move to Illinois for college on a soccer scholarship. They chatted and she was nice, and after a few drinks at the party, she said, "Look, Vinny, I'm not looking for anything serious before I leave or anything, but I'd like to have some fun my last couple weeks, so if you want to hook up, I'm down."

They went straight to Blaze's bedroom and locked the door. Michelle knew what she was doing and led the way, though Vinny was a quick learner. Michelle also had been her team's captain, so she had no problem telling Vinny exactly what to do. Vinny was so caught up in the moment that he was afraid he wouldn't remember the details later, but as they emerged from the room thirty minutes later, Vinny recalled every second. His body tingled everywhere.

"Look at you, grinning like an idiot," Blaze said.

"I'm just a little buzzed from all the tequila," Vinny said, which made him burst out laughing.

Michelle came over to the apartment the next night and was there every day and every other night for the last week of September and the first week of October, before fall quarter started.

"If you ever find yourself headed out to the Midwest, make sure you let me know. You were an amazing student," she said, laughing, and then kissed Vinny goodbye.

They called a few times, and Vinny kept track of her team's wins and losses for the season, but already at Halloween, there was Amanda, who was at a party Vinny was supposed to break up in Joe's neighborhood.

"Look," Vinny said, "you have to keep it contained inside the house or the neighbors freak out," he told the homeowner's daughter.

"You're a little young to be on the neighborhood SS," the party's host said.

"I have no desire to shut you down. Or spy."

"Didn't answer my question," she said, not without a little flirtation. "Want to stay?"

Vinny smiled. "Ma'am, I can't do that. But I can come back after the party's over, if you need help checking around, making sure everyone's gone and all your property is protected."

He handed her the card with his number on it. Two hours later, he got the call from Amanda, who needed help looking for her shoes. "Someone might have taken off with them," she said.

Amanda never came to the apartment—Vinny only saw her when he was on duty. She was the kind of girl who took to Vinny as a dare, imagining she was slumming it with the security guard. She was from Joe's world and attended Boston College, though she didn't live on campus. Vinny definitely knew he was being used, but he was up for the reciprocal using, in addition to getting to see the inside of the giant house whenever her parents were away. Another fantasy Vinny had: buying the house directly across from Amanda's and hosting parties there. In some variations on this fantasy, Vinny wouldn't invite her over, but in others, she'd come over and watch the other girls around Vinny. He was not above being vindictive, especially in his daydreams.

Vinny did contact Carlos's colleague, who coordinated for the Boston Vegetarian Society in a church basement. A woman named Nataly invited Vinny to a meeting that Thursday evening, and it was much as he expected—intellectuals in cardigans and hippies in hemp clothing.

Nataly was somewhere in between—a physics professor with a mess of frizzy curls pulled into a ponytail and a long floral skirt and a cardigan sweater. And Birkenstocks. She shook Vinny's hand and said she was so glad he came. "Now, Carlos called you Vincent, but do you prefer Vinny?"

"Yes, but you can call me whatever."

"No, names are important. Vinny, then. And you can call me Nat. I know most of us are going to be old fogies for you, but you won't have to socialize more than you want."

Vinny was back in his quiet, observational mode, but that didn't stop plenty of people from chatting up the new guy. A half-hour lecture on factory farming led to an exchange of vegetarian and vegan recipes, as well as someone hoping to invest in a vegetarian grocery in town. The society also had brought plenty of food for the gathering. There were crackers made from seeds that Vinny could live without, but there was a stockpot of an Indian lentil dish that Vinny could have eaten until it was gone. He'd never had Indian food, so he tracked down the cook—an Indian woman who was an economics professor at MIT and married to a banker. So when they invited Vinny to a group dinner at a Thai restaurant the following week, Vinny didn't hesitate to accept another evening with the fogies. He left with three recipes and the name of the best brand of tofu. He hadn't known there was a difference before.

After a few months, Nat invited Vinny over for dinner, and that became a regular tradition. Her domestic partner, Harv, was twenty years older than she was and could barely hear a thing anymore, but he had been a jazz musician and still knew music. Vinny wouldn't have said that his weekly visits with Nat and Harv were replacement parents. He wouldn't have presumed to be that close to Nat, though he always felt better in her presence. She knew not to pry into his business but was an intent listener to anything Vinny had to say. At their second dinner, she'd asked him what opportunities he'd had in Keystone, if they were sufficient, and if he felt there was anything lacking in his education, and if so, she'd be happy to steer him into the right direction. He couldn't think of anything offhand—"Reading's always been my thing anyway, and I'll read pretty much whatever I can get my hands on," which gave Nat license to hand him a small pile of books every time he came over. Novels, histories, biographies, economics, living a plant-based life, reducing the carbon footprint, how every day of living a plant-based life saves one animal's life—Vinny absorbed it all, then exchanged notes with Nat the following week.

Being at Nat's house did provide a stark contrast to anything he'd had growing up, but it was easier with people who weren't relatives. There was no history, no guilt, just an easy relationship. He did feel accountable to Nat, and, in his own way, to Harv, who would play Coltrane and Monk records that he'd memorized. He had people who cared what he thought in a way that was different from his friends and his job. All this time spent at their house reminded Vinny of the one thing left behind at his parents' house. He hadn't forgotten about it, but he hadn't been ready to go back there for what he figured would be his very last time.

The chest buried under the house.

By now, the money in there was chump change, but there were still a few personal effects Vinny needed in his possession. So shortly before

Thanksgiving, on a day off work, he made the fifteen-minute trek to the neighborhood he hadn't seen in nearly four years, to the house he couldn't wait to never see again. His dad's car was in the driveway, and Vinny wondered if he was retired already, though that didn't seem likely to Vinny. Work was the only bright spot in his dad's day, and besides, his dad was only forty-eight.

A cop pulled up behind Vinny's car and got out. Shit, Vinny thought. He got ready to show his security guard's license, but otherwise couldn't think for the life of him why he was of interest now, of all times.

The cop tapped on Vinny's window, so he turned on the engine to roll it down. "Is there a problem, officer?"

"Huh. I was just wondering why a big thug-looking motherfucker like you would be sitting in his car on this street?"

"Sorry, sir, I'm a security guard, I have a license—"

"Don't tell me you forgot me, Vinny Bruno."

"What the fuck? How did you know my name, sir? My parents live here, and I am not bothering anyone, so stop harassing me."

"You going to talk to an officer of the law like that, Vinny Bruno, fresh out of the big house?"

"All right, what is this?" Vinny said, ready to get out of the car. His reflexes were taking hold and he wanted to smash that busted-up nose under those cheap aviators with the mirror lenses of this clown who knew him. He looked directly at the cop again and realized that the nose and glasses aged him, but otherwise, he was only a few years older than Vinny. Vinny recognized that nose. " Steve Fucking Davis," he said, nodding his head. "Well, I'll be. Typical, street hood becoming a cop. Seems just about right."

Steve Davis laughed. "All but one thing—that's Officer Davis to you, fucker."

Vinny got out of the car, and the two shook hands. "Shit, man, I thought you were going to try to bust my balls."

"I was, a little. You deserved it for turning my nose sideways with that fucking bat."

"Shouldn't go around stealing little kids' bikes, especially when they've just lost their sister."

"I know. And man, thanks for giving Angela's bike to my sister. I don't think I ever thanked you properly."

"I never said it was from me."

"Yeah, but I saw you roll it up to the driveway. I just didn't want to say anything."

It was all true. About six months after Steve Davis had stolen Vinny's bike and Vinny had reclaimed it with a knockout swing, he heard about Davis's dad dying by suicide, leaving his mom to raise him and his older sister with Down syndrome. Once the old man kicked, Vinny started seeing the sister more, and the word about the neighborhood was that Steve's dad had been ashamed of her, which made Vinny ashamed, especially when he figured out that Steve had been wanting to teach her how to ride a bike and their old man had broken his bike. Angela's small purple bike had been up in the rafters of the garage, one of the few things Vinny's parents hadn't trashed in the move for whatever reason, so he found the old training wheels, screwed them in, and took the bike to the Davis house. It was the one nice thing he did during those rough years.

"How is your sister?"

"Carrie's doing all right. She's in a group home with about ten other people, and honest to God, she has a boyfriend and it's driving me crazy. I call her, and she tells me she's too busy to talk."

It was hard not to think of Steve's sister and what she was up to without imagining what Angela would be up to, if things hadn't happened the way they did.

"So you back for a visit?" Steve asked.

"Me? Hell, no. I'm not even going inside. I do have something I need to pick up, though. Hey, how did you know this was my parents' place?" It wasn't like this was the house Vinny had lived in when he'd rearranged Steve's face.

"Yeah, I got on the Stoneham PD, and everybody knew about your story. And once I was on the force, we had to start kicking your pops

154 | Anthony Bucci

out of bars for getting drunk and starting fights. I've brought him home four times, now."

Vinny felt like he had been belted in the face. His dad? Getting drunk and getting into fights? "Do—do you know how my mom's been? He's not touching her, is he?"

"No—I'm pretty sure that's not the problem. I think he's getting it all out in these bar fights, though."

"Yeah, but psychologists often say it's just a matter of time before violent men become domestic abusers."

"Jesus, Bruno, psychologists no less?" Vinny nodded his head. That was a Keystone book, but then Nat had talked about it as well—one of the members of the vegetarian society had to leave her husband, who ate bacon at every meal.

"It's a known fact," Vinny said, the old rage at his father swelling up.

"I haven't heard anything—and it's a small neighborhood. People talk. But I'll keep an ear out, okay? If we hear about him doing anything to her, I'll take care of it."

"*I'll* take care of it," Vinny said.

"No, Bruno—I'd better do it. I got this, okay? You need to keep your nose clean."

Vinny shook his head, but then said okay. He didn't want to get sent up on account of *that* asshole, of all people. "Look," Vinny said, "I need to get into the back without them knowing I'm there."

"Digging up a body?"

"What?"

"I'm just joking with you, Bruno. Sure, what do you need?"

"The old man home?" Vinny asked, pointing to the car.

"No, he has a red Lincoln now, fairly dinged up, but it's only a couple of years old."

His dad in a red Lincoln? Had he stepped into some *Twilight Zone* version of his old neighborhood?

"Your mom has his old car now. Want me to go knock on the door, keep her distracted?"

That could work, although he was sure he could handle his mom.

Still, it would be good if she never knew he was there. "Tell her you're doing a welfare check and see how she reacts."

"Man, you're a cold motherfucker."

"No—those two are the cold motherfuckers," he said, thumbing toward the house. "I'm ready to be done with them."

"How much time you need?"

"Ten minutes?" He hoped that would be enough.

Vinny went around to the fence and waited for Davis to knock on the door to unlatch the gate. He heard his mom's voice through the door and Davis calling out, "Mrs. Bruno, it's Officer Davis here, just want to do a welfare check." His mom sounded confused, tired. He wouldn't lose time or sleep over why. He had to get under the house.

The crawlspace still had a latch—fortunately, that hadn't been boarded up. He'd dug out the hole in the back, but rather than filling it all in, he had covered it with a board and then put old lumber in front of it. That was easy enough to move aside, and he could do it quietly enough. There was a ton of dried raccoon and cat shit everywhere, and a fresher pile that stank. Soon, though, he uncovered the old footlocker. He dragged it back the length of the house, and when he got back into the yard, he listened for the voices—his mother was inside, and it sounded like Davis had gone into the house, as well. Perfect. He carried the footlocker back to his car, brushed off the dirt and animal shit, and once he was all set, he hit his horn twice. He might as well wait in his car to thank Davis. See if he had anything to say about his mom.

Davis was out the door in two minutes, thanking Mrs. Bruno, and then the door shut. He gave Vinny a salute and Vinny got back out of the car.

"All set?" Davis asked.

"All right. Now I owe you one."

"Hmm—maybe we're sort of square. A nose for a bike—"

"And now a distraction makes it 2 to 1."

"Yeah, but I started it with stealing your bike."

"Shit, who knew becoming a cop would make you less of an asshole?"

"Not much less," Davis said. "Hey, here's my home number. Give me a call sometime. You can buy me a beer, if nothing else. A beer for a distraction is definitely square."

"Sounds good, I'd like that, Davis."

"See ya later, Bruno. Stay out of handcuffs."

"They won't be catching me again."

"Let's hope not," Steve Davis said, getting into his car.

Vinny took the recovered locker to his real home and up to his room. He wasn't sure if he was ready to open it. No, now was as good a time as any, he figured. He needed to see her face again. It had been too long.

Other than cash, what he really wanted were the pictures of Angela he'd saved, the ones his parents didn't want to put up in the new house. He'd removed the few photos from old albums, anything that had Angela, and took those, too. They didn't want her, so he'd take all of her. Every single photo taken of Angela was now spread out in front of him. As were the stack of her favorite comics, and her stuffed clown, though he never knew why the fuck she'd liked clowns. The thing was creepy as fuck—but it was hers. Now, it was finally his. "Angela, you've been under the ground too long. You'll never go back there again."

Vinny would never have admitted it to anyone, but he took ten minutes in the privacy of his room in an empty apartment, and he wept for all that had been lost for the two of them. Afterward, he hung up her picture, then went out to get frames for the rest of the photos. As he drove home with the new frames, he felt a brand-new lightness. This was his life, now. Everything that had to do with that life at the house of Bruno misery was done. With that locker dug up and in his possession, it was as if a piece of his soul was restored to him.

∞

The crew were all annoyed that they would have to work through the holidays, but as a consolation, Vinny, Blaze, Whispers, and Tommy would get a break—together—the first week of December. It was a bone thrown to them, but they were going to make it count.

"It's the first time we can finally take a vacation together," Blaze said. "Man, this is going to be out of sight. Let's go to Puerto Rico."

"Let's consider all the options, first," Tommy said.

"Options, what, it's a fucking island in the Caribbean, we can go to a resort, it will be in the eighties, I got family that can show us around, and man, the girls. The fucking girls who will be there…" Blaze trailed off, a light in his eyes.

"It's not a bad idea," Whispers said. "I've never been on an island before."

"Have you ever been in the ocean before?" Vinny asked.

"Have you ever worn shorts before?" Tommy asked.

"Shit, man," Whispers said. "When I was ten—we all had to in phys ed."

"I don't know if I want to see your legs," Blaze said.

At first, Blaze showed them a picture of his town and talked about the people who would put them up, before Tommy said, "I'm sure that's great and all, but—we can afford the best hotel."

"But, so like," Blaze said, "a heads-up, my family is in the mountains. Kind of in the center. It's a small island, though, and the lakes are beautiful, and you can swim in a waterfall."

The complaint was over wanting to lie on beaches with lots of girls and swim in the ocean, so eventually, Blaze put in a call, and a cousin made plans to meet them in San Juan and ended up booking two extra hotel rooms for them. Vinny didn't care. He wanted to feel warm sand in his toes. Do that grounding thing he heard about. After being cooped up, he wanted to look out at the endless ocean.

They got so drunk on the plane, they would have crashed at the hotel and missed an entire day if it hadn't been for Blaze's cousins, who picked them all up at the airport in San Juan and brought them to the party-in-progress at their hotel rooms. They spoke in a whirl of Spanish, broken up by sentences of English in which Blaze's cousin Lui translated, but the topic was mostly about hooking up with girls. Word in Blaze's family's hometown got around that The Party was Going Off in San Juan, and Vinny sobered up just in time for more frothy booze in tall glasses served with pineapple and a diet consisting almost entirely of plantanos and the pineapple off the top of every-one's daiquiri. Almost every dish ordered had pork in it, and every time Vinny backed off, saying he was vegetarian, someone handed him fish or shrimp.

Dietary restrictions aside (though Vinny was used to being the odd one out), Vinny saw plenty that was wonderful about the world. People who treated him like they'd known him all his life. Fine grain sand. Warm, clear ocean water. This was the kind of life Vinny Bruno should be living—if not full-time, as nearly as possible to that. It also didn't hurt that every couple of hours or so seemed to bring a different girl into Vinny's lap, most of them five or so years older than Vinny, all of them cute and chatty and teasing him about his American accent. Vinny decided to hold back and kept speaking only gringo Spanish, even though, as long as they weren't all talking over each other a mile a minute, he could mostly follow the conversation. So he had to pretend to be shocked when Blaze and Joe were behind him, telling a couple of girls to meet them all up in their hotel rooms later and to make sure they had at least three other friends. Tommy was half-faithful to Carla, afraid to do anything but get blowjobs because he said that with AIDS and all, you never knew. Joe gave him shit and called him a racist, and besides, Joe had a whole carryon full of jimmies and didn't want to bring a single one home, and after that, Tommy went up to his room with two girls. Vinny hoped Carla was a patient girl.

Whispers had seemed to attract every Dominican woman on the island, and after the second day, the guys never saw Whispers without an entire entourage of Dominican women around him, rubbing oil on his skin and teaching him to snorkel. Though there was a whole lot of lap sitting in the snorkeling Whispers was doing, Vinny noted.

Whenever Vinny spoke with the other guys other than "Where to next?" or "Catch you in the morning, but not too early," it was to express dismay that they had to return to the coldness of Boston and work in a few short days.

"*Coño*," Blaze said, "it's like Batman having to put in time at his day job. It's like the worst undercover situation."

"Not quite the same," Vinny said. "Billionaires don't do much work, so Bruce Wayne just had to show up a few places for meetings." He was increasingly annoyed that at nineteen, with the money they already had, that they were acting like working stiffs.

"I know what you're thinking," Joe said.

"What am I thinking?" Vinny asked, and then the girl who was nibbling Vinny's ear said, "I hope you're not thinking much at all," and then rubbed her hand on his erection.

"A group like us with all our old ties? And at our age? Only works if we have a good cover story," Joe said, not even hiding the fact that his hand was so far into the bikini of the girl on his lap that they might as well have been conjoined.

Right. Their cover story. Former troubled kids making good, working hard in their blue-collar life. It wasn't far from the truth. They worked hard at planning jobs. Maybe one hundred percent of their blue collars might not be honest work, but then, how much honest work swindled money from good people? Displaced people? It was easy to rationalize what they did because of how much the ruling class kept the rest in a tough situation. He'd even overlook the fact that Joe was part of that ruling class.

Before this trip, the good life was a hypothetical. Hell, even Vinny's youth was hypothetical. If he was being reckless now, it was recklessly giving up his body for pleasure, which, shit, was half of British literature from the nineteenth century. That Oscar Wilde guy had a whole chapter of a horror novel devoted to a picnic where servants removed the seeds from strawberries, all in pursuit of a life of pleasure and decadence. He bet Keystone kids had no fucking clue what was actually in their library. Beyond that, though, nothing Vinny had done had harmed anyone but insurance companies. That was something that Blaze had insisted on up front, and Vinny was pretty sure they'd been able to keep to that. If they hit the drug dealers, well, then, fuck the drug dealers. As the girl nibbling on his ear turned around and faced him, her skirt up over her ass, Vinny's shorts down around his, Vinny had the fleeting sensation of being something other than Vinny

Bruno, and his cover was this teenager working hard to go straight—
Vinny Bruno was the mask. Really, all this time, he was meant to be
someone else, and that real person ached for the thrill of the score, the
perfect plan, the chess match against a crooked system that he would
beat. That was the goal. To make money, but mostly to win—because
he could.

Chapter 12
Blood and Ice

Everybody but Whispers came home darker-skinned, and Whispers came home with the smoothest, most well-oiled skin that ever had been seen. All were more than a little hungover and in need of a good soaking of their groins in cool water. Carla immediately suspected Tommy's dalliances, so they broke up, leaving Tommy not much in a mood for anything else.

"What you need is a job to focus your attentions," Vinny told him. "It just so happens, we've got one in the pipes."

They'd had two more big scores given to them by Nicky Wrists, but none as tough a nut to crack as the alligator truck. Also, things were easier when they didn't have to sneak out of Keystone and back in by a certain time every night. If they had to make the heist the night before a big work day, there were always at least two of them on duty at the same time, so they could trade off sleeping while on shift.

Vinny was looking forward to his dinner at Nat's house at the end of the week, an early holiday celebration, since Vinny would be with Joe's family for the holiday, then over to Blaze's family for New Year's before going back on duty. He could finally stuff himself on real food and not just scraps from the tops of drinks, overloading on potassium and fiber, but then Nicky called. When Vinny went to the warehouse with Blaze, while Whispers waited in the car and Tommy was working his security shift, Nicky said, "Thursday night, I got a job that only you can do."

While Vinny loved hearing those words, he also had his Spidey senses on high alert. What Nicky Wrists might have meant was he had a job only Vinny *would* do. "How many guys you ask first?" Vinny said right back.

"Vin, why so uptight? This is a great chance, and the payout—oof, the payout," he waved his wrists. "It's the type of take that kids your age would give their left nut to have."

"So you're saying I'm the lucky one."

"Damn right, that's what I'm saying."

"All right," Vinny said. If this was a test for Vinny, it was also going to be a test for Nicky. He felt Blaze's barely perceptible nod in Vinny's direction, a subtle cue that he was marking everything and that there were eyes on them they couldn't see. "Let's hear the plug."

"Big returns make big rewards. A guy's flying in from Lithu-fucking-wania, which, as you may or may not know, is a republic newly independent from the USSR."

"I watch the news," Vinny said.

"That's great to fucking hear. Anyway, lots that's new. Stuff you don't really need to know, but an Antwerp diamond dealer had some black-market stuff with the Reds of Lithu-fucking-wania, which is now closing up shop, but he also has been filtering in some diamonds from Sierra Leone that couldn't be sold in Antwerp and were getting filtered back and forth to obscure the origins, and in the meantime, some get filtered to a—let's call him a competitor, over here. Turns out, though, the competitor also has a few other enemies who would like their hands on these Sierra Leone diamonds and would pay top dollar for the particular set, which, as you may have gathered, is being brought in on..." Nicky checked his yellow legal pad, "the Aeroflot flight from Vilnius, Thursday night at eleven. All you have to do is find a way to intercept him and get me the diamonds. And for that, gentlemen," he nodded at Vinny and Blaze, "you boys will receive two million dollars in cash."

Exactly $400,000 for each of them. Now, that was a price tag worth the gamble.

"All right," Vinny said. "Who else is going to be looking out for this guy?"

"Well, Vinny, it's hard to say. Like I said, there are competing interests."

"Meaning, the airport is going to be a hot spot of traffic on Thursday night."

Nicky Wrists waved his wrists and shrugged. "Probably, yes? Maybe, no? You're smart boys. Figure it out and watch your backs."

"Gonna tell us who we're looking out for?"

"Glad you asked." He pulled out a printout of someone's business photo. "Edgar Murray. Jewel wholesaler, of sorts. Mostly a gofer for people above our pay grade."

Reddish hair, but otherwise, a guy who did not stick out in any way. The exact type of guy who'd be on a couple of payrolls.

"All right," Blaze said, "so what do we do, go up to him and say 'Give us all your diamonds'? Or is there a case we need to swipe?"

Nicky waved his wrists. "Supposedly, he travels with a briefcase. Figure it out, boys, and we'll see if you're as smart as you claim to be."

Vinny nodded and turned with Blaze to leave the warehouse with the picture of Edgar Murray, wholesaler of sorts. "By the way," Nicky said, "no sampling of the merchandise. I got specific counts coming in, and my guys are going to know what's there and what isn't."

"Nicky, I'm insulted at the suggestion," Vinny said, walking out without another word.

They waited to get back to the car with Whispers before Blaze let loose. "Two million? Two million, motherfuckers!"

"Wait, what?" Whispers asked.

Vinny let out a whistle. "Two million is the take, easy job, all we gotta do is kidnap a diamond guy at the airport, while two different crime families are also trying to get to him, and I think Nicky's looking to double-cross us."

"Fuck," Whispers said. "That's—a lot to think about all at once."

"But come on, we can be a little excited about the two million," Blaze said.

"Fuck, yes we can," Vinny said. "We just have to make sure we can do the job."

"Sounds like we're going to be doing three jobs at once, and in three days," Whispers said.

"Priority One for this week. Everything else is second, everyone needs to focus."

Every guy had his duty, which was double-duty for each of them. Nicky Wrists had been sure that Edgar Murray would be taking a cab, as he always did when he came into town. They had to ensure he would take their cab, so Whispers toured the cab stand at Logan Airport and walked the route from arrivals.

Joe holed up in his personal tech lab, even calling in sick to his IT job, while Whispers made some calls about getting his hands on a cab, and Blaze visited one of his father's old friends. They all met up in Joe's room, and Blaze returned with a small plastic cylinder of lab-grade chloroform.

"Where'd you get that?" Tommy asked.

"It's not illegal to own it," Blaze said, "only to knock people out with it. But since we're in a rush, I called in a favor. So, just make sure your cab has the divider between your seat and the passenger seat. Have the body shop guys work their magic and put silicone seals in."

"Why don't we just hold the chloroform up to his face quickly?" Tommy asked.

"Because, my movie-watching friend," Blaze said, "in the real world, it actually takes two or three minutes for chloroform to knock somebody out. Now, I can hold a guy down for two to three minutes, with my hand to his face, but really, A, I don't want to have to get that close, and B, how am I going to get into the backseat without him freaking out, and C, if, say, someone is following us and they see a scuffle in the backseat, we're marked immediately. So," he said, holding up a length of coolant hose from a car, "we rig this up so the fumes blow into the back of the car and knock him out in a way that we don't have to touch him. Then, when we're ready to pull him out, we roll down the windows first wearing hazmat masks so we don't get our fucking throats burned. Cool plan?"

Tommy nodded.

"Yo, Tommy," Vinny said, "tell us what you and Joe ran down." Vinny wanted to make sure Tommy had his time on the floor.

"All right," Tommy said, "Joe? Tell 'em."

Joe pulled up a screen on his computer. "I started tracing Nicky's calls, in and out of his office. Easily found a fucked-up number that was definitely from Lithuania. That number made a lot of other calls to a Boston number, and then I cross-referenced that number with all the flights Mr. Murray has made back from Europe to Boston. Sure as shit, every time he comes back, he's been in touch with someone from the Matera family. And, Tommy?"

"Why, thank you, Joe," Tommy said. "See, the Matera crime family is expecting one of its regular hand-deliveries from Mr. Murray. They deal in a lot of black market stuff, including but not limited to diamonds and Mexican heroin. And, Joe?"

"*Gracias, Tomás,*" Joe said, on cue. "Funny thing, the O'Malley crime family seems to be dabbling in the Mexican heroin trade, as well. Funny enough, they seem to have been offloading a bunch since right after our little highway job."

Vinny knew what was next. The papers were saying plenty about the escalation in the war between the families. "And Nicky's chosen a side," he said.

Joe clicked his tongue. "Ah, not necessarily. Tommy?"

"Ah, yes, our good friend Nicky. I've seen him meet with some of the O'Malley men at the warehouse, off and on, because you know how much time I've had to spend casing the place. Comes with its benefits. Cars get familiar. In my off time, though, I've tailed Nicky's little bodyguard or whoever the fuck he is, and that dude has gone to Frankie Matera, nephew of Big Daddy Matera. So, whatever Nicky is doing, he is playing *both* sides."

"Or he's playing his own side," Vinny said. "Which means we don't fall anywhere on that spectrum. Motherfucker."

"So what now?" Joe asked.

"We proceed just as we were," Vinny said. "This is everything we suspected. Blaze, Whispers, you take the canister," he nodded at the chloroform, "and make sure there's a good trigger installed in the cab."

Vinny had one final trip to make on his route to check all their drop spots. The Boston Diamond Company on Washington Street. The woman who buzzed him in the door sized him up. "And what are you looking for today, young man?" She was mid-thirties, almost pretty, and worked off other people's dreams. She had diamond studs in her ears but no wedding band herself.

"Yes, miss," Vinny said, full of charm, "I'm getting ready to propose to my girlfriend, and I want something real special."

"Ah, congratulations. Do you know what she likes?"

"Well, she normally wears simpler styles—like your earrings there," he said, and Veronica of the Boston Diamond Company automatically touched her left ear, and then brushed the side of her neck. "What I want is a quality diamond in a simple setting."

"How many carats are you looking into?"

"Well, I've saved up quite a bit, and of course I came into my inheritance," and as soon as he said that word, Veronica's entire demeanor changed.

"Congratulations again," she said.

"Sort of—I mean, I'm really going to miss my grandfather."

"Oh yes, excuse me, of course. Please, let me show you something in the two-carat range."

"That's just it," Vinny said. "If we're talking about high-quality stones, what is it? The clarity—what's it called when they're flawless?"

"Certainly, most internal flaws aren't noticeable to the naked eye—truly flawless diamonds are rare, but you can also get internally flawless stones, which increases the price, naturally. We call those IF diamonds. Now, many that you will see here have a VVS1 and VVS2 rating, which are difficult to see under a ten-times magnification."

"Uh huh, and what would be the price difference, exactly? Do you think you could show me some examples?"

She brought out several loose stones, in two- and three-carat range, rated VS1 and 2 and VVS1 and 2. "Depending on your price point— many younger couples start off with the VS1 or 2, which are still very good. If size is what you're looking for, a VS1 in a three-carat range is comparable to a two-carat VVS2. This three-carat will run one hundred thousand, and the two-carat will be eighty-five thousand. And also—we haven't yet talked about color quality. The more yellow in the stone—that means more nitrogen in it—the yellower the color will be."

"And yellow means cheaper?"

"Generally. Some people prefer the color, especially if you want a gold setting. Platinum settings, well, you'll want a K color rating or better."

"Better, like A, B, C?"

"D, E, F," Veronica said."

"May I see?"

Veronica handed Vinny the loupe. "Here's a color rating of E. Now, you'll be able to see the slight inclusions inside the stone—there are three, can you see them?"

Vinny strained with the magnification, but he could see them. "It's a beautiful stone."

"Very. That one is one hundred two thousand dollars. Of course, with a stone like that, we throw in *most* settings gratis."

Vinny whistled. "That's a pretty penny. But well worth it."

Veronica smiled. "Do you want to see more of the VS1s, perhaps?"

"What if I were to bring in my grandmother's stone? Would you be able to rate that for me, just to see—sentimental value—and then set that?"

"If you have your own stone already, sure, we can put that into an updated setting for you." Veronica looked disappointed but not surprised.

"Veronica, are you here most days of the week? I'd love for you to continue to help me with this."

"I work Monday through Friday."

"Then I'll try to come back in a week or so. Oh, in the meantime, do you know where I can pick up one of those little monocle loupe things?"

Veronica smiled. "If you're very good and promise to come back next week, I will let you borrow this one."

"Veronica, you just found yourself a loyal customer."

Vinny pocketed the loupe and made his next round to Radio Shack to pick up some CCTV wires.

∞

"Nat, I'm really sorry, I can't make it tomorrow night—a work thing came up, and my buddy wants me to cover his shift."

"Don't worry, Vinny, we can postpone. Do you want to do the weekend? The groceries will all keep until then, and then Harv and I can just have some tempeh tomorrow."

"Uh, sure—will Sunday work?"

"Sunday will be great."

He already hated lying to her, though lying and covering had become as standard as breathing to him. He had one work shift to go, overnight, and every hour inched along, making Vinny more agitated. He even turned down a booty call from Amanda. He got home at 8:30 a.m. and crashed for five hours, before getting up, making himself a smoothie with extra protein powder, then doing five hundred pushups.

"Damn, sweaty," Whispers said, coming in from his shift. "I'm going for a nap, then I pick up the cab at eight. Everything okay?"

"Yeah, you?"

"I'm just the wheels."

"And the trigger," Vinny said.

"All passive. I do what I do. You got the rest?"

"Yeah. Yeah." He didn't have doubts, but he had a foreboding. There was a lot, and it all had to go down perfectly.

∞

At 10:30, they pulled into Logan and circled around. Only Whispers held back, to ensure no one climbed in the cab and killed the plan all together. They all had their walkie-talkies, and Blaze and Vinny dropped off Tommy to wait for the Aeroflot plane to land. They didn't know if he'd be stopping at baggage, so Tommy would have to wait at the gate for him, Tommy standing out far less than Vinny and Blaze did.

The back of Vinny's neck prickled, sweaty and cold. "Man, you good?" Blaze asked.

"Fuck, I'm fine."

"No, bro, it's okay. I'm a little jumpy too."

"We can't be fucking jumpy at Nicky's."

"No shit. I'll be good as soon as we clear this part."

As long as Edgar Murray got into the right fucking cab, the first part would be a breeze. During the week, they'd done recon on the O'Malley and Matera henchmen, and Joe hacked into the DMV to get the license plate numbers and makes of the known card members. Too many to count, but there were a hell of a lot of Lincoln Town Cars between the two factions. Which also happened to be the most popular car of choice for Greater Boston livery companies. They would just have to be on top of any car following for more than five minutes. Fortunately, Whispers' friends had gotten them an old Sentra, the most nondescript car of all time. At eleven, Vinny drove Blaze to the parking garage, where a Mitsubishi bike was waiting for him. He'd be tailing the crew, an extra pair of eyes for anyone following the cab. It would be up to him and Vinny to serve as distractions.

"All right, boys," Whispers said through his walkie, "I'm making my circle. Tommy, it's up to you."

"Plane has landed, but it's not at the gate," Tommy said. "Four other planes have also landed, so keep sharp, there's going to be a crowd."

Ten minutes later, Tommy clicked the walkie three times to signal that Aeroflot was disembarking. Vinny felt his chest tighten. He was waiting at the loading curb a hundred yards behind the taxi stand. Then, he saw Tommy. Tommy had marked a red-headed man in a blue suit, no tie, otherwise unremarkable except for what was in his possession. "There he is," Vinny radioed. "Just ahead of Tommy. Whispers, he's coming toward you."

Vinny started up his car and merged into the minimal traffic, slowly. As he passed, he saw Edgar Murray headed to the taxi in front of Whispers. Fuck. But then Tommy pushed ahead of him and jumped in the cab. In his rearview, Edgar got into Whispers' cab. "Got him," Vinny radioed to Blaze. Vinny held back, watching for the cab to pull out. He crawled forward, pretending to look at terminal numbers, and then waited for Whispers to pass him. He sped up a little, and then waited to see which cars seemed in a hurry after the cab. There were three other Lincolns, but two of them had TCP stickers. He'd watch the ones that didn't, especially if there was more than one guy in the front seat. The third fit that bill. Another cab was coming up, so Vinny waited for it to pass, then cut off the Lincoln. The driver flashed him, and Vinny flipped them off and sped forward. As they went to swing around Vinny, Blaze roared up on his bike and they had to swing back behind Vinny quickly. Whispers had gotten lost among the other traffic, and there were three other cabs nearby, which helped create confusion. The Lincoln swung around at the next chance and went after the wrong cab. Vinny relaxed, and then he and Blaze made a beeline for their rendezvous point, an old parking garage with no CCTV on the premises, recently closed and sold to a commercial construction company to build a business tower. No one cared about the building that was still there.

The taxi was waiting in a dark corner, Edgar Murray passed out in the back.

"How did it go?" Vinny asked Whispers.

"Where's Tommy?" Whispers asked. "He saved the day."

"He sure did. We didn't follow his cab—he'll be okay," Vinny said.

"Man, that was close." Whispers shook his head. "But it was cool, because Mr. Murray was all about the small talk when he got in, talking about what a creep Tommy was and how Boston was changing too much. He didn't notice that I'd locked the doors. He was still talking when he started choking and then asked if I could turn off the air because he was getting too much exhaust. I said it wasn't from us, and then it finally dawned on him that things might not be all right, and by then, sleepytime."

"Phew, fuck yeah," Blaze said. "So, where's the score?"

"All he has with him is this tiny briefcase," Whispers said. "Figured we could open it all together, since it's the holidays."

"Merry fucking Christmas," Vinny said.

They opened it to find another loupe, some cleaning clothes, jewelry cleaner, and a couple of rings. "That's not fucking it," Blaze said.

"Nah," Vinny said, feeling around the sides of the case for a false front. He found one spot in the case lining that felt softer and stuck his finger through. The whole lining popped off, and in a manila envelope lined with bubble wrap, folded in a cloth, were forty diamonds, all roughly two and three carats.

"Holy San Antonio," Blaze said.

Vinny grabbed the loupe. "Whispers, give me a light over here." Whispers got a flashlight out of the back of Vinny's car and held it over Vinny's shoulder while he examined a few of the stones. Tiny blemishes, maybe—by his best guess, all VVS 1 and 2 range. These were great diamonds. He wished he could determine the color grade. "Wicked pissa."

"Is there maybe like a paper in there that says how much they're worth?" Blaze asked.

"Genius, why would a diamond expert need a sheet?" Vinny said. "He's the sheet."

"Unless Nicky has a sheet," Whispers said.

"Fucking Nicky," Blaze said.

"How much you think is there?"

"Based on what the jeweler told me? Sixty thousand minimum, likely eighty thousand, and over a hundred G's for the bigger ones."

"Fuuuuuuck," Blaze said.

"Wait a minute," Whispers said. "Let's say for shits that each of those stones is a hundred G's. That would be four million. Isn't that half of what Whispers said he's paying us? Come on, now, when the fuck has

Nicky ever gone fifty-fifty with us?"

Vinny shook his head. "Damn. You're right. Unless these diamonds are worth more than that."

"Or unless Nicky was expecting there to be more diamonds," Whispers said.

Shit. Nicky didn't know how the jeweler would be bringing these in. "Quick, Blaze, pull our friend Mr. Murray out of the car and set him down here."

"*Coño* is dead fucking weight, yo," Blaze said, pulling the body out of the back of the cab. As his feet hit the ground, the heel of his shoe clicked open and a pile of diamonds spilled onto the concrete garage floor, some rolling under the car.

"Holy fucking shit!" Blaze said. "What'd I do?" He laid Edgar Murray onto his back, and his head lolled to the side, while he, Vinny, and Whispers scrambled on their hands and knees to gather all the diamonds. Vinny pulled off the shoe and inspected the trap compartment on the heel. The thick soles, hard heels, were hollow. He tipped the shoe over, and four more diamonds fell into this hand.

"It's like that Paul Simon song," Vinny said, but Blaze and Whispers didn't know the one he was talking about.

"There's the rest of the money," Whispers said. "Check the other shoe."

Vinny slipped off the second shoe and felt the tiny release latch, which sprung open, spilling diamonds into Vinny's palm until they overflowed and fell. "Shit."

"I got it," Blaze said.

"No, shit as in—there's close to a hundred fifty stones."

They each took a handful and counted to be sure. One hundred fifty-three, including the forty from the case. "All right, so if we were to say fifteen million for the whole take, that two million makes a lot more sense."

"Okay, so what would Nicky have done if he only got the briefcase?" Whispers said.

"That's some pretty fucking interesting food for thought," Vinny said.

Blaze looked out the door of the garage, then came back and said, "Just checking. All clear."

The three of them all looked at each other. "Seems like we may have leverage," Whispers said.

Vinny looked at their piles of diamonds. It was a dangerous game, but he also saw an opportunity. "Look, very little of what we'd planned is going to change. But we can come out of tonight ahead in more ways than one." He put the envelope of the forty diamonds back in the case. "Nicky asked for the case. We'll give him the case."

"*Oye*, and do what with the other hundred thirteen?" Blaze asked.

"First thing's first," Vinny said. "Take off his socks." They divided up the diamonds left from the shoes, though Vinny may have placed more of the two-carat diamonds in the briefcase than Edgar Murray had wrapped in there, and put the remaining mostly three-carat diamonds in Murray's socks. They tied the tops off with knots, and Vinny and Whispers stuffed the socks in their pockets. "Take the rest of his clothes off," Vinny said.

"Bro, why?" Blaze asked. "That's fucked up."

"Because, when he wakes up in some random-ass stairwell, and he doesn't have his clothes, he won't be a hundred percent certain that the diamonds in his shoes were found."

"Where do we put his clothes, then?" Blaze asked.

"We burn them," Whispers whispered.

It was set. They stripped all the clothes off Edgar Murray and loaded him into the enclosed stairwell of the garage. Tommy radioed on the walkie-talkie that he'd had his cab drop him off at a Dunkin' Donuts a few blocks away from Nicky's warehouse, so Joe could pick him up on the way. Whispers would drop off the cab at his chop shop, where it would cease to be a cab, then circle back to Nicky's.

"So, we ready for this?" Vinny asked. "Because once we go in, there's no going back on the plan." Whispers and Blaze nodded. "We're crossing that line, most probably. We call Nicky's bluff. If he turns out to be a big fucking pussy, then great. If not, watch who comes from the back. Blaze, you good?"

"Fuck off, you know I'm solid, I was born ready, bro," Blaze said, though he kept shifting his weight from foot to foot.

"Whispers?"

"Fuck, man, I'm with you all the way."

"All right, all right."

As he drove to the warehouse, Vinny once again felt a change inside himself. It was as if he was no longer in his body but instead watching himself from above. It was some other twenty-year-old who was driving that stolen car, scrubbed by Whispers' friends. It was someone else pulling the hood of his sweatshirt over his head, making sure not to get in direct view of the CCTV cameras, though he was sure Joe had that all taken care of. He watched from above as he pulled Murray's briefcase out of the backseat, the envelope of diamonds hidden in the compartment. It was someone else marking where Joe and Tommy pulled up around the corner before knocking on the warehouse door with Blaze.

The henchman with the cinnamon-roll face answered the door and led them past the familiar stacks of small containers and boxes on pallets, the place now emptied of workers, toward the back office on the bottom floor, though there was another office upstairs that Vinny had never seen. He didn't know how many other guys were waiting upstairs, but a good bet was more than one. If he really was floating above his body, he wished he could move through the warehouse, invisible and ghostlike.

"Here's the briefcase," Vinny heard himself say. "Let's see the money."

"Right, about that," Nicky Wrists said. "There's been a renegotiation of things on my end. I had to take a cut, which means I can't give you the original amount."

There it fucking was. Part One of the double-cross. "No can do," Vinny heard himself say. "We did the job for a price. That was the agreement. No price, no job."

"What do you think this is, a fucking union job? You think you're at the docks working some kind of collective bargaining agreement? You kids are working for me."

"Actually, we're independent contractors. We work for ourselves."

Nicky Wrists shrugged, looking unimpressed. "Why don't you be a good boy and set the briefcase down right here on my desk."

"I'd be happy to. As soon as you put out the two million we contracted for."

"Well, see, that's not going to happen, but I'm offering you one million, which is still the most you've ever gotten for a job. I don't know exactly how many people you have to pay out of that one million, but that's on you."

"That's a pretty tough argument to make, considering we have the diamonds in our possession," Blaze said.

Nicky Wrists waved his hands in the air as if swatting away flies. "Do you think you kids can come into my warehouse and make demands of me? Do you not think I got you on tape? Do you not think I can share these tapes with other interested parties and make sure they make you hurt? That I wouldn't tell them you're the ones who've been screwing them over and tried to use me as your fence? Do you not think I could say whatever I want? I'd hate to do such a thing, because I was a young punk like you once, but I always knew my place."

This time, Vinny was very much in his body. He felt the smile creep across his face. "These interested parties—would they be the Materas or the O'Malleys? Because you know, it's just so hard to keep track of all the people you're double-crossing these days, Nicky, I gotta say."

"What?" The smugness on Nicky's face gave, just a little, as his eyes flickered wide for a split second. "What are you talking about?"

Vinny must have been back in his body because he could feel the sweat trickle down his spine. No one else knew about that sweat. To the rest, he was ice. Maybe he was. "Why don't you look at your tape, Nicky? See what it is you got there. Maybe you should make sure you really have what you think you have before you go spouting off."

What Nicky didn't realize was that Joe had hacked into his CCTV and recorded every event with the O'Malley and Matera representatives, that he had made recordings of those, and that he and Whispers and Tommy had broken into the warehouse two days earlier to switch out all the tapes, managing to wipe clean every recorded meeting with Vinny, Tommy, and Blaze. Nicky scrambled for one of the tapes in his desk, and when he pressed play, all he saw was himself with one of the O'Malley men.

"Merry Christmas," Vinny said.

"You little fuck," Nicky said, and it was the first time fear and anger showed on Nicky, the first time he bared his teeth like a dog about to bite.

"See, you call me names, but I'm not the one who was going to double-cross ya, Nick," Vinny said. "But I catch wind of a double-cross against me? I'm going to do something about it. Like make my own copies of your tapes."

Vinny heard the click of the gun first, before he understood what was happening. Blaze was aware, though, and before anyone could blink, Blaze had thrown a knife into the throat of Nicky's bodyguard.

"What the fuck!" Nicky shouted.

"'What the fuck' is right," Vinny said, as he and Blaze drew their guns. Two more of Nicky's guys came around from the back of the warehouse, drawing on Vinny and Blaze.

"All right, assholes, I'm going to ask you once. What did you do with my tapes?"

Vinny laughed. "That's not the question you should be asking," he said, and let out one quick whistle. Two shots rang out in succession, and Nicky jumped. He smiled, looking at Vinny and Blaze, but that smile fell as soon as it was clear that Vinny and Blaze weren't the ones who were hit. Nicky's other two bodyguards dropped, holes in their heads.

"I keep saying not to take us for some street punks," Vinny said, "though I wouldn't underestimate street punks the way you've under-estimated us. Quite the gamble, being Italian but moving behind the Italian mob's back and making deals with the Irish."

"I'm sorry, Vinny, I'm sorry," Nicky said, waving his wrists a little higher. "You made your point." There was a sob choking Nicky's throat. "You can have the two million. We can let bygones be bygones."

Blaze looked at Vinny, laughing. "Damn," Blaze said, "people really say that? I thought that was just in the movies."

"This clown is a movie character," Vinny said. He looked back at Nicky. "Let's see the two million you got in that safe of yours right now."

"All right, Vinny, all right." Nicky knelt by the safe, scrolling the dial back and forth until it unlatched. He pulled out five stacks of bills, using both hands to load them up on the table. "Can I see the diamonds?"

"Absolutely," Vinny said, setting the briefcase on the desk next to the pile of money and flipping it open toward Nicky. He then popped open the hidden compartment, revealing the envelope, which he opened, then unraveled the cloth, letting the diamonds spill out on the desk. Nicky picked one up between his thumb and forefinger.

"Beautiful," he said. Then he looked at the pile. "Is this all? I thought there should be more here."

"That was all that was in the briefcase," Blaze said.

"You idiots—he could have had more on him! What did you do with Murray?"

"We stripped him down—he wasn't wearing them in a belt or anything," Vinny said.

"Then I don't think it's fair, I mean, this wasn't what was—it's just that," Nicky fumbled for words, his eyes occasionally darting between his dead henchmen and Blaze's itching trigger finger, and the dark space from above where the shots that killed his henchmen came from. "Look, Vin," Nicky pleaded.

"Look, Nick," Vinny interrupted. "You thought you could fuck us. Now you're getting fucked. I know it ain't fun, but you reap what you sow."

"Don't patronize me, you little fuck!" Nicky said, and without another word, Vinny pulled the handgun from the back of his waistband and shot Nicky through the throat.

Chapter 13
Aftermath

"Whoa, Vin," Blaze said, as Vinny stood over Nicky, grasping at his wound that gurgled blood and bubbles, pouring over his bank teller's suit. Blood spilled down his wrists as he gasped for breath, like a fish pulled onto dry land, already dead but the body still fighting the inevitable shutdown.

Whispers and Tommy jumped down from the upper warehouse office. They'd come in the back way, found it clear, and watched for the likelihood that more of Nicky's henchmen would attack. Whispers had also found the backup safe and had popped it open. "What do we take, and what do we leave?" Whispers called down.

"How much money?" Vinny asked.

"Another three million in cash. There's also a ledger."

"Bring it all down, then," Vinny said. "Joe, you got all traces of us gone? No backup tapes?"

"We're all clean up here," Joe called down.

"Everyone else, look around, make sure there's no trace of us left."

Tommy, Whispers, and Joe packed up the cash and ledger from upstairs, while Vinny handed Blaze the money Nicky had pulled out of the safe.

"Okay, what next, Vin?" Blaze seemed lost, shellshocked, unable to act on his own.

"Hey, Blaze, stuff the cash in your sweatshirt and tuck it into your pants."

With the command, Blaze kicked into gear and was back to being his normal self. Vinny was looking at Nicky Wrists' bloody body. He could smell the blood, though. Warm and metallic, mixed with the foulness of fear, like an animal. Vinny made sure he got the diamonds wrapped up and back in the briefcase.

"All right, everyone upstairs, let's leave out the back, and quietly. Blaze, you and I will head out the side. We don't look around. We walk south, then back to the car."

"Check."

They drove back to the chop shop to switch out their vehicles, and then Vinny and Joe piled into Tommy's BMW E30, while Blaze hopped into Whispers' Trans Am to follow Tommy to the apartment.

They were mostly quiet in the car, and Vinny wasn't sure where he was—if he was in his body or in some limbo somewhere above his body still. They'd crossed the line now, and there was a before and an after. They'd killed Nicky Wrists. They'd killed three of his henchmen. Mexican Joe was the only one who didn't fire a shot. Vinny was the only one to shoot a guy begging. "Tommy, pull into Burger King. I'm starving, I want some fries."

"What the fuck?" Tommy said.

"Dude, pull the fuck into the drive-through."

"How can you eat right now?" Joe asked.

"Huh? How can you not?"

"Whatever you say," Tommy said, changing lanes to turn into the entrance at the next intersection.

Joe's walkie-talkie crackled. "Bro," Blaze's voice said from the car behind them, "what the fuck's going on?"

"Vinny's hungry," Joe said.

"He's what?" Blaze asked. "*Pinche pendejo.*"

"Tell him to fuck his *coño* self," Vinny said. As Tommy pulled up to the speaker to order, Vinny shouted over him, "Two large fries, and a large Pepsi."

"Is Coke okay?"

"Why?"

"We switched to Coke now."

"Fuck yeah? Since when?"

"Since last year."

"Well, what do you fucking know," Vinny said, then turning to Tommy and Joe. "Did you guys know that?"

Joe shrugged. "It was a minor news item, but I don't really eat here."

"Hell, then. Sure, give me a Coke."

"Will that be all?"

"What are you guys having?" Vinny asked.

"I'm good," Joe said.

"Nothing for me," Tommy said.

"Come on, seriously? Am I the only one having something?" Vinny said, his voice higher than normal.

"We're good, bro," Tommy said. He looked at Vinny and nodded.

"All right, then," Vinny said, sitting back in his seat.

They were up at the window to get their food when Blaze knocked on Vinny's window. "Jesus, fuck, Blaze, what are you trying to do?" Vinny said.

"Joe, switch with me. I wanna talk to Vinny."

Joe got out of the back seat of Tommy's car, and Blaze squeezed himself into the back. "Jesus, Tommy, you ever get a car that can fit real people in the backseat?"

"What is it, Blaze?" Vinny asked, as Tommy passed him the bag of food. The bottom was already soaked through with grease.

"Fuck, bro, you really gonna eat that right now?"

"No, I'm going to spread it over Tommy's dash. What the fuck you think I'm going to do?" He pulled out a handful of fries and shoved them into his mouth. The whole car filled with the smell of hot oil as Tommy pulled out onto the street.

"Bro, stop," Blaze said.

Vinny pulled out ketchup packets and squeezed them into the bag of fries, making a big production of holding the packet high up and squirting a long stream of it into the bag.

"Oh my god, bro, I'm going to be sick," Blaze said as he watched the blood-red ketchup.

"You fucking got in the car!" Vinny said, while Tommy said at the same time, "Not in the fucking car!"

Blaze pushed at the back of Vinny's seat until Tommy pulled to the side of the road as Vinny opened the door. Blaze leaned out his head and puked on the pavement.

"Fuck, Blaze, watch the door!" Tommy shouted.

Blaze wiped his mouth with the back of his sleeve. "Goddamn, Vin, you cold."

"Because I eat?" Vinny said.

"Because, after, *you know.*"

"Some tough guy you turned out to be," Vinny said, laughing.

"Look, I'm cool with what we did. But it ain't nothing. It ain't nothing." He shook his head and stared out the window.

Vinny rolled down the window to air out the car but kept eating the fries, and Tommy waited to start driving.

"Everybody good?" Joe crackled through the walke-talkie.

"Blaze got a little-girl stomach," Tommy said, laughing.

They got to the apartment and Whispers unloaded the duffel bag of five million in cash, then went to the fridge and pulled out a case of beer, passing the cans around. Vinny opened up Nicky Wrists' ledger and thumbed through the entries.

"Joe, you taking care of this tomorrow?" Whispers asked, nudging his toe at the pile of cash.

"Well, Nathan Franklin will be."

"Who the fuck is that?" Tommy asked.

"Nathan Franklin is a successful trust fund manager, with multiple accounts in the millions, which can easily be funneled to five accounts in the Caymans."

"Does Nathan Franklin have convincing ID?" Vinny asked.

"Nathan Franklin has state-issued ID, though the state doesn't remember issuing it," Joe said. "Amazingly enough, he shares a marked resemblance to me, though he's a little fatter and older."

"I thought you needed a shave, *coño*," Tommy said.

"Bro," Blaze told Tommy, "when you say that, you only sound whiter." Tommy flipped him off.

"Do you just take it into a bank?" Blaze asked Joe.

"*Carajo*, you really have no idea what it's like to have money, do you? Remind me to teach you assholes how to have money like a responsible adult millionaire sometime, okay?"

"*Capisce*," Vinny said. "All right, so the money is taken care of, but gentlemen, if you want to hold it in your hands and take big sniffs, go ahead."

"Watch the prints, though," Joe said.

"Seriously?" Whispers asked.

"Everything can be potential evidence," Joe said. He looked at each of them. "What, somebody has to think about these things."

"This is Joe's first job, everyone, let's welcome him to the club," Vinny said, giving a phony applause.

"¿Que pedo, güey? Sheesh."

"Easy, Vin," Tommy said. "We're just decompressing."

"Hey, what, fine, I'm cool."

"So what about the diamonds? The briefcase?" Blaze asked. "We divvying those up as well?"

Vinny opened the briefcase onto the coffee table, then pulled the diamonds from the sock in his pocket and tossed them in the open briefcase. "We each keep three. Call it a nest egg, do with them what you want, but, you know, not all at the same time."

"Come on, Vin, only three?" Blaze said.

Twenty-five missing versus fifteen, Vinny thought. Would those extra ten matter? "Fine. Five each."

"Why don't we just keep them all?" Blaze asked.

"Because people are going to be coming for them," Vinny said. "People with bigger resources than we have. People who are blood-thirsty. We draw blood, but we don't drink it." It was a good rationalization for Vinny. It kept him separate from the mobsters. He could do what needed to be done, but he didn't have to do more. There was no question Nicky had been planning to roll on them, for his own self-serving purposes. Fuck him, he had it coming.

"What's the plan, then?" Tommy asked.

Vinny sat up, fingering through the pile of diamonds. "I've been thinking a lot about this. Nicky was baiting a turf war and was going to use us as the fall boys. Well, nobody knows who we are, not even Edgar Murray. He get a good look at you, Whispers?"

"Not enough for that white boy to tell me apart from any other black man," Whispers shrugged.

"Good," Vinny said. "And Joe, you can make it so that we can call somebody and they can't trace it back to us?"

"Easy," Joe said.

"All right. We give the diamonds back to the Materas."

The crew all jumped. "What the fuck, Vin?" Tommy said.

"What game you playing?" Blaze asked.

"Think about it. They were supposed to go to the Materas. Nicky was going to sell them to the O'Malleys, then set us up as the thieving middlemen. Someone's gotta take the fall for Nicky's death. The diamonds could incentivize the Materas to go with the story that the O'Malleys popped Nicky in a deal gone wrong. They get the diamonds, they get to go to war with the enemy."

"And what would they do with us?" Tommy asked. "They could always roll on us."

"They won't know who the fuck we are," Vinny said. "That's the whole point. We tell them we stumbled into this, and like good Italians who were being double-crossed, we wanted to give the heads-up to fellows in a similar predicament. I have no intention of ever meeting with them face to face."

Whispers nodded. "I've heard crazier plans. Shit, we've pulled off crazier plans."

"We do a favor for the Materas in the form of property return, and they do us a favor by putting the word on the street that the O'Malleys are responsible for what went down at the warehouse. No one has any reason to suspect any of us."

"Oh," Joe said, "I forgot, I have an early Christmas present for everyone. I hacked into the security footage outside Pop's Liquor, and I can easily splice in old video of us out front, so if anyone asks, of course we were there at the time of the killings. It should never come up, but if it does, we have an alibi. Video evidence."

They all clinked their cans, and even Blaze was able to drink, though he still looked a little green to Vinny.

"Now," Vinny said, holding up a three-carat diamond, "take your pick before we say goodbye to these babies." He took out the loupe and flashlight and tried to select five of the biggest VVS1s he could find.

"I can't believe we're giving these all up, though," Tommy said.

"Yes, but we're each getting a million from tonight, plus whatever we can get from the Materas as a reward, so I think you can let the diamonds go."

"But Vinny," Blaze said, "what if we take a couple more? Just think, I could make earrings for both my mama and my sister for Christmas. I would be the best brother ever."

"Fuck anyone else, I'm making earrings for myself," Whispers said.

They laughed, but Vinny's heart sank. He'd had Reina in mind when he was picking perfectly matched diamonds for a set of earrings. Fuck it, he was still determined to give her a diamond of some kind.

∞

Vinny didn't want to waste time. He went over to Joe's with Whispers the next afternoon, after Joe got back from work and before Vinny and Whispers had their security shift in the neighborhood.

Joe dialed up Frank Matera, nephew of Big Daddy Matera.

"They won't be able to trace this?" Vinny asked.

"Oh, they'll trace it," Joe said. "To Manitoba."

"Frank Matera?" Vinny said.

"Who the fuck is this?"

"Don't worry, I'm a friend."

"Don't tell me not to worry. If you're a friend, why the fuck don't I know you?"

"I prefer not to be known, but we have a common rat in our kitchen, if you read me."

There was silence on the line before Matera said, "Nicky Fucking Wrists."

"So you read me," Vinny said. He nodded to the crew. "We happened upon something of yours when we were settling a score of our own."

"Oh, did you?" Matera said.

"Turns out, ol' Nicky had an arrangement with some Irishmen." This was Vinny's biggest risk. He didn't want anyone coming after him from the Matera family, which they might have done if they were out looking for the diamonds. Granted, they might have blamed the O'Malleys anyway, but he wanted to set up the direct link. And get compensated.

"So what's in it for you?" Matera asked.

"I'm glad you asked, see. Because we got some CCTV tapes of Nicky, on top of the recovered property belonging to you, that was mixed in with stuff he was trying to pull over on us."

"This property you mention," Matera asked. "Is it a person or a bag?"

"A briefcase," Vinny said. "A heavy one."

"What are your plans, then?" Matera asked.

"To disappear. We ain't competition. Think of it as a one-time exchange of mutually beneficial services. You get what's yours, at, say, two-thirds your original asking price, and then you point the finger directly at your enemies, and you can forget we ever existed."

"Can I count on that?" Matera asked.

"Presumably. As long as one day, you don't run across some small, independent establishment and try to cut in on a mom and pop making a buck."

"So that's what you are? A mom and pop?"

"Semantics, sir."

There was a pause, and then Matera asked, "Where do we meet, then?"

"Not meet," Vinny said. "We're going to wire you an account number for a transfer. As soon as that money is in, your property will magically appear in your possession."

186 | Anthony Bucci

"And if I transfer the money and don't get my property?"

"Wouldn't that be fucking stupid of me to do?" Vinny said.

"When do we get the account number?"

"Tomorrow. Be ready with the funds, and we'll supply you with the where. It would be mutually beneficial to have the transfer made within an hour of that call."

"Don't you worry about that," Matera said.

Satisfied, Vinny wished Frank Matera a merry Christmas and hung up.

"Joe, how much of this manipulation can you do on this thing?" Vinny asked, pointing to the desktop.

"What kind do you mean? The video editing? The accounts?"

"Any of it. Like, how much of our business can we end up doing by computer?"

Joe shrugged. "It's getting easier all the time. Of course, new tech means better security, but that's not a big deal. I have to say, Vin, there's a lot of opportunity with the corporate world and banking. If you didn't bring it up, I was going to mention it, because I've already been testing some theories—"

"You've already tried?"

"Well, yeah. An experiment. This last month, I made a million dollars just pulling rounded-up change from insurance companies— the thing is you have to do it randomly, invisibly, from a lot of different sources, otherwise, you get a lapse of millions of dollars instead of a few hundred here, a few thousand there, which all gets lost in the accounting, anyway. These fucking companies are so sloppy."

"I like it, Joe. When were you going to let us in?"

"Well, at our next accounting meeting. By the way, I wrote an algorithm to test out the stock market and pooled some of our collective money, and now we're up, all together..." and he paused for effect, "ten million."

"What. The. Fuck. You shitting me, Joe?"

"Merry early Christmas?" Joe shrugged.

"You evil fucking genius," Vinny said, kissing Joe's head. "Ten million?"

"Divided five ways, so not bad."

"You have that much money and you're still living at your fucking parents' house?" Vinny shook his head and they both laughed. Yeah, Vinny was feeling better about things.

Besides, he had a plan to finish. Joe took the briefcase to work in a postage box and had their corporate courier, who delivered parcels for ten different Boston companies, take the case full of almost all the diamonds to one of Matera's shell companies, the one where Frank Matera usually spent his time. Joe faked the receipt so that they couldn't trace the origin, and the courier sure as shit wouldn't remember from which box pile he'd picked up the nondescript package or at what time.

Joe raced home on his lunch break to coincide with the delivery, and Vinny stopped by with a veggie pizza and made the call, giving the number for the account in the Caymans that would only exist long enough to receive the money and then pass it off to a handful of other accounts.

"So how much money do I have now?" Vinny asked Joe, and Joe typed away at an encrypted web page and pulled up Vinny's holdings. "Across three accounts, Vinny Bruno, aka Desmond James, aka Lonna Turner, you have eight million, five hundred forty-eight thousand and…six hundred twelve. Give or take."

Vinny almost pissed himself. Vinny fucking Bruno. A goddamn millionaire. "It's definitely time for an upgrade in domestication."

"Yeah, but we still have our cover."

"Hard-working guys all living together don't need to be crammed in an apartment or at Mom and Pop's. It's time."

Joe nodded. "It's time."

∞

Vinny wasn't bothered at all that night by the events of the previous days. As far as he was concerned, Nicky got what was coming to him eventually, and they all had acted in self-defense. That didn't stop the nightmares or waking up sweating, though. Images played of Nicky pulling out a gun, and then Blaze turning his gun on Vinny, and then Tommy, and then Whispers and even Joe, all firing into Vinny at once, while Nicky Wrists shook his wrists. He fell back asleep only to see Nicky on the floor, a gaping bullet hole in his throat, standing up and climbing onto Vinny, his blood burning Vinny's skin like the xenomorph's blood in the *Alien* movies. In his dream, Vinny was scared. Scared at what he had done, at what he was capable of doing. He thought back to Chencho's warning that they don't go down that road. Being twenty years old and taking a life, even a corrupt life that was a threat to his, was no small thing. In his dream, Nicky was a stain that wouldn't go away, something that everyone else could see on him, wherever he went.

Vinny woke from the second nightmare pissed off. He shouldn't be pissed off or scared for killing that no-good, backstabbing son-of-a-bitch. It had been Nicky's time to go. He had tried to use them to start a mob war and make a shit-ton of money for himself. Fuck that guy. Still, Vinny was pissed that the shaking of his hands wouldn't stop. He got up, and there was Whispers, coming home from his shift.

"Jesus, you look like hell," Whispers said. "Have a beer."

"Do you think we should get a dog?" Vinny asked, opening the can.

"What, like a Doberman or a German shepherd or some shit?"

"Maybe. But not really for protection. Like, aren't pets supposed to make you feel good?"

"They shit a lot," Whispers said. "And I don't love dogs."

They sat together while Whispers finished his beer and went to bed, but Vinny couldn't go back to sleep. Something was wrong, these chills kept coming back, and he felt in turns this tarry rage seeping up with nowhere to direct it, and then tremendous guilt that he was somehow disappointing someone, though he couldn't figure out who he gave a shit about disappointing. That wasn't true. He'd almost, but not quite, forgotten the dinner he was supposed to have at Nat's that night. At eight in the morning, he called her and told her he was sick and didn't know if he was contagious. "I can't get you sick before the holidays," he said.

"Oh, Vinny. You just get well, and I'll make sure we have a great dinner the minute you're feeling better."

It was good to hear Nat's voice, and then he felt awful for lying. He ate everything in the cupboards and fridge, including two fried eggs and the last third of a tub of peanut butter on celery sticks. Fuck it, he thought, and he drove to Hardee's and ordered a burger and fries. He was just going to do it. Fuck everybody and every goddamn thing. He practically ripped the greasy bag out of the cashier's hand and pulled into a parking spot, fiendishly unwrapping the burger and shoving it into his mouth. The second he took that bite and the juices of the beef patty bled onto his tongue, Vinny woke up to his mistake. He thought about spitting it out, but someone was getting out of the car parked across from him. He swallowed the too-large bite, and immediately his body rejected it. He gagged twice, and as soon as he opened his driver's side door, he threw up the bite, barely chewed. He threw the rest of the burger out the door, then felt guilty and got out of the car and threw it away in the trash next to the walk-in doors. He got back into his car and drove down to the Charles River, watching the Harvard crew teams row in their sleek little boats. Fuck them, he said, his eyes fiery hot. Fuck them! He punched his fist at the dashboard, popping the button off his tape deck. What was he doing? He wasn't going to cry. He was beyond being capable of that, but still, there was a brief moment where he felt the meat still in his throat. That wasn't it. "Angela," he said to his radio. "Angela, I'm sorry," though he wasn't sure which part he was most sorry for. All of it, probably, somewhere along the line. He wasn't sorry for the eight-odd million, though, and that settled him. "I'll do better, Ange," he said. "I promise you. I haven't kept you with me enough lately. But, big sister, you gotta watch out for me, too. Maybe you are." He thought of that feeling he got, that awareness that he was on Nicky's chopping block. "I miss you, Ange, but I'm not ready to see you again, not just yet."

It was a moment, just a few minutes, and then he mastered himself. That cow that suffered because of him and now in the trash, he was going to make it up to that cow. He'd donate some money to the ASPCA. To the World Wildlife Fund, whoever was protecting animals. Hell, even the crazy bastards at Greenpeace. He'd give them a thousand apiece. That's what you were supposed to do at the holidays.

Later that day, he called Nat again, telling her whatever he was feeling had passed and it must have been something he ate.

"If you're feeling up to it, you know you're always welcome."

That night, he was mostly feeling normal, though he felt like he had to cover up something, as if Nat had some insight directly into his brain.

"You still feeling a little down?" she asked.

"No, no, I'm good. I've been thinking I need a dog. You know, I've never had one, and they're supposed to be good, loving, you know, give you the good vibes."

"They do," Nat said. "You have the lifestyle to take care of one? I mean, I'm not saying you couldn't do it, Vinny. I think you have a lot of love to give. I think a dog would be a great place to start."

"I mean, a cat could be good, too. Or a fish. Or an iguana. I knew a guy once who had an iguana for a pet, and he loved the hell out of that scaly thing."

"Is that really what you're looking for?" Nat asked, getting him some ice water.

"No, you're right, it's a dog that would be good." He drank down the water, feeling his face getting hot, unable to regulate himself—his flushing or his speech.

"Oh, Vinny—what is wrong?"

"I can't—I'm okay. I'll be okay."

She sat down next to him and leaned in. "You're not in trouble, are you?"

"No—no, I'm not."

"You sure? Look, I'm going to tell you something, and not even Harv knows about it. I got one guilt pass, and I haven't used it."

"A guilt pass?"

"I told myself when I was younger, I'd do one bad thing in my life. Now, I've been holding off on using it, saving it up. But if you tell me I have to…dispose of a body, say, I'll do it, and we won't speak another word about it."

Vinny looked at her in horror. Why did she use that example?

"Relax, Vinny, I didn't mean literally. Unless—you know. I just mean that if you did something, maybe slid into something, and you need someone to vouch for you, I will, one hundred percent."

"Why—I mean, I don't need it. But why would you do that?"

"Because, Vinny—you've never had anyone do one unselfish thing just to protect you. And I think if you'd had that, it would have made a difference in your past. But it doesn't have to be your future. There, that's it, I'm done preaching, I know you don't come here for that."

"True," Vinny said quietly. "I come for the food." He smiled at Nat, knowing she understood that wasn't the full truth. "One thing you can do for me," he said, "I want to go full vegan. No more animals at all."

"Good for you, Vinny," Nat said. "It'll be an adjustment, but you can do it. Pizza will be hard, and soy cheese is lousy, but I just pour tahini sauce on everything, and I haven't missed dairy in a decade."

Chapter 14
Two Years, and a Different Life
1993

Keeping one's head low for a couple of years turned out to be intolerable, though not impossible, for a group of young men just out of their teens with millions of dollars in their collective onshore and offshore accounts. Instead of going crazy, they kept busy. They were, for any outsider, the model success story of the system. They were each released from probation, their records sealed. They bought a beautiful estate in Boxford. They advanced at the security company, slowly taking over operations, as they had planned with Joe's father, Carlos.

Then, Carlos had invested his recommendation and fifty thousand dollars to help his son and his friends buy out the security company for the community. Joe had said it wasn't necessary, but Carlos said the boys needed an outside source keeping them accountable at the start of the business. Vinny, Tommy, Whispers, Blaze, and Joe were equal owners of the company, with Joe's father as a silent partner who would stay in long enough to recoup his investment.

Whispers came up with the idea to have automated calls for any security issue trip a series of video cameras to record and send the images directly to the office. He and Joe took three days to make it work and, within two months, had already sold twelve homes in the community on the upgrade, which would be installed as soon as their ownership transferred.

In preparation, they hired new drivers to patrol the community and monitor the cameras, and with the hope of their eventually handling the new orders. They opened a second office in Marblehead, fully staffed with lower-income family men who would be making a living wage for the first time. Blaze was especially pleased when he got to hire two former truck drivers, telling Vinny it was like paying back the community.

Carlos's only hesitation came when they announced they were buying a house together in Boxford.

"My dad is worried that you're taking advantage of me and my money," Joe said, sheepish. "Can you guys just, I don't know, go out of your way when you see him to talk about work, like that's what we spend our time thinking about?"

"That kind of is what we spend our time thinking about," Whispers said, though he'd recently been spending a lot of time with one of the Dominican girls they'd met in Puerto Rico, as she and her mother had moved in with their relatives in Chelsea. He spent a lot of time thinking about her, Vinny figured, because he spent half his time talking about her.

"Don't worry, *pendejo*," Vinny said, "we'll make sure Papa Carlos knows we're all mooching off you."

"Cocksucker," Joe said.

They were toasting to their new business venture, twenty-one and twenty-two years old, the age of college graduates, all those fancy barneys in their six-hundred-dollar business suits whose parents had always given them more than they ever needed. Vinny and his friends were self-made men, with help from Carlos's money and expertise, but otherwise, as a crew, no one had managed what they'd managed.

Whispers lifted his glass of Laphroaig single malt. "Man, I have to say. I know it doesn't seem like that big of a deal to y'alls 'cause of what we're doing, but when I was a kid, I always wanted my own business. This is a real moment for me."

"Cheers to that," Blaze said.

Vinny, too, felt the importance of this moment. "So, you know, I've been thinking," Vinny said. "How about rebranding the company, with our own name and logo. That way, it really is ours."

194 | Anthony Bucci

Whispers nodded. Blaze took a shot of Don Julio Real, which he wouldn't let anyone else drink.

"How about Pendejos Protectors?" Joe said, sputtering a laugh into his own drink.

Blaze picked up from there. "Culo Chasers?"

"Spinner Hawkers," Tommy said, and when Blaze and Joe stared at him blankly, he said, "You know, 'cause we're protecting the spinners. The cute girls."

"I know what a fucking spinner is, but what the hell is a hawker?" Joe said. "Like a dude who watches birds?"

"Hawking, like hawks, they have good vision and they spot and track their prey."

Joe shook his head. "No. Nope. Eh, wrong answer," he said, pressing down on his knee like he was pushing the stop button.

"Fuck, you drunk bitches," Whispers said, laughing.

"Fine," Tommy said, "but what about Night Hawk Security?"

"What's this shit with you and birds?" Joe asked.

"*Nighthawk* is a comic," Vinny said.

"Boy," Blaze said to Tommy, "you have an infinite amount of bad ideas."

"Fuck you," Tommy said.

"Fuck You Security? Sounds like a bad business model," Joe said.

"Infinity of Bad Names Security," Blaze said, pouring another shot as carefully as he could, trying not to laugh and trying not to spill from the three hundred fifty dollar bottle.

"Wait a minute," Vinny said, "Infinity Security. Now, that has a good ring to it."

"Good alliterative quality," Joe added.

"You two fuckers," Blaze said, "sound like the fucking college boys up the street. You going to be those hoity-toity barneys?"

"Wait a minute, shut up, shut up," Vinny said. "Infinity Security. It sounds good, but also, and hear me out—" Vinny hiccupped, though he wasn't too drunk, not yet. Pieces of an idea were coming together, like a puzzle. "You guys, it's us. Like, our inside thing. Our crew."

Blaze got down on his knees, laughing but trying to stay serious, and said, "Vinny Bruno, I love you to infinity, brother." Then he moved to Joe. "Joe, I love you to infinity, brother." Then to Whispers. "Whispers, I may love you even more than infinity." To Tommy, "Yeah, you're all right, bro."

Tommy laughed and snorted out his Jack and coke, which only made everyone laugh harder.

Joe gasped. "I have an amazing idea. Let's get tattoos. Infinity symbol tattoos, we'll each get them."

"All right," Whispers said, "I'm in."

"Yeah?" Blaze said. "But like real tattoos, not Joe's rub-off decals."

"*Chingáte*."

"Naw, but let's do this. Joe, you got your tattoo guy's number?"

"I'll call him tomorrow," Joe said.

"Fuck tomorrow," Blaze said, "bring him over here tonight. He can do it right in this living room!"

"Dude, he's not going to come at eleven-thirty," Tommy said.

Blaze looked at him. "Do you know what people will do when you throw money, booze, and weed at them? Call that fucker up. He'll come."

Joe's artist, who went by the name Mongrel, was there with his packets of needles in forty-five minutes flat.

They each picked their spots—Vinny and Blaze, on the middle of their backs, Joe's on the back of his neck, Whispers' just below his stab wound on the soft jugular notch. Vinny knew he was tough, but pound for pound, it would be hard to imagine a tougher motherfucker than Whispers.

They all laughed as Tommy took a shot of Jack, wincing as Mongrel tapped the needle into his left shoulder.

Tommy sat next to Vinny, his head leaning back on the top of the couch. "Man, Vinny, I love ya like a brother."

"Ditto, Tommy," Vinny said back.

He looked over at Blaze, shit-eating grin on his face, half asleep. They all had their tattoos bandaged, the patches marking each of them. The problem with getting tatted when drinking was forgetting to be careful and lying down or rubbing against something. To some, a tattoo may be nothing more than a symbolic gesture, but for Vinny, it was a big fucking symbol. Here were five guys who looked nothing alike, one Mexican, one Puerto Rican, one Black American, one Italian American, and a half-Irish, half-WASP from the 'burbs, but they were family, and now they had one defining external trait that was the clear link. That symbol meant the world to Vinny Bruno.

∞

Being finally settled into the new house, the only logical step for the Infinity Crew was inauguration by house party. They argued over whether to make it a family party or a hookup party, but living with Blaze meant that his family would come no matter what, despite Blaze's telling Tommy to invite all his spinners and "have them bring their friends." Whispers and Tommy groused a little, but Vinny was A-okay with Blaze inviting his family if there was even the outside chance that Reina would come.

He'd seen Reina once in the last two years, on Christmas night at Blaze's mom's house. He wasn't going to bring her the diamond earrings he'd made for her because that would be too soon and forward. Didn't mean he didn't have them wrapped in a box with her name on it, stashed in his gun safe. Unfortunately, Reina was leaving on the train that night to go back to New York. Had he known this, he would have gotten to the house hours earlier. Now, it would be having to get familiar all over again. What he needed was a concrete plan.

"Hey, so your sister, she got that job in the big New York gallery, right?"

"Yeah, man," Blaze beamed, "she's going to be tearing it up."

"Absolutely," Vinny said. "So don't you think we should support her endeavors? Maybe buy some artwork from her, help her make a commission, she can tell us what's what?"

"Vinny, you are my bro. I love you, you fucking *cabrón*. Well, we'll ask her at the party."

"She's coming?"

Blaze smiled. "Yeah. I think Chencho's picking her up at the station. Don't worry, I'll give her some of my good tequila, none of that shit booze you guys drink, and then I'll smoke her out, and she'll be cool. Score us a discount."

"I thought the point was not to cost her money," Vinny said. "We can afford to pay full price."

"Oh, yeah. But whatever, it's not her money, it's the gallery's."

"Not if she makes commission of the total price."

Blaze nodded as if half-thinking about the math of it. "Jesus," Vinny said, "you need to go back to school and take another fucking math course or business class, something."

"Fuck you," Blaze said, "I'm a business genius."

"Maybe the business end of a gun, *cabrón*."

"Your family is my family," Vinny told Blaze, "and so Reina is our family. We gotta do right by her, support her business."

He would have invited Nat to come to the party—she was his family, in a way, but since Joe's father bowed out of coming, he decided to arrange a special vegan potluck just for Nat, Harv, and Joe's parents. Blaze asked Chencho if he wanted to come to that dinner, but Chencho said that Carlos made him nervous during the couple of run-ins they'd had, so he'd stick to bigger parties with more people to run interference.

Vinny hired housekeepers to clean up the entire house and the backyard and pool, and he still went through every corner of the house with a vacuum and dust rag the morning of the party. As soon as Tommy opened the packs of hot dogs, Vinny grabbed the wrappers and threw them in the trash. Noticing the trash was now half-full, he pulled out the bag to take to the bins outside.

"Man, calm the fuck down! Everything is fine," Tommy said. "Since the fuck when have you been such a neat-freak?"

"No, I'm just—look, it's all going to get busy later, so we'll start with an empty bag, so things won't pile up when everyone is here."

Tommy shook his head.

Blaze yelled at Vinny for wiping the condensation ring off the glass coffee table under Blaze's beer.

"Things are going to get fucked up when everyone gets here—let's start with a clean house so people don't think we live like pigs."

"Vin, there isn't a crumb or speck anywhere in this place. Calm your shit!"

He wouldn't be calm, though, until Reina got there, and not even then. All the women that Vinny had ever been with didn't give him a tenth of the thrill he got just from thinking about Reina. He'd managed to—mostly—put her out of his mind since last Christmas, and he certainly hadn't been a monk in the meantime. There was a neighborhood girl who went to Emerson that he hooked up with a couple times a week, and he liked her a lot, but there was no room on the pedestal of his heart except for the one true queen.

He knew he couldn't bring out the diamonds that were in his personal closet safe upstairs, hidden behind the false wall that wasn't in the blueprints, but it gave him a warm feeling to know Reina's earrings were there, waiting for her.

He hoped Blaze had mentioned to her already about the art, so it would seem natural for him to ask about it. He'd done his homework, spending his recent downtime enthralled by street artists like Basquiat and Haring, but was really into Ed Ruscha from California—those were his rehearsed names to drop, at least.

Except that when Chencho brought her to the party, she wasn't alone.

Vinny walked up to Reina, who'd come in a sexy black sundress and Mary Jane Doc Martens, and then up next to her swung a pale, skinny guy all in black—black jacket, black ripped jeans, black boots with silver chains and buckles on them.

"Reina—hi."

"Hi, Vinny."

Vinny let the sound of his name on her voice ring in the air for a minute, despite the speakers pumping out Tupac all around them.

"Vinny, this is Hector." She put her hand on his chest. Vinny wanted to rip the heart out of that chest. His shirt looked like it was doing its best to hold in a Manhattan oil stain. "He's a brilliant artist, and my gallery is producing a big show of his work in a couple of weeks."

"Oh, really?" Vinny went into boss mode. "That must be very exciting for you, Hector. What kind of art—sculpture, painting? Street art? Neo-pop? Neo-expressionism?"

Hector stepped past Vinny to take a sweeping view of the living room. "I don't believe in labels."

Vinny wanted to punch this guy.

"Hector, Vinny and my brother are actually looking to invest in some art for their new place, and I was thinking of your *Ticonderoga* piece."

Hector raised a thick, manicured, possibly-dyed eyebrow.

"Or maybe *Aztec Bloodletting*?" she suggested.

"Wow, those are quite the names," Vinny said.

"They were quite the historical references, too," Hector said.

A quiet several seconds passed. "Well, we got a bunch of food out back," Vinny offered.

"No, thanks," Hector said. "I don't imagine you'd have anything vegan here."

"Actually," Vinny said, "I'm vegan. I make my own vegan burgers, plus I'm grilling about ten pounds of organic vegetables."

It was as if suddenly Vinny had told Hector he was descended from Moctezuma II. Hector's face lit up. "Really, Vinny? How long have you been vegan?"

"For a couple of years. But I've been vegetarian since I was a kid."

Reina smiled.

"Actually," Hector said, looking around again, "there's a piece not in the show that might be perfect for this room." He looked toward the empty thirty feet of wall across from the fireplace. "*Radioactive Halflife of Earth*," he said, nodding, as if it made perfect sense to everyone there.

"Ah," Reina said. "I think, Vinny, you and Blaze will have to come up to Hector's opening in two weeks, and then maybe we can make an appointment for a private viewing the next day."

Vinny's disappointed heart swelled back up. Two weeks, for two days. "Absolutely," he said.

Reina looked at him, that deep, Blaze-style look, that sized up his soul, his very intentions. Fuck, Vinny thought. She probably already knew about the earrings in his safe.

He guided Reina and Hector to the backyard to get stocked up on food. Chencho had already gotten into the pool with his shorts that came down almost to his ankles, and he was splashing around with seven of the girls Tommy had invited.

Blaze had about ten family members there, and, other than the food for grilling Vinny and Tommy bought, they had single-handedly supplied food enough for a small army. Reina went straight for that table, while Hector followed Vinny to the grill.

"You get it," Hector was saying, "the body's got to stay in its purest state. The flesh or milk of creatures interferes with that."

Vinny didn't want to agree with him. He was pretentious as fuck, but when talking about his veganism, Vinny knew that Hector meant it. And now, Hector was acting like they were bosom buddies. They'd both lost Reina to her family for the moment, and Vinny realized that Hector didn't know any of them, and Reina wasn't introducing him. And Hector wouldn't leave Vinny's side. So now, Vinny was the babysitter for his true love's pretentious artist boyfriend whose art he had to buy.

Hector was quoting from the same *New Yorker* article on veganism that Nat had given to him, so now Vinny had to keep talking to Hector. He didn't know, Hector wasn't his type, but he tried to gauge if the only reason for his aversion was his blocking Vinny's path to Reina.

"So," Vinny asked, since he wasn't getting away from Hector, "what is your approach to making your art?" He wasn't entirely sure what he meant by this question, but it was a start.

"Vinny, I'm going to tell you something. Straight up. My process is life. I experience it. If something in the world moves me, if I see something, read something, news on the TV, that's all been processed, filtered, used for mind control—to keep us placid like sheep. I have to go out into the world, experience it, see a homeless person in the street experiencing injustice, or an animal being slaughtered, and that might make me think back to the way the native peoples of this country were raped by the European colonizers, how this land was raped, just as the streets of Manhattan are raped by the Fortune 500 companies, and it is my duty to respond, as an artist and as a human who has finally opened his eyes to the world, you get me?"

"Uh, yeah. Absolutely."

"...and so from this new state of consciousness, I join my soul, and my body, with the canvas, and I act out my emotions."

Fuck, Reina, Vinny thought. Was she as crazy as Hector was? Vinny was at a loss for what Reina saw in this guy, but he knew that Reina was in a pretty top gallery in Manhattan, and if Hector had a show there, then maybe he was for real. However, he now had his doubts on the sanity of the art scene overall.

"I guess I'd really have to see your work to fully grasp what you're putting down."

"Oh, you must," Hector said, all sincerity. "Come to my studio the next time you're in the city, and you can watch me work."

"Thanks, man, that's great. So, I'm going to go check on the ice, but I'll catch you in a bit." Vinny hoped this would be his chance to lose Hector.

"I can help if you need it," Hector offered.

"No, relax, enjoy the party."

Hector had nothing to say in reply, though he looked in the direction of Reina, surrounded by her mother, grandmother, and cousins. Reina looked over, and then turned away. Hector didn't join her, but Vinny didn't stay to check out what he'd do. He went into the kitchen, opened and shut the freezer, and then found some bags of chips to restock.

Whispers was on the couch with Daniela, his girlfriend, and though there were other people in the room, the couch was their own isla. Everyone else was in or hanging around the pool. Vinny Bruno was not a man to give up, but he knew when he had to be patient, and right now, his patience was wearing out, at least as far as Hector was concerned. Really, he'd buy a fucking painting just to make Reina happy—he wouldn't have to display it, but he had hoped to get something he liked from a guy who wasn't an entire douchebag.

"Hey, there, Bruno." Reina had snuck up behind him. "Care to refill a girl's drink for her?"

"Yeah. What are you having? You know, I think Blaze has some expensive tequila hidden in his room, and I know you have permission."

"I'll take you up on that offer," Reina said, smiling. "So, do I get a tour? Blaze has his hands full."

"Yeah. Of course." Vinny showed her the house, then finally took her upstairs to Blaze's room and opened his in-room liquor cabinet.

"Ohh," Reina said, "bro has been holding out on us." She grabbed an unopened bottle of Don Julio. "To be safe, should we take this into your room?"

Vinny might have had a heart attack. "You sure you feel safe alone in my bedroom with me?" He hoped he didn't sound like a douchebag, although maybe that was Reina's style.

"Oh, Bruno," Reina said. He loved the way she was calling him by his last name. "I'm sure I can handle myself with you."

As they got into his room, Vinny ventured to ask, "So are you and Hector serious?"

Reina threw back her head and laughed. Then she leaned in and kissed Vinny long and deep. He almost came right there.

"I guess that's my answer?" Vinny asked, before kissing her again.

"Not serious, but he's exciting."

"Hell, I'm exciting," Vinny said.

"Yes, Bruno. I bet you are. But a girl like me has to do some chasing, test out all the waters. And besides, Hector? He's going to be a fucking famous artist."

"And you like the fame."

"I don't want to be with him once he is famous—can you imagine? Fucking intolerable."

"Hector, then, is just one wild oat. How's the rest of the field looking after that?"

"It's looking solidly planted, at least for the most part," Reina said. "But I can't make any promises." She kissed Vinny again. "We'd better leave it at that for now," she said, pulling back.

"Kind of like an I.O.U.?" Vinny asked.

Reina stood up and moved toward the door. "Call it foreshadowing."

Vinny collapsed back on the bed. It wasn't everything, but it was the beginning. Hector wouldn't be in his way for very long.

Chapter 15
The Hector Problem

Two weeks later, Vinny and Blaze rode the train to Manhattan. They'd gone to a few clubs in the past couple of years, along with trips to Vegas and Miami and the U.S. Virgin Islands, but something about New York thrilled him in a different way. He had enough Boston pride to think of all the ways he preferred Boston, but he liked the no-bullshit attitude, the scrappiness, and just all the different types of people living on top of each other in one place. And of all those people, he was about to see Reina.

The gallery was one street down from Fifth Avenue, on 77th, in the heart of everything showy and pretentious but still vibrantly alive in the city, and Vinny felt a thrill that he would not have called nerves as he approached the door, already crowded with artsy people dressed to show off their wealth but not to be confused with the kind of people who walked around with blue poodles.

"Ready to go buy some whack shit?" Blaze asked.

Reina was near the front, speaking to an older white couple. They both wore black turtlenecks, even though it was eighty degrees with sixty percent humidity outside. "*Puñeta*," Blaze muttered.

Reina finished her conversation and came over, hugging Blaze and then Vinny. Vinny inhaled her perfume and hung on two seconds too long.

"All right," Blaze said, "break it up."

"So welcome," Reina said, "we're all excited because Hector's show just got written up in today's *Times*. That's a big deal for the gallery."

Blaze had on his rabble-rousing face. "Well, if the *Times* says it's a good show, then I'm all in."

Vinny was ready to step in, but Reina also seemed to recognize her brother's mood. "Did I mention there's free wine, beer, and heavy hors d'oeuvres?"

"The fuck are 'heavy hors d'oeuvres'?"

"It means a shit-ton of finger foods," Reina said, putting her hands on Blaze's shoulders, spinning him around, and pushing him to the side table with the food and booze. "Come find us again when you're happy, *mamabicho*. Come, Vinny, I'll give you a tour."

The piece in the center of the main gallery was a black acrylic sculpture that looked like it had been semi-melted, mounted on a red pedestal, and with one drop of red paint on it meant to look like it was dripping blood. For fuck's sake, Vinny thought.

Reina popped up behind him. "So what do you think?"

"It's interesting," Vinny said.

"Not a modern art fan?"

"No, it's not that I don't like it. I like the idea that you have to think about it, interact with it a little bit. I'm always up for a good challenge. But this whole bleeding rock thing, like, really? Come on." He leaned in to look at the title. "*The Rape of the Iroquois Women at the Hands of the French Trappers, 1798.* Okay."

"Come on, let's check out the paintings," Reina said, steering him toward the back of the gallery. Vinny stopped her and looked back at the rock. "So, is the red paint on the rock, is that from the assault, or is that, like, just a symbol for tragedy?"

"Hector would insist it's not at all a symbol. Also, it's not paint."

"What the fuck is it then?" Vinny looked back, studied the crackled surface of the red. "That shit ain't blood, is it?"

"It's Hector's blood, all right, mixed with lacquer, in a technique from the Renaissance."

"But that's not hygienic, is it? Like, we shouldn't be touching that, right?"

"Well, no one should be touching art, Vinny."

"But that's fucked up."

"It's not the only piece with his blood in it." There was a small installation video on loop showing him working on a different sculpture, with him cutting his chest with a razor and letting the blood drip down his chest dramatically before collecting it in a mortar and mixing it with other liquids and powders.

"This is your boyfriend?" Vinny said, without thinking to stop himself. "I mean, sorry. But does this guy have a death wish or something?"

"It's not like that. Hector can be very sweet. He's just intense. The art scene can do that, sometimes. He's just caught up in the whole persona, feeling like he has to be this one thing."

"Yeah, but—at what point is it an act, and at what point does the person become the persona? That kind of person can turn into a black hole, swallowing up everything—everyone—around him . He better not ever mistreat you."

"I appreciate it, Vinny, but don't start sounding like my brother, or I'll have to put you in a headlock."

"Well, now you're talking," Vinny said, smiling.

Reina smiled, too. She had her brother's smile and his strong brow, but her smile didn't make her seem like she was contemplating how to kill you. Although Vinny still felt slayed by her.

"So these were the two I was thinking of for your house." On the back wall were four large paintings, about ten feet across each, all similar but in four different color tones.

"So is one of these *Ticonderoga*?"

"Ah, you remembered," Reina said.

"I listen to every word you say when you talk," Vinny said, standing back and examining the green-toned canvas, brown and black and gray oil lines moving through it.

Vinny hated that he sort of liked *Ticonderoga*—in part, he was relieved that he could live with something he was buying, but his pride at appreciating anything a prick like Hector was capable of making sure stung.

"Where is the great ar-teest?" Vinny asked, looking around. "You know, my new vegan best friend?"

"He's talking with some buyers from Germany right now. I'll bring him over to say hi. I know how much you're looking forward to that."

"What about the Aztec piece? Is that the red one?"

"Actually, no, it's not in this series." Reina took him to a smaller room behind a false wall. "This is his most neo-expressionistic piece." There was an Aztec pyramid, and a body laid out before it, a hole in the chest, and a heart floating high above the pyramid. It wasn't graphic, though—Vinny loved it. Goddammit, he thought.

"Yeah, I thought you'd like it," Reina said, smiling at him, reading him, he realized.

"I love that you thought it would be a good choice," Vinny said.

"It's a steal at forty thousand," Reina said.

"Forty thousand?"

"Hey, in a few years, I'll make a wager with you that it'll go up to ten times that. Shit, by the end of this show, it's likely to go up to eighty or a hundred."

"What? For this?"

"What, Bruno, you got the money." She gave him a coy look.

Vinny nodded to the painting. "Do I get a special gift bag with it?"

"How about a hand-delivery when the show ends?" Reina pulled a little red dot out of her pocket and put it next to the title plate. "Vinny Bruno, art collector. There you go. Oh, hey, look, Hector!" she called out. "You just made a sale."

"Hector, some fine work here," Vinny said, reaching out his hand.

Hector looked at Vinny's hand, then at Vinny, then shook the hand reluctantly. His eyes were black-rimmed, and also sunken in. Not quite the reunion Vinny had been expecting after Hector's fawning at the party.

Hector looked at the painting. "This will be worth millions after my death."

"Hec," Reina said, "Vinny is still interested in seeing your studio tomorrow."

"Don't call me Hec, Rei. If you can't use my full name, don't address me at all." He turned toward another patron behind him and said, "I have something that will show you the true modern-day colonial sin, which is Capitalism," Hector said, going off with the other man.

"Jesus," Vinny said, "What's his deal? Upset that he sold a piece? Is that too colonial for him?"

"Don't judge the message by the delivery," Reina said. "Anyway, he's a channel swimmer about to reach the French shore."

"Huh? A what?"

Reina looked at Vinny. "He shoots up. Heroin. Big H. All the love he was full of this morning has run its course. Watch, he'll start acting like an even bigger asshole, and then he'll disappear into the back, and when he comes out again, he'll be your absolute best friend. Anyway, it's a tossup between heroin and his own ego."

"Whoa, shit. You okay, Reina? I mean, does he share needles, 'cause you know, you can get AIDS from sharing drug needles."

"Vinny, I'm fine. I'm good. I'm protected. But I appreciate your concern and your health lesson."

"So again, I have to ask, I mean, I'm sorry if I'm butting in, but what are you getting out of it? Is he really that great of an artist?"

"You'd do well to pick up a couple of his pieces tonight. Scope out another one or two you like best. I'll make sure to hold them for you. And you and Blaze can come sign the paperwork and hand over your money, Mr. Big Shot Security Company Guy," and as she said it, she held Vinny's hand. But when she touched him, Vinny almost died from the electric shock of her touch.

Begrudgingly, Vinny let Reina go and wandered the gallery. The art was not subtle. And there were five pieces that Vinny hated to admit he found more than a little compelling. Blaze rejoined Vinny, a napkin of tiny pizzas stacked in one hand, a plastic cup of wine in the other, his face much more relaxed than it was when they'd gotten to the gallery. "We just bought this one," Vinny said, pointing to *Aztec Bloodletting*.

"Really? Sweet." Blaze held up the napkin and pulled a tiny pizza off the stack with his teeth. "These gallery shows ain't no joke, huh? The art's weird but kind of cool, you know?"

"Reina wants us still to come to Hector's studio tomorrow to look at another piece."

Blaze shrugged. "Fine by me. We going to get dinner somewhere? Reina said she'd call us later for us to meet at some club she knows."

That was all right by Vinny.

∞

At his studio the next day, Hector was once again a different person, lively, catering to any need Vinny or Blaze might have. They were all a little hungover from clubbing the night before, but then Reina met them for brunch that morning at a place with a whole vegetarian menu, including vegan options. Vinny had three orders of Tofurky bacon.

They went up to the studio, where Hector brimmed with energy and love. Vinny suspected that Hector was likely doing speedballs, because that energy wasn't coming from heroin.

Blaze hit him up for a blunt and said he'd be down to buy whatever. "Let's be a little choosy," Vinny said to Blaze, not wanting to go overboard for Hector.

Hector hadn't come out with them the night before, and Reina had been quiet, saying she was tired, but Vinny was suspicious. He noticed she was still quiet around Hector this afternoon, and neither one of them spoke directly to each other, it was always, "Oh, I'll have Reina write up the sale," or "I'm sure Hector has beer in the back if you want one." Something was up.

Vinny and Blaze didn't end up going with *Radioactive Halflife of Earth*, which had been Hector's recommendation at the housewarming party, but Vinny did kind of like the neo-expressionist *Divorce of My Parents, The Soviet Union and Lithuania*, despite the precious title. For Vinny, it was an inside joke that made him remember the diamonds they'd gotten from Lithu-fucking-wania. Reina said it was inspired by Dmitri Vrubel's famous graffiti mural on the Berlin Wall, *My God, Help Me to Survive this Fatal Attraction*. When Hector denied he had any true inspiration, Reina went to his work table and picked up the torn-out magazine page that showed the image, two Soviet leaders in a seemingly passionate kiss. Vinny had seen that image in the same magazine. He thought it was great, and he liked that *Divorce of My Parents* referenced something political.

Hector then said that Vinny could write him a personal check, but Vinny said he could get a business receipt if he went through the gallery, then looked at Reina. She smiled at him. Her commission was fifteen percent, which she said was great for someone her age.

"So you're not going to take it home today?" Hector asked.

"The gallery can store it for us until the end of the show," Vinny said. "It would be hard to take it on the train."

"Oh, yes, sure, the train, of course," Hector said, though he wasn't angry or annoyed. Just shirtless, sinewy muscle stretched over a thin frame. Small cuts were scabbed and scarred over his torso. He wore bracelets up his wrists, but a few times he moved his arms around, Vinny saw the track marks. Nothing was outright bad about the encounter. If it weren't for Reina, Vinny wouldn't have spent more than a few passing seconds thinking about Hector's behavior. Vinny also realized he was looking for any reason to hate the man. The small passing comments, though, were enough to crack open a solid dislike.

"Yeah, someday, I'll be dead—when that happens, people will truly see what was lost in this world." Hector looked at his own painting of Soviet soldiers, one he was calling *Russian Republic's Prenuptial Agreement*. It was still in progress. All of a sudden, Hector picked up a small razor blade and sliced a one-centimeter cut just under his right nipple. Then he ran toward Russia's Prenup and pressed his torso against the face of the soldiers, smearing the blood around, making sounds that sounded close to an orgasm.

"The fuck?" Vinny said as it happened, while Blaze choked on his beer, trying to catch the beer dribbling out of his mouth. "¡Puñeta!"

The only one not impressed or shocked was Reina, who seemed only to be marking time that morning.

"Shit, man," Blaze said, "there ain't no blood on our pictures, is there?"

Reina shook her head no.

"Only the blood of my labors," Hector said. "My very soul. But for these pieces? Yes, when I am gone, they will remember that I actually bled for my art."

"You got a death wish or something?" Vinny asked.

"Don't we all wish for death, one way or another, Vinny? No, it's not a wish."

Vinny wondered if this guy was at all attached to reality, or if he thought about the shit he was saying. His worry, though, wasn't that Reina would stick around with him much longer; he was worried that Hector would somehow take Reina down with him. He didn't like the smell of what he was seeing.

"I think we should leave you to it, then," Reina finally said, grabbing up her purse. "I'll have our intern Tran come by tomorrow to pick up *Divorce*."

"Yeah, sure," Hector said, still enthralled by the wet blood on the canvas.

"See ya, Hector," Vinny shouted.

As soon as they were down the stairs, Blaze started in. "Reina, what the fuck? No, I put my foot down, that guy has got to go."

"Baby brother, you're the boss of me now? Don't tell me what to do. And without me, you wouldn't have scored those pieces for such a great price."

"Fuck, we get our art from the next dude who shows at your gallery," Blaze said.

"Good point," Vinny said.

"*Oye, bichos,* trust me. I know what I'm doing. Hector's crazy as fuck, but he's smart and talented, despite the bullshit he babbles, and rich art collectors are wetting themselves over him right now, all scrambling to snatch up his work. If you don't like the paintings, you don't have to hang the stupid things up in your house, but fucking listen to me when I tell you to hang onto them for at least five, ten years. Most artists were crazy fucking assholes, anyway. He cuts himself, Van Gogh cut off his fucking ear. In the Renaissance, they made their paints with blood and piss, so this is not an original concept, he's just, like, combining visual and performance art."

Blaze and Vinny stood there like two schoolboys getting their lecture.

"Okay, Reina."

"Sorry, Reina."

She looked stressed, though, and it was a new side to her. Later on that day, once Reina went into the gallery and Vinny and Blaze were on the train back to Boston, Vinny asked Blaze if she had seemed unusually stressed or in any way that was atypical.

"My sister's dating a fucking vein rotter," Blaze said. "*Esta loca.*"

"You think she's in trouble, though?" Vinny asked.

"Nah," Blaze said, suddenly relaxing back into the seat. "I gotta be pissed since I'm her brother. But Reina is my sister *and* my father's daughter, ¿entiendes?"

Vinny nodded. Yeah, he could see that. Still, he thought Blaze should be a little more concerned. "That fucking guy, though," Vinny said, shaking his head.

"Think he's going to be super famous?" Blaze asked.

"Everyone seems to think he's gonna be."

"Hey, Vin—" and Blaze laughed to himself, "this is what it means to have disposable income." He laughed like it was the silliest idea in the world. "Us two wicked *bellascos* fuckers—investing in art. On some guy we've never heard of! Did you see all those rich old fuckers in there last night, trying to jerk Hector off to buy one of his little Etch-a-Sketches?" He was howling, tears streaming down his cheeks, and Vinny had to laugh, too, that they had once again beaten the bigwigs to the proverbial punch.

Chapter 16
The Final Masterpiece

One thing Hector did get Vinny thinking about was more of the Soviet breakup. Every day, the news was filled with stories of Yeltsin's liberalizing of the new Russian Federation, but also how the former Soviet Union had been tanking well before the breakup.

Joe's algorithms had continued to make them all more money than they'd ever expected back at Keystone. They had their legitimate stocks, but then Joe had been using the latest technology to track down corporations' records and caught three Fortune 500 companies that had been moving their dividends around between quarterly reports.

"These fuckers have been cooking their books for eighteen months, but they won't be able to hide these debts any longer. So I'm going to short them, and in, I'd say, give or take three weeks, a month, they're going to tank and probably take down..." Joe clicked on three other names, "these three companies with them. The trick then is to figure out what companies will benefit as a result, which takes a lot of extra research, and we buy their stock before it shoots up."

Joe scratched down a few more notes, looking quite satisfied with himself. Vinny realized that Joe couldn't help himself—he couldn't not do this kind of figuring and mapping and strategizing, and likely would be doing it even if there was no money involved. He was always staying ahead of the system, having all the world's knowledge at the click of his button. Joe might just be one of the most powerful men in the world, and nobody would know it.

"I've been thinking, with Russia," Vinny said, "would there be a way, then, with all the taking of their economy right now, the hyperinflation, to figure out who is actually making money over there? Because someone's gotta be benefiting, especially since they've been privatizing everything and then still have all those resources."

"Vin, I like where you're going. And it's like a patriotic duty or whatever, right?"

"Absolutely."

This was it—it was security with his place and situation in life. Vinny was excited about the future, feeling as mellow as he'd ever been.

∞

Blaze was on his way to Puerto Rico. One of their offshoot operations, since they had accumulated so much money with the investments, they wanted to clean a bunch of it, and Blaze's contribution was to get them all invested in Puerto Rican real estate. Being older, being established, having a shit-ton of money, meant that the Infinity Crew finally had something to lose, and they had no interest in losing everything they'd worked so hard to get.

Vinny made *nopales* and grilled veggie tacos and *tostones* for Blaze to send him off to Puerto Rico the next day, this time for a couple of weeks. They were both surprised when the knock on the door came, and they found Reina on their doorstep, shaking with rage but also crying.

"*Hermana*?" Blaze said, and Reina fell into his arms.

"Hector," Vinny said.

There was a red ligature mark around her neck, and her wrists were raw. "He fucking tied me up while I was asleep, then took Polaroids of me. Then—" she looked down, "he raped me like that, like I was a prisoner or sex slave. He kept me like that for two hours. He said he had to know what it was like to be a colonial oppressor."

"You are not going back there," Vinny said.

"No shit," Blaze said, bringing her into the house. "¡Puñeta! That's it, I'm canceling the trip. We are going to New York, Vinny."

"No," Reina said, "don't do that on my account."

"How can I leave?"

"I'll watch out for her. Then we can decide what we're going to do about it," Vinny said.

"Damn right," Blaze said.

Vinny offered to put her up in the extra bedroom, but Reina asked if she could sleep in Blaze's bed, like when they were kids. "As long as the sheets are fucking clean," she said, trying to laugh. Though Vinny asked, she didn't want to see a doctor. "It's not the first time—it's just the worst time. I'd never been tied like that. I was scared."

The next day, they drove Blaze to Logan, and Reina made sure he got on the plane.

"I'll take care of her," Vinny said. "I'll guard her with my life."

"Yeah," Blaze said, his brow knit but his expression relaxing, "I bet you will. I'm watching you."

When they drove back to the house, Vinny asked, "When was the first time Hector assaulted you? If you don't, you know, mind me asking."

"I know you knew I was acting weird the night of Hector's opening. I went to find him in the bathroom at the gallery, thinking he was shooting up. He was doing a speedball, but then he threw me over the sink in the office bathroom. I was fucking dry as a bone, Vinny. It was awful."

"Why didn't you say anything then?"

Reina squeezed her eyes shut and shook her head. "I kept saying I could take it, that it wasn't that bad. It was just my body. But it wasn't, Vinny."

They went back to the house and he put her on the couch, wrapping her up in a blanket.

"Vinny, will you lie here with me?"

"Of course." He climbed next to her and held her tight.

"I want you Vinny, but not right now."

"I know, *cariña*." He didn't want their first time to be tainted by rage and hurt and assault.

She was quiet for most of the week, making a couple of calls to the gallery or to clients, and then Blaze called at least once a day to check in on her. A week later, though, they were having a quiet dinner, and Reina was back to teasing Vinny, laughing about life, and then Reina asked Vinny to tell her about his sister.

"What can I say, she was the only thing from my childhood that I loved. And now all I have of her is here," he said, pointing to his chest, "that, and a few pictures upstairs." Reina listened as he described stories of them reading comics, and she asked questions about what Angela was like, how she would have liked a certain movie that was out this last year, what her favorite color was. Vinny soon remembered things he had thought were lost to time. He had no hesitation in telling Reina everything. "She was the one thing I truly loved—until you came to Keystone that day. I fell hard, and the next time we met, I knew it wasn't just because of how you looked. It was everything."

Reina got up from her side of the table and came over to Vinny's side, sitting on his lap. She kissed him, and he kissed her back. Then she said, "I'm ready, Vinny. I don't want to wait for you anymore."

They'd both been hurt, they'd both taken risks, they both understood loss and pain, but together, they made something damn near perfect. Vinny couldn't believe it was happening. He'd played out how she'd feel, how she'd taste, in so many different scenarios, from in a hotel bed lined with rose petals to the sandy shore of a private tropical island. There wasn't ceremony to it, now that it was finally happening. It was just the two of them. And reality left everything Vinny had ever imagined in its dust.

The next morning, before Reina woke up, Vinny got out the earring box. He couldn't wait to give them to her and was actually shaking.

Reina opened her eyes. "What's that stupid grin, Bruno?"

He handed her the box. "I had these made for you," he said. "Maybe a while ago, but it would have been weird if I had given them to you before."

When she opened the box to see the earrings, she threw her head back and laughed. "Oh, my God, these are fucking gorgeous!" She put them on immediately. Then she looked at Vinny. "They look suspiciously similar to earrings Blaze gave to our mama last Christmas," she said.

"Possibly," Vinny said, shrugging, "except yours have more carats and a better rating. Shocked the hell out of the jeweler when I brought them in. She said she'd never seen diamonds so perfect. I think she was reluctant to give them up when I came back to get them."

The rest of the week went by in a snap—perfect things usually do, Vinny thought. But Blaze was returning, and they had business to attend to. The night Blaze got back in, Vinny had already been forming a plan on what to do about Hector.

"We breakin' his legs?" Blaze asked.

"We're past that now," Vinny said. What he needed Blaze to do now was procure a machine gun.

∞

Blaze didn't go with Vinny to pick Hector up from his studio in Manhattan. But Hector was loaded up on another speedball and was thrilled to see his favorite investor.

"You haven't, by chance, seen Reina over with her brother, have you?"

"Why? Is Reina not around?"

"Oh, I think she said she was going to her mom's for the weekend," Hector said.

"That's probably it. Anyway," Vinny said, "I actually have a surprise. I used some of our security company connections to arrange something with the city council in Poughkeepsie—but they don't know what they're in for."

Hector looked intrigued.

"Bring some of your paints," Vinny said. "And a roller brush."

Hector's eyes lit up. "Graffiti mural?"

"Total guerilla style," Vinny said.

"And I can do whatever I want?"

"Fuck, yes," Vinny said.

"Aztecs in Poughkeepsie," he said. "But why there? Isn't it a little… provincial?"

"It's the heart of colonial New York," Vinny said.

"Righteous. And then afterward, they can appear everywhere. I want a dead Aztec on an Amish farmhouse, Vinny. Let's do that."

"First things first. We're headed to Poughkeepsie."

The drive in Vinny's borrowed car was tedious, as Vinny had to pretend he was interested in the temporality of all things, and how it was up to art to be both temporary and permanent, so some such bullshit. Vinny gritted his teeth, pretending like this piece of shit hadn't assaulted and tortured Reina.

"Ooh, you wear driving gloves," Hector said, noting Vinny's brown kid-leather gloves. "You got style."

"They're comfortable," Vinny said. "Oh, speaking of, can you hold the wheel, I gotta reach back quickly." Hector grabbed the wheel, then when he overcorrected and veered into the next lane, he leaned way over and grabbed the wheel with both hands, bringing himself in deep next to Vinny's ear.

"Don't worry, I got this," Hector said.

"Wonderful," Vinny said. "Thanks, I got it from here."

They parked near the rail line and under an overpass, along a section of back road that wasn't well trafficked, except by the occasional junkie. It was nine at night when Vinny drove up with Hector. Blaze was waiting near a wall, a drop cloth on the ground, a portable spotlight against the wall.

"Wow, you were eager," Hector said. He gathered his paints from the trunk. "Normally, I'd like to plan this out, but I do have ideas." He looked around at the emptiness of the scene. "I guess if it stinks, no one will have to see it. It'll be my dry run. Then one day, when I'm dead, they can find my work here, and when they realize the provenance, this will become a pilgrimage site."

"Isn't that for religions?" Blaze asked.

"Well, for some people, art is a religion."

They let Hector paint for two and a half hours, a weeping Aztec pulling out the heart of Stalin.

While Hector worked, Blaze went on patrol to make sure no one was around or coming up on the bike path. They'd picked the perfect site. Not a soul. Even the rats seemed to have stayed clear that night.

"What we should have done," Hector said, while finishing coloring in Stalin's beard, "was to set up cameras to record while I worked."

"Oh, I brought a camera," Blaze said. "Not to video, but to document. I'll get it set up while you finish."

"Well, I still have a few more things to do," Hector said. "And really, a piece is never truly finished. Sometimes, you just have to step away."

Vinny nodded. "Truly."

Blaze took a tripod out of his car. There was also a pedal, attached to a pneumatic pump.

"What's that for?" Hector asked, when Blaze put the pedal on the drop cloth, near Hector.

"Step on it," Blaze said.

Hector did. "Oops, got a little paint on it from my shoe."

"That's fine," Blaze said. "It will clean off later."

"Oh, good."

"It's so you can take a self-portrait," Blaze said, smiling.

"That way, it'll all be your work," Vinny said.

"Great. Beautiful," Hector said. While Blaze went to patrol and Hector splashed paint over Stalin, Vinny wiped down the car, just in case. He'd worn gloves and a heavy shirt. There was no dust from his feet on the driver's side, but he wiped the floor mat and pedals, just in case. Not too well, but enough to make sure his generic shoe print didn't leave a clear mark. All that was left were Hector's own fingerprints on the steering wheel.

Blaze came back and smiled at Vinny. "I'll do one more sweep," he said.

Twenty minutes later, Blaze came back and gave the okay.

"So, that looks about finished to me," Vinny said.

"How can a work ever truly be finished?" Hector said.

"How, indeed. But it's getting late," Vinny said.

"Man," Hector said, starting to look a little sad. "Just between us. You wouldn't, I don't know, know where to score some horse?"

Vinny looked at Blaze, and Blaze at Vinny. "He means heroin, Vinny," Blaze said.

"Oh, okay, thanks. Actually, believe it or not, we've done the recreational channel swim," Vinny said, "but only on weekends."

"In fact," Blaze said, "I got a setup in the car. I'll go get it."

"You two," Hector said. "You are dolls. I'll give you another painting," Hector said. Blaze brought out the needle and a small bag of heroin, which Hector set up, sitting cross-legged on the drop cloth, in the halo of spotlight.

"It's really quite a touching silhouette there, isn't it," Vinny said to Blaze.

They watched Hector shoot up, then close his eyes for a moment, letting the drug wash through him. "Thank you," Hector said, his eyes full of love.

"This guy," Vinny whispered. "Okay," he called to Hector, "now you got to stand up for me."

"Okay," Hector said, slowly standing.

"Trunk, please?" Vinny said, and Blaze opened the trunk of the car to reveal a machine gun. From where they were standing, they would be barely visible to Hector, who was off on his own plane of existence, anyway.

"All right now, tap the pedal again for us," Vinny said. He held the machine gun close, just over the tripod.

"Remember, Vin," Blaze whispered, "no more than forty-five degrees. It'll be enough. Watch the kickback."

"Thanks. Hey, asshole," Vinny called to Hector, "I have one more thing to add to the mural. I call it *Human Graffiti of a Completely Pretentious Fucked Up Rapist Who's About to Get What's Coming to Him.*"

"Huh?" Hector said, and as the machine gun made its first click, Vinny saw the briefest streak of realization in Hector's eyes as his blood and guts were splattered on the wall behind him. He emptied the thirty-round magazine into Hector, then they wiped down the gun and set it up on the tripod, making sure it spun correctly to match the path of the bullet spray.

They both left in Blaze's car, leaving behind Hector with everything, including the heroin kit and machine gun.

The body was found by a cyclist five hours later. On the news, they mourned the shocking death of the fastest-growing successful artist, who had so much left to give but who also had a known obsession with death.

"It makes sense," one art critic was quoted as saying, "that with his themes, he would choose to put all his blood into his final artwork. Tragic, though. But we knew how haunted he was. Now, all that's left for us is to decipher what this final work truly represents."

By the end of the day, collectors were burning up the gallery's phone lines, trying to get their hands on anything of Hector's they could. His agent locked down his studio and hired security to prevent break-ins. By the end of the week, pieces with Hector's blood were selling for close to a million dollars.

The pneumatic pedal was Blaze's special touch, making it seem like Hector had set the whole thing up himself. But Vinny wanted the final piece of the mural to be his own, not Hector's, even if no one else knew about it. Nearly no one else. He was glad he didn't have to fight Blaze for that right.

But on the drive home from Poughkeepsie, Blaze had asked Vinny, "You're not going to tell my sister it was us, are you?"

"I don't have to say anything if you don't want me to," Vinny said.

"Okay." Blaze was quiet for a minute. "But you two are together now, right?"

Vinny smiled. "It just...." He was trying to find the words. The two of them hadn't yet broken the news to Blaze when he arrived.

"I'm not fucking stupid, bro," Blaze said. "But if you fucking hurt her, you also will be human graffiti."

"Not on your life. Or mine."

"Shit. Well, that means we are fucking brothers. I mean, you are going to make an honest woman out of my sister, right?"

"That's the plan."

"Damn fucking better be." After a minute, Blaze asked, "Shit, does this mean the two paintings we have are going to go up in value?"

"I guess we'll have to wait and see, bro."

Chapter 17
A Very Good Year
1994–1995

Vinny had the happiest year of his life. Reina took the train into Manhattan when she had to work, and sometimes Vinny would ride the train and meet her for dinner, then they'd ride the train home together and spend the rest of the night naked and tangled in each other's arms.

It was a time for growing up for all of them. Tommy spent time in Marblehead and Providence and then bought himself a house in Marblehead. He was seeing an Italian woman but didn't talk much about her, other than to say she was great, and he was hopeful for the future. Vinny understood—he was in his own world with Reina and was pulling back himself. He and Reina had weekly dinners with her family, including Blaze and Chencho.

Whispers still technically lived at the house, but he'd bought a triple-decker for his Dominican girlfriend and her mother and was spending most nights there.

Joe bought himself a big house in Cambridge and sometimes lunched with the MIT computer science department, pumping them for information on the big computing questions that were coming up.

Though Vinny spent less time with Nat, they still had monthly vegan dinners, and Nat joked that Joe was gaining a reputation for being a gentleman dandy around the MIT campus, acting more like a Jane Austen character than someone from Boston in 1995. A Jane Austen character with a giant Mexican flag tattoo and a small infinity symbol on his neck.

Despite his gentlemen lunches, Joe was not having the best year of his life. He had become increasingly paranoid, mostly because he could see other hackers trying to hack him. He had to constantly maneuver around a series of IP addresses in Moscow and Kiev. He had become addicted to pills, a cocktail of uppers just shy of amphetamines. Vinny told him what he needed was to smoke a fat jay, but Joe said what he needed was to stay sharp.

"Vin, you don't know what these people will do. Did you know that Russian mobsters are coming to New York, and to Boston? They aren't the old-school-style Italian versus Irish mobs. There is no fucking negotiation. Between them and Yakuza, I don't know who I'd rather face less."

"You wouldn't want to face any of them, and so far, you haven't," Vinny said, trying to lighten Joe up.

"You don't understand. They have billions of dollars in assets through all these corrupt Russian businessmen who had all these assets in all these old Eastern Bloc countries, and now they're putting their top money into hacking. Their whole goal is to take over the world—this isn't neighborhood crime anymore."

Vinny could imagine, based on what he'd read. They were getting sophisticated. "Joe, buddy," he said, "I trust you. Nobody's smarter than you are, and that's coming from me."

Still, he worried about Joe's increasingly erratic behavior, though it was never downright reckless or Vinny would have said something. It shocked the hell out of him to get a call one day from Carlos, who fished for a few minutes before asking if Vinny knew what was up with his son. Vinny was grateful he was on the phone and not in person, facing Carlos. It was hard to lie to that fucker.

"I know he's more likely to tell you what's going on than he is to tell me," Carlos said. "And I'm sure if you knew, you likely wouldn't tell me. But if you tell me you aren't worried, then I won't be. I trust that you care about my son."

Well, shit. Vinny would have to thread that needle carefully.

"I have to say, I have noticed that Joe has seemed stressed out, which is new. I did ask him about it, and while I couldn't understand everything he was talking about with all the computers and algorithm-whatevers, I think he's just launched himself into some project and is frustrated that he hasn't figured it out as easily as he normally does. It reads more like frustration to me than anything to be worried about yet—but I promise, I'll keep checking in on him."

"Vinny, I appreciate that," Carlos said, and took a breath. "That eases my mind a little. Just make sure he's eating, okay?"

"Absolutely."

Vinny hedged for a day before he decided to tell Joe that Carlos had called him. "You need to get your shit together, bro, because your dad is noticing and he's worried."

Unfortunately, this only made Joe freak out. "Fuck. And if he tries breaking into my hard drive—"

"Can he do that?" Vinny asked. "Is he a better programmer than you?"

"Probably not, but shit, anything is possible."

"Joe, fuck, a giant fucking meteor killing us is possible, but we can't lose our shit over it. Get yourself together, bro. Man the fuck up."

"Shit. Fuck. No, you're right. I know."

"Just quit the fucking amphetamines, okay? You're going to give yourself a heart attack."

∞

The only meetings Vinny regularly kept on the down-low from everyone were his weekly meetings with Detective Steve Davis. They had become good friends over the years. Often, if Vinny needed a word on the street, or if Steve needed some investment advice, they would meet for coffee or a couple drinks.

"So, funny thing," Davis said, as he sipped his drink, "our division has this big fucking rivalry softball game every year with the local Feds, and those fuckers always win because they cheat."

"I'm sure they do, all cops cheat," Vinny said, laughing.

"Yeah, thing is—a couple of the Feds were talking to one of my colleagues in homicide about that Hector Ramos suicide last year, you know, the artist?"

"I remember."

"And I paid attention because I know you've been spending a lot of time with the gallery woman he used to date."

Vinny bristled. Something was up. "Her brother and I are business partners at Infinity Security—known each other since Keystone."

"That's what I thought," Davis said, nodding. "I don't know what's up, but I heard them say they were reopening the case all of a sudden, new information that had come to light, something about the gallery. They're looking into it as a homicide."

"Whoa, fuck," Vinny said. He tried to contain the heart attack he was about to have, no amphetamines needed. "That would be bizarre—he paints a mural and then gets killed right after? Do they think it was a drug thing?"

Davis shrugged. "I'll keep my ear out, but I didn't know if maybe you'd heard anything from the sister."

Vinny shook his head. "All I know is he was a fucking pretentious fuck, always talking about death, and a shitty boyfriend. Reina had stopped seeing him before he killed himself or whatever."

Davis pursed his lips and took in a deep breath. "Just, you know, know that people are nosing around in something that may peripherally affect your situation."

Vinny held up his cup in a salute. "Point duly noted." He slid over the monthly envelope, which Davis put into his pocket. Davis nodded and finished his drink, and asked the waitress for the tab, which he paid. "Walk out with me," he told Vinny, and they rounded to the back. "If Feds are involved, it's serious shit."

Vinny nodded and gave half a smile. Then, to change the subject, he said, "Davis, you get a nose job recently?"

"Fuck you, Bruno," and Davis took the money out of the envelope Vinny had given him and threw the empty envelope on the ground.

"Fuck you for littering," Vinny said. "Pick that shit up or I'll do a citizen's arrest."

"You first," Davis said, and after Davis pulled away in his car, Vinny did actually pick up the envelope and throw it in the trash. Fucking cops these days, Vinny thought.

The fuck were the Feds doing, reopening Hector's case? All he wanted to do was to take Reina to dinner, and then fuck for hours afterward. He didn't know if he should warn Reina or Blaze, though he couldn't imagine Blaze getting sloppy with the gun or the heroin. Did the gallery suspect something happening with Reina? He wouldn't let her take the fall, that was certain. He could ask Joe to hack around, maybe, but going into the Feds' database? That's the shit that got him sent up in the first place. Besides, Joe knew nothing about Poughkeepsie, nor did Whispers or Tommy, and Vinny wanted to keep it that way, plausible deniability for them, though it felt weird to keep it from Tommy and Whispers.

The next few months flew by, and there was nothing, and Davis said he hadn't heard any news on that front. Life was perfectly normal. Vinny didn't want to turn paranoid like Joe, so he let it go and kept his nose cleaner than usual around town. Instead, he put his focus on popping the question to Reina. So he was really taken by surprise when there was a pounding on his door just before Thanksgiving.

"Vincent Bruno, you're under arrest for the murder of Hector Ramos."

Chapter 18
Federal Correctional Institute, Otisville, New York
1997

Vinny had almost forgotten what it was like. During his first time, that first year when he was fifteen, he'd been in an extended depression. He had little real hope in his life. Now, things were different. He'd seen the life he wanted. He'd had the most amazing year with Reina, and now—he didn't want to think about it. He had made something wicked beautiful. He couldn't let this place turn him into something else. It was hard, though, when everyone around him was trying to bring Vinny into their world.

Vinny couldn't figure out why the fuck the Feds had decided to reopen Hector's case, which had been an open-and-closed suicide case.

Vinny was extradited to New York. He wasn't granted bail, but he got one visitor while he was held in MDC Brooklyn. Davis came in, granted a professional courtesy as a fellow officer because he said he had news about Vinny's estranged family and their parents had been friends.

"I had no idea, Vin," Davis said, and Vinny only shrugged. "Or are you just covering for someone else?" Vinny shrugged again.

"Look, I found out a little more, not much, but I wanted you to know. The Feds only reopened the Ramos case because someone gave you up, as a trade to get himself out of a jam. One of the Feds was joking about you being given up by one of your crew members. I think it was one of your friends who rolled."

Vinny slammed his handcuffed fists down and almost broke the table. "Which one?"

"They didn't say, and I couldn't ask. But I'll keep my ear out, okay?"

Vinny trusted Davis. There was no reason for him to lie to Vinny.

"Oh, but I do have some family news—that wasn't bullshit," Davis said. "I'm really sorry, Vinny—your mom had a heart attack when the news came out. She survived, but she's not in good shape, Vin."

Well. What was there for him to do about it? Did she care now about his life? She hadn't once reached out to Vinny in the last five years. No contact between them at all. "I lost my mother a long time ago, Steve."

Steve nodded. "I hear ya. Still, I'm sorry, Vinny."

∞

Vinny was slated to go to trial, but the prosecutors said if he pled out, he'd get a shorter sentence. "Plead to what? I didn't do anything!" Vinny said to his attorney, Allison. Vinny had immediately put Allison on retainer when he got arrested, and she'd fought tirelessly for him.

"Unfortunately, Vinny," Allison said, "the prosecutors claim there is a tape. A recording of you that night that Hector Ramos was murdered, showing you with him. With the tape, and if there is an informant, Vinny, the judge is going to want to send you up for life if you are convicted. They're trying to crack down on violent crime here in New York."

The tape. Would it show Blaze? Fuck. Why hadn't they gone after Blaze? That's right, Blaze wasn't with him when he picked up Hector. Vinny wasn't going to talk, and he'd let everyone know he wasn't. Any connection to Blaze would connect to Reina, more heat on them. If Vinny copped to it, that would be it, end of investigation, end of story.

"I don't like this video, Vinny," Allison said.

"Why can't we see it?" Vinny asked her.

"Federal trial." Allison shook her head in disgust. "Federal rules say they don't have to give us the tape until three days before trial, so we won't be able to gauge what they do have versus what they don't have. It's a really shitty part of this system. Do you know what could possibly be on the tape? If we push to trial, the prosecutors said all deals are off."

"I have no idea, and I can't imagine what they'd think they have. What should I do?"

Allison looked at Vinny. She wasn't one to tiptoe around. "Vinny, you're a great guy who has donated a lot of time and money to the community ,with your veganism and animal rights donations, and you've run a successful business. Everyone I've interviewed, including your friend's father who's the professor at MIT, spoke very highly of you. You'd have great character witnesses. But you also have this high-profile victim whom people are enthralled with. This case has only made Hector more famous, and now, no one's talking about what a shit he was as a person. The media are totally sanctifying him. Only you know what they could have."

"So you're saying I should take the plea?"

Allison sighed. "It's a gamble. I hate the thought of you going away for this, but going away for *life*? As opposed to a few years? This particular prosecutor is out to get famous. I don't like the guy, and I don't trust him. But once again, I must stress the fact that only you know what they could possibly have. Vinny, I will defend you with everything I got if we go to trial."

Vinny pled out, avoided trial, and *voilá*, two years later he was in Otisville. But still, who the fuck had rolled? Blaze? He couldn't believe it. He wouldn't, no way. Was it?

He had a twelve-year sentence to figure that out.

What hurt most was losing Reina. Maybe not forever, but for twelve years. He had told her to leave the house as soon as he was arrested, but she was questioned anyway and let go. Then, when Vinny called her from jail, she'd screamed at him, loud enough for the officer next to him to hear. All calls are taped, so the federal prosecutors had a good laugh.

"How could you have done this to me, Bruno? You fucking betrayed me. This whole time, I thought Hector had taken his own life, but it turns out Hector had more to give. I'd believed in him, and you took that away from me, you fuck."

His crew members were questioned about Vinny's potential motivations, and they all said they had no clue, and that was that.

A crime of passion, the prosecutors called it. Hector was in the way, and Vinny had gotten Hector out of the way. Vinny never admitted to any motive—only copped the plea, to the frustration of the prosecutors, the art world, and the general media. The news sensationalized the romance of it. "Lethal Love," one headline read. "Vegan's Vengeance," read another. The entire world was left intrigued.

Vinny shrugged. He'd do his time, fine. They sent him for the first year to a maximum security prison in Lewisburg, Pennsylvania, for a year, then to a medium security prison called Otisville in Upstate New York. At Lewisburg, he picked up the nickname Vegan Avenger, which was intended as a slight until Vinny owned the name outright. Adolescent testosterone and fully grown adult testosterone are two very different entities. It's true that plenty of guys in there had the stunted maturity of teenagers, or maybe the system itself had caused that regression. So when one Puerto Rican gang member tried to goad Vinny by calling him that and then tossing Vinny's tray of vegan dinner on the chow hall floor, Vinny had punched him so fast and so hard that the guy didn't have time to reach for the knife he carried and was knocked flat-out for three minutes. That was the first time Vinny landed in the SHU, the segregated housing unit. There were a few other incidents where he was tested, but then plenty of the other inmates came around. Vinny wasn't out to make friends, though.

His friends didn't come to visit him. That was the way Vinny wanted it, not until he figured things out. Especially Blaze. Vinny sent word to Blaze to never visit—he couldn't show any connection to Vinny, and Vinny wanted it that way. Blaze had to take care of Reina.

Nat came to see him, though. They sat together at a conference table in the visiting room.

"You should have come to me. I still have my guilt pass. I haven't used it."

Vinny hadn't thought of that, but at the time, he certainly hadn't taken her offer seriously or as anything more than a nice gesture. She'd grown older in the last few years, in a way that showed in her eyes and around her mouth. Over her flowy brown and gray hair, she wore a floppy straw hat with flowers on the front of it. Dressed for a summer dinner party in her backyard. Vinny would give anything to be in her backyard again.

"How's Harv?" Vinny asked.

"He can't hear for shit," Nat said, rolling her eyes. "I wished I could have brought you some food. I want to be the one to cook for you, the second you're out."

"Nat, you're really sticking by me?"

"Oh, Vinny. You're a good man. The murder thing, well. I don't care that Hector Ramos was a vegan or a famous artist, I read all about him, and I'm sure that if you did have anything to do with it, there was a very good reason, just between you and me and everyone at the Boston Vegetarian Association."

Vinny laughed.

"Vinny, you're the guy who saves animals. Vicious killers, they don't give a shit about life. I know that you're a good man." Nat grabbed both Vinny's hands in hers. "How the hell did you get caught?" she suddenly asked, sitting back in her chair.

"Nat, that is something I would love to find out."

She shook her head. "Get in line."

"That's not for you to poke around looking for."

Nat squeezed his hands again. "Vinny. Remember. Twelve years is terrible. But it's almost been three years. Figure out a way to pass time. But most importantly, once you can make the next nine years seem like a blur, remember that you have a life to go back to. You don't need to make things worse by, you know. Doing something afterward that can come back to bite you."

"Thanks, Nat." He wanted Nat to leave feeling better. "So how did Carlos take all this?"

Nat shook her head. "Man, is he fucking pissed at you."

That was to be expected, Vinny thought. He didn't care, per se, what Joe's father thought of him—well, he did, more than he'd ever cared about his own father, but Carlos was a tough nut.

It was funny the way a family could be shaped. Vinny's blood was in no way relevant to him. Angela was it, but she was Vinny's soul, grafted onto him. Anything truly called good that Vinny had done, had come from Angela. But Angela was gone from this world, and for the rest of Vinny's life, he had chosen his own family.

Now, though, it was going to be up to Vinny to make one very painful cut.

No, he told himself. Whoever had betrayed him had already made the cut. This wasn't coming from Vinny. But he sure as shit was going to clean up the mess.

∞

Time did pass for Vinny. He had made a few friends, if not for life, then people willing to go to bat for him. Early on, when Vinny was still getting harassed, always by the newcomers who wanted to prove themselves by going after one of the bigger guys on the compound, and who usually went after Vinny the second they saw his vegetarian meals. There was always some version of "pussy" or worse thrown around, which didn't usually bother Vinny, but words were never enough for the new punks. So in the first two months, when Vinny's chickpea dinner wound up on the floor, a one-hundred-eighty pound Irish guy with three shamrock tattoos sat quietly at the end of the table, occasionally taking glances at Vinny. The new punk of the week took his swing at Vinny, landing on his jaw, and then Vinny laid him out flat with one punch. At that point, two more guys from the new punk's gang started after Vinny, but the Irish guy was a boxer and hit them both with a combination so fast no one saw anything, and they both fell on their faces. After the action ended, the guards came in swinging their clubs, and Vinny and the other three guys were sent to the SHU.

The next month, when Vinny was back in Gen Pop, he saw the shamrock guy reading a book at one of the tables, so he sat down across from him with his own book.

"Thanks for keeping me out of it. I saw your 038 number," the shamrock guy said.

"Bro, I'd never tell. Yup, from East Boston, then moved to Stoneham."

"I'm from Lowell. I'm Shane."

"I'm Vinny. So you got a beef with those guys?"

Shane sniffed. "Nah, I just didn't like 'em trying to jump my homie."

"Well, thanks for the help. What are you in for?" Vinny asked.

"Eh, I owned a pub in Lowell, and a certain group liked to use my back room, and then I did some things to help them out and the Feds didn't like it."

"Well, you kept quiet, so I like you, bro. And I see that you got hands like lightning."

"Thanks. I was a boxer back in the day. I really miss my pub. All the people. Someday, when I get out, I'd like to open another one, or a boxing gym, but I think a lot of my investors won't be around. What are you in for?"

"Conspiracy to commit murder. How long you been down?"

"Been in for four years, been here for two," Shane said. "I got eight."

"So you know what's what around here, then."

"For the most part. It'd be nice to have a solid homie around I could talk with about Boston now and then. Let's meet later and swap paperwork."

"Yeah, I got mine, so I'll meet you in the yard tonight after chow," Vinny said.

Vinny met Shane that night, and they officially broke bread. He found his way into the system and had a great ally, and anyone in Otisville longer than a month knew not to fuck with Vinny Bruno and also learned that he was a good guy to have on your side. He knew a shit-ton about most everything, having read upwards of ten thousand books in his life, and was a keen problem solver and logistics planner. Though he didn't go in for any plans, he was happy to run through other guys' plans and point out ways they would succeed or fail. As a result, he wound up with quite the following.

At night, though, he had nothing to do but think of what Steve Davis said, that it was one of his roommates—his crew—who'd rolled on him. The rage churned in Vinny—around this world, it was hard to stay calm, even though his required counselor, a woman named Wendy, ran him through some silent meditations he could do to lower that rage.

"Wendy," Vinny said one day, in the last year of his sentence, "I appreciate what you're trying to do here, but I can't let this go."

"Tell me more about it."

"I just—it's someone I trusted like family," Vinny said. "I thought he was family."

"How do you know it was someone you know?"

"Because, an acquaintance told me that one of the Feds let slip the word 'roommate' when discussing who sent me away. I used to live with four other guys. They were all my brothers."

Wendy nodded. "You know it was just one of them?"

"Well, don't get me suspecting it was the whole lot of them. One's bad enough."

"What do you think happened?"

"One of them got pinched for something, and to take the heat off himself, he rolled on me for the bigger crime. That's how the Feds operate."

"So all you have to do is figure out which one of them was doing something illegal."

Vinny raised an eyebrow.

"Aha," Wendy said. "Which one do you think would be the one to rat you out?"

"None of them. I mean—" Vinny went quiet and thought about this. Blaze was the only one who knew, but he felt in his gut that Blaze would be the last one on earth to rat him out. Besides, why would the Feds choose to put Vinny away instead of both of them? Usually, they would both get arrested, and then someone in Blaze's position would plead out to a lesser charge. That hadn't happened. No, Blaze was in too deep. It wouldn't have made any sense on any level for it to have been him. Who, all things being equal, because of Reina, was actually a brother in all but the legal sense. Blaze would be hurting both Vinny and Reina.

Whispers? He thought again. It would be just like Whispers to get caught up in a totally petty bullshit crime and get pinched for that. Except, Whispers had a code. And he never talked. He'd taken a knife in the throat, for fuck's sake. Then again, his girl was pregnant. She probably didn't yet have the hundred percent legal paperwork, although they could easily have figured out how to do that.

Tommy? Tommy was his oldest friend. His blood brother. It had always bugged Tommy that he'd let Vinny take the fall and get sent away the first time. The other guys had never trusted him for it, but he knew Tommy had come back for him and would never betray him.

That left Joe. His heart broke to think about it. Joe? Really? If anyone wasn't acting like himself, it was Joe getting all banged up on pills.

"Whoever it is," Wendy said, "I can see how he'd deserve to die, betraying you like that."

Vinny did a double-take. "I—I'm glad to see you trust me, because you wouldn't normally say that to an inmate, would you?"

Wendy shrugged. "I know you're solid, Vinny, I've checked out your case, and your file here, and I personally like you." She sighed. "I'm not saying it's right, but shit. A brother who betrays you is the enemy. You know about Dante, Vinny?"

"Like the *Inferno* book?"

"Yeah, you read it?"

"Actually, no."

"Well, you need to. So most of what we think of Hell comes from that book, and with the circles of Hell. There are nine, and the deeper you get, the worse the crimes and the punishment. You know who's in the bottom circle?"

"Gotta be murderers?" Vinny guessed.

"Nope. Betrayers. Traitors. Traitors to family, like Cain and Judas, and Brutus, who betrayed Julius Caesar."

"Fucking serious?"

"Fucking dead serious."

After that, he didn't mind his sessions with Wendy. Just having someone who wasn't inside, in khaki, justify Vinny's feelings was enough to relax him. Justification, commiseration. It made Vinny feel seen, at least.

He still couldn't figure out the cameras, and he mentioned to Wendy that it was bugging him, that he'd been caught on tape.

"Have you seen this tape?"

"No, I took the deal before we got to the trial discovery stage."

Wendy shook her head. "Oldest fucking trick in the book. There was probably no fucking video. Damn."

"I had a great attorney. She explained there was a chance that the government could be bluffing and left it up to me. I've always wondered what my life would have been if I went to trial. What do you think?

She shrugged. "Depends on what they really had. It sounds like they were protecting someone's identity. If there was no tape, and just the word of someone who's never been named or brought forward, they would have had to produce them at trial and they would have had to testify against you. Vinny, your destiny would have been how believable the traitor was."

"I could not take that chance, I had other people I love that would have certainly been dragged into it. The decision I made was for everyone's safety. If I had to do it all over again, I would still make the same decision. But it doesn't soften the blow of knowing someone I loved put me here."

Just talking about it made Vinny enraged. Pick-a-fight enraged. Someone sent him here, all right. He needed to be one hundred percent sure who it was, because this was his crew, his brothers. There had to be something he was missing.

Chapter 19
The Other Side of the Wall
2008

"Jesus Christ, Vinny," the guard named Max said, sliding his last meal through the door slot. "Only you, a week away from release, would get fucking sent to the SHU. And then get this fucking vegan cuisine sent from the kitchen." Vinny just smiled.

An Asian garlic tofu meal with broccoli over white rice. His tiny cell filled with the savory smell as soon as it came through the small rectangle slot in the door.

Now on his last day, Max and Santos joked with him as he changed out of his khaki shirt and pants, saying they should dip them in bronze and rename the SHU the VBSHU, the Vinny Bruno Segregated Housing Unit.

"The Plant-Based Bruiser," Santos said, laughing.

"You're the toughest sonofabitch I've ever seen, especially for a grass-eater," Max said.

Vinny laughed. "What do cows eat?"

Santos shrugged. "Grass."

"So, cows are vegetarian. I just cut out the fucking middleman and spare the animals. Always do the work yourself, fellas. The only thing I eat with eyes are the souls of my enemies."

He handed over the khakis, and they handed him his new clothes. The belt was tight, Vinny had to buckle it on the last hole.

"You gain some weight, old man?" Max asked.

Vinny pulled up his shirt, revealing his eight-pack. "I know this gets you off," Vinny said. "Take a good last look."

The *GQ* version of Vinny Bruno passed through the halls one last time to catcalls but also to the shouts of all the guys who'd come to rely on Vinny. They shouted out various promises to look him up when they got out, hoping for his help or friendship on the outside. One guy Vinny waved to that he knew for sure he would see on the streets was an Indian named Qualls.

The final outer doorslid open with a whine, and there was the limo, as arranged, and all the old faces he'd been waiting for, all a little older. It was a shock to see them, the same but each different.

They all hugged, and then the driver opened the back door so they could pile in, Vinny holding back and waiting for the others. Blaze scrambled to the front, so that his back was to the driver and he faced the rear of the limo. Whispers and Tommy stretched out next to Blaze, and Joe filled the last spot on the long J-shaped seat. Then Vinny climbed in, sitting by himself on the separate bench seat so he could face everyone and stretch out his legs.

Blaze adjusted himself in the seat and exhaled. He must have gained about forty pounds, Vinny thought, laughing. He caught Blaze's eye and nodded at his paunch. "I know, man," Blaze said, showing his dimples, "a few too many *tostones*."

As they pulled away from Otisville, Vinny took one last look, then reached for the decanter of whiskey.

"Man, you don't want that shit," Blaze said, pulling a bottle of Jose Cuervo Reserva de la Familia out of a bag on the seat next to him.

"Ah," Vinny said, "good to see you didn't lose all your money in the crash."

Joe jumped in. "Fool, you think I wasn't completely aware that these fools were backing unstable subprime loans and that everything was going to come tumbling down? Bitch, please. I would never let you guys down like that. Maybe we're not quite as rich as we might have been, but we are not broke like a lot of people, and we'll make it back.

240 | Anthony Bucci

They toasted, and Blaze told him that he divided his time between Massachusetts and Puerto Rico and how some *flaca* was finally making a family man out of him, so he was going to get married in the fall. They toasted again, although Tommy didn't take this shot.

Sitting nearest Vinny, Joe shifted in his seat, crossing and uncrossing his legs, and wiping the dampness from his five o'clock shadow.

"Joe, would you like the air turned up?" Vinny asked.

"Sorry, this fucking humidity is killing me," he said, smiling.

"Oh," Blaze said, "so I let your friend Nat into the house yesterday—she dropped off like four fucking vegan dishes of food for you or whatever. Three of them are in the freezer."

"Good ol' Nat," Vinny nodded.

∞

There was a carryon bag that had been tucked under the bar, and Vinny marked it. They were out near the destination now. It was getting to be time.

"I don't know whose bag that is," Joe said, toeing the side of the bag.

"It's mine," Vinny said, reaching for it and putting it on his lap.

The limo took its exit and continued its trip past the refinery, and turning onto the small side street lined with warehouses.

"Man, this has been a long time coming," Vinny started. He looked at each of them in turn: Blaze, Tommy, Whispers, and Joe. "I don't know what to say, but I've had a long time to think about it, how I got locked up for some bullshit that no outsider could have pinned on me." Vinny shook his head. He recounted his reading of Dante, about his discovery of how the worst crime that Dante could imagine was betrayal. Murder, and for a guy like Hector? "I took the fall. It finally made sense when I found out about the rat."

Vinny pulled the 9mm out of the bag.

"Dude, fuck, bro! Watch out with that, there are bumps in the road! What's up?" Blaze asked.

"This is what's up. I've been waiting for this day," Vinny said. The air was thick and hazy, and the smoke from the refinery blended with the colorless sky.

Vinny took one long look at Joe, who shifted in his seat. "Man," Vinny said. "You always said you loved me like a brother. I bought that. And it took me too long to see the difference. These guys here," he nodded at Blaze and Whispers, "they've always called me brother. Not *like* a brother. For them, hurting me would be like tearing off their own flesh. 'Cause we've got the same flesh. We're one." He then looked at Tommy. "And I thought that fucking meant something to you, Tommy, but really, after all these years, the only thing that mattered to you is *you*. You couldn't do a little punk-ass sentence? I would have held you down while you were away." He pointed the gun straight at Tommy.

"Whoa, shit!" Blaze said, and Whispers did a quick double-take, then, getting the picture, leaned in close to Tommy, putting his hand firmly on Tommy's thigh.

"Vinny, come on, what are you talking about?" Tommy said.

"Don't play that with me. I know you rolled on me to get out of your own jackpot. The case on Hector was closed. You had them reopen it."

"What?" Blaze shouted.

Tommy's eyes darted to everyone in the limo. "I—no, of course it wasn't me." His voice was already cracking, though.

"You took twelve years from my life. I did those twelve years *for you*. After the three years I did protecting your ass when we were kids, and you still did this *to me*?"

"But—but it wasn't me! I swear on my mother!"

"You sit there, looking right at me, and you lie to me? You betray me and you lie to my face, after hugging me like we were brothers."

"Vin, we are—I'm not—I wouldn't!"

"Tommy, Tommy, ssh, stop. I know all about the Feds picking you up 'cause you got caught dealing cocaine and selling guns. I read the paperwork with my own eyes."

∞

It was Davis who'd come to see Vinny on a private law enforcement visit a month earlier.

"I found him," Davis said. "Thomas Harris is the guy."

Vinny's heart dropped. Tommy? "Are you sure?"

"The Feds were all over him, and I saw the file because they asked a detective at our station what they'd had on him, and there was nothing much—except that the girl he was with, Francesca, her father is a soldier for the big Providence crime family. Tommy was trying to branch out on his own and was moving cocaine and guns through a strip club. His phone was tapped by the fucking Feds, but Francesca's daddy has a Congressman and the state prosecutor on the payroll, and so when Tommy got picked up, it soon became clear he was connected. The Feds were pissed that the wagons were circling around him, and they leaned on him hard. So he said he could give you up for the murder of a famous artist. The Feds wanted something sensational to be attached to, so they threw their weight into the Ramos case, which they knew would be in all the papers. Fucking Christ. I risked my job for this, but I wanted you to see it with your own eyes, Vinny, because I care and I know you need closure." Davis pulled out the paperwork. "Here, read it, quick."

So Vinny's twelve years were all so the Feds could save face and because Tommy couldn't keep his shit together and man up. Because Tommy was in over his head. Again.

"Fuck!" Vinny had slammed his fist down on the table as he read the DEA6 interview report. "Do the other guys know?"

"Just you."

"Let's keep it that way. This is going to end, once and for all."

∞

When Vinny looked across the limo at Tommy, who was starting to blubber, he wasn't sure if he wanted to beat the shit out of him before he killed him. But he was trying to rein in his temper. This was cleaning up the final mess. The false brother. The Cain, the Judas. Those fucking angelic blue eyes as he whimpered like a little bitch. Like a rat.

"Vinny, I'm sorry, give me another chance, I had no choice," he whined.

"Everyone's got a fucking choice," Vinny said. "That's the whole point."

"Vinny, please! Please, guys!" and Tommy looked around at Blaze, Joe, and Whispers, but they were all stonefaced.

"You're not getting help from any of us, you traitor motherfucker," Joe said.

"Shit," Blaze said. "Goddamn, I can't believe it was you. Did you know?" he asked Whispers.

"If I'd known, do you think this fool would have lived this long?" Whispers said. "Christ, Vinny. This whole time."

"Look, you were all right about him, from the get-go. I thought he was a true brother."

"He probably thought he was, too," Blaze said. "But I don't think he knew what it really meant. Shit, Tommy, how did you even pin Hector on Vinny?"

Tommy covered his face with his hands.

"I asked you a fucking question," said Blaze.

"I figured it out when you bought the machine gun from me," said Tommy.

"What?" Blaze's face went white.

"What's going on?" Vinny asked.

"Fuck, no. No. That was it?" Blaze shouted. "Fuck! Tommy had stolen some guns and was trying to offload them. He called me up and asked if I knew anyone who was looking, I said no, then I told him actually, I told him I was looking to pick up a machine gun for you, Vinny, for a project. I didn't say what it was." He turned to Tommy. "I was fucking trying to do you a solid, Tommy, you piece of shit! Vinny, I'm sorry. I'm so, so sorry. I didn't want to bring your name into it, but I thought you'd be happy I was throwing him a bone. I never would have thought—and then you went away, and now I'm always going to feel like—"

"Don't," Vinny said. "It wasn't your fault, Blaze. It was this traitor, and this traitor alone."

"Fuck you," Tommy yelled, "you've all had it out for me, from the beginning."

"Now, hold up," Whispers said, his hand still tight on Tommy's thigh. "Had it out for you? We were a crew. I even covered for your punk ass the night at Nicky's warehouse and never told anyone that you froze up like a little bitch and couldn't pull the trigger and I had to shoot both of those goons so Vinny and Blaze wouldn't get wasted. Should have known then you were a little bitch coward who wouldn't step up and be there when it counted. Vinny, kill this piece of shit, already."

"Vinny, no, please!" Tommy begged. "I'll do whatever, but come on—"

Vinny couldn't believe Tommy's lack of brotherhood, ethics, and, now, dignity. "Damn, I've been waiting for this day. There's only one thing better than freedom, and that's revenge. Time's up. Enjoy the ninth circle of Hell." He fired the bullet right into Tommy's forehead.

They were pulling into a factory yard, through a broken fence. The road was lined with weeds. It was an incineration plant. The limo finally came to a stop, and the window separating them from the driver rolled down.

"Fuck, Vin—the driver," Blaze said.

"Don't worry," Vinny said.

Steve Davis turned around. "We're here, Vinny."

"Friends," Vinny said, "I'd like to introduce my dear friend, Detective Steve Davis. He's someone you can all trust."

"Damn," Blaze said, "I guess we've all got our secrets," and then shrugged.

Vinny gave a knowing smile. "Yes, we fucking do, don't we?"

They all got out of the limo, and Davis got out, walked over, and removed the cover from a limo that looked identical to the one they were in. Then he took a screwdriver out of his coat pocket and threw it to Vinny.

"Vinny, do me a favor and take the plates of that limo and put them on this other one while I get your friend to start the steam boilers and get them heated up for the barbeque."

"Okay, I got you," Vinny said to Davis. "Let's make sure this piece of shit burns just like he would in hell."

After removing the plates, Vinny got into the driver's seat of the limo, and Davis directed him to a pulley system like you would see at a car wash. Both front tires caught onto pulleys, and Vinny put the car in neutral, got out, and joined the crew.

Vinny looked at the guys and said, "I think this is something we need to do as one," and he walked over to the control lever and put his hand on the start button. Whispers walked over and put his hand over Vinny's, then Blaze, right on cue, put his hand over Whispers' hand, and last was Mexican Joe.

Vinny looked at the guys and said, "Are you all ready?"

"Hold the fuck on, I'm part of you all, now that I'm not a secret," Davis said, smiling and walking over to them. He put his hand over Joe's. This was the new crew.

Together, they pushed down the start button, and the limo was slowly pulled into the burning fire with Tommy in it, soon to be reduced to ashes.

They stood there, watching the limo as it was pulled into the inferno. As it cleared the entrance, a man in a low-brim baseball cap walked out of the incineration plant office and waved to Vinny.

"Hey, my friend, get on your way. I'll handle the rest for you, Vinny," Aaron said. He was a stock guru with a dark side, a dear friend of Vinny's from Otisville. The plant was Aaron's family business.

"I'll see you next month in Boston," Vinny yelled to Aaron, as they all piled into the second limo. They had made plans to have dinner at a predetermined restaurant.

"Does anyone know Tommy was with us today?" Whispers asked.

"No," Davis said. "I went by his house this morning, unannounced. It was just him there. He was the only one who didn't know we were coming to get you today."

"Man," Whispers said to Vinny, "you know I would have made him disappear for you, if you'd asked."

"I know you would have, even without me asking to, 'cause you're a real brother. But I wanted the satisfaction of seeing his face when his fucking rat-fuckery finally caught up to him."

They all had dinner at one of the best restaurants in Boston. They agreed to never speak of Tommy again. When they asked Vinny if they should come home with him, he said, "Tomorrow. There's someone I gotta spend tonight with."

Blaze smiled. "We won't be far, bro."

∞

Davis pulled up to the old house in the legit limo. The stolen limo was burned to ashes. Although it was a bit risky if they had ever gotten pulled over, they hadn't, so it was all history now. Vinny's heart surged. He and Reina talked on the phone every month these last three years, but still, he never let her come up to see him. He knew now he didn't need to worry—no one was sniffing around about Hector, it had been many years since he was put away. No one suspected a thing about the paintings.

Reina ran out the front door, her black hair falling over her shoulders.

"Have fun," Davis said, as Vinny jumped out of the car.

Reina. It was years, eons, a split-second, and she was in his arms. They went inside the house, which had been completely renovated and modern. The furniture was new. Vinny was amazed. In the living room was a new painting, an Ed Ruscha, and across from that, the familiar Red Aztec.

"*Ay, papi,* you better get ready for the ride of your fucking life." Before she'd finished saying it, her shirt was off. She wasn't wearing a bra, and Vinny's mouth was immediately on her hard nipples.

"Oh, my God, Reina," he said, grunting as he unbuckled his fancy new belt. They couldn't wait for each other. In two seconds, he was hard as a rock, and Reina was reaching for him, rubbing him with her hand, then pressing her pelvis against him. She ripped the button off her own pants yanking them down, and Vinny helped her pull them off the rest of the way. He buried his face in her nest of sweetness, and she was already wet for him. He was inside her a minute later, and they both groaned at the familiar feeling—a distant memory that came flooding right back.

"I want all of you right now, and I also want to hold off," Vinny whispered hoarsely.

"Fuck, Bruno, I've worn out seven vibrators waiting for you—give me whatever you got."

"You going behind my back with a vibrator?"

"I had to get the biggest ones, and they still don't move like you do."

He pushed into her, and they both came in a matter of minutes, Vinny falling onto her mouth, her tongue penetrating him, and then he rolled onto his back, holding her in his arms. They stayed like that for a few minutes before Reina was on top of him again, rocking her wetness that belonged both to her and to him along his cock, waking him back up, rubbing him hard again, and then putting him inside her. Vinny smiled at her like he was seeing her all over again for the first time. She dangled a breast in his face.

"*Ticonderoga* sold last week at auction for $2.5 million. The paintings actually went up more after the story of your killing him and staying silent spread throughout the world," she said.

"Nice work, baby. Although I'm kind of sorry to see it go." He pushed up his hips, reaching as far into her as he could go.

"That makes twelve of Hector's works. *Ay, papi*, you're going to break me with it if you keep doing that."

"Oh, sorry, it's just been so long—"

"I didn't say stop," Reina said, coyly. "I want you to try to fucking break me." She reached behind her round, perfect ass and squeezed Vinny's balls to make him harder. "The paintings are off with Chinese coal and tech billionaires now. All the high rollers who didn't get hit are buying up everything now."

Sixteen paintings Reina had taken from Hector, before and after his death. All saved for the making of a legend. The man who was blown to bits on the wall of an overpass in a final work of art. All Reina's idea. The perfect plan.

It was the day he knew he would kill Hector. They were lying together in this room, Vinny holding Reina. They'd just dropped Blaze off at Logan Airport.

"Don't worry, I'm going to make him pay," Vinny had said to Reina.

Reina smiled. "Bruno—I've already made him pay. It's up to you to cash the check."

"What do you mean?"

"Look, I would guess that in your line of work, it wouldn't be the first time you've killed someone. And if it was, so what? It's time. Wouldn't you do that for me? For us?"

"I'm not—" Vinny stammered. Only fucking Reina could make him stammer. "So. But. How? Did Blaze tell you something?"

"Vinny. Come on. You know how much money Blaze has given me over the last couple of years? My Manhattan apartment? He is not getting that money from your security company—no offense, but come on. You guys all got matching fucking infinity tattoos. That's not because you love your that company, ¡chacho!"

"Then you came here…"

"Because I knew you'd take care of it. Besides, that crazy fucker said his work would go up in value once he was dead. It just so happens that I have receipts dated a couple of months ago for, like, ten more of his paintings, which, according to these receipts, the straw buyers paid for in cash. Hector signed off on all of these."

"He did?"

"The fucker would sign anything when he was high. If he said I could have something, I took it immediately to my apartment." She laughed. "One, I even got him to sign on the back, in his own blood, 'To my muse and goddess, Reina.' Fucking hilarious. No one's going to think I stole them, mostly because I didn't have to."

"Is that true?"

"For most of it, yeah. There might have been a few times he left his work out where I could get it while he was on a three-day bender, and which he forgot to look for afterward. How much fucking blood he put onto his art."

"You've been planning this since you first met Hector, haven't you?"

Reina laughed. "Well, maybe not exactly this. I was going to have him sign over a bunch of paintings, but I fully expected him to die of a heroin overdose in the next few years. That fucking death wish. But now, after—you know. He takes what he wants, and he calls himself a fucking Aztec king who scoffs at the world, saying only the weak would refer to his brutal nature as brutal. That we're all cannibals. Some bullshit like that. So I got to thinking, wouldn't it be fucking poetic, and fitting, and infamous, if he was splattered on a wall somewhere?"

"Fuck, Reina," Vinny said, shocked, a tiny bit horrified, but also deeply impressed. He was willing to bet she had a stronger stomach for this business than her brother did.

"But one thing," she said. "I know Blaze is going to want to be a part of ending Hector—but don't tell him about the paintings, okay? And don't tell him I know what you're going to do. I don't want Blaze to know that I planned this."

"You have my word. And I live and die by my word."

"I know you do, Bruno. That's why I love you."

Vinny had told Reina two things before he got sent up, as a contingency. Not to sell the house, and not to come visit him. "I don't want you seeing me that way."

"Fuck, I've already seen you that way, if you recall, Bruno."

"Still. I want you to think of me here. Not there."

"That's going to be hard, Bruno."

"You have to make it look like you hate me. That's the only way this is going to work. That way, they can never bring it back to you. I can't let you get sent away for this."

Thirty-eight-year-old Reina rode him faster now. "I had the money directed to the three account numbers, just like you'd arranged," she said, "and then I closed those out, and Joe arranged the account for a sale. Got us a nice penthouse on Fifth Avenue, *amor*. Next to Jerry Seinfeld's building. It was a great investment."

"Fucking straight?"

"Previous owner was underwater, and we could pay cash. In three years, it'll double in price—I beat out the Russians for it."

"That's my girl," grabbing her ass, feeling the swelling mount inside him.

"The only ones left are *Aztec Bloodletting* and *Divorce of My Parents, The Soviet Union and Lithuania*," Reina said.

"I want to keep those," Vinny said.

"I thought you would, my fucking warlord. *Ay.*" She squeezed her eyes shut, then cried out, and it was all Vinny could do to wait for her to come before he did again. It was Reina's turn to collapse onto Vinny this time, and she rubbed her nipples over his face, gently across his eyelids, and then held still over his mouth so he could take turns sucking on each one. "You didn't break me, though."

"There's always tonight." They lay there for ten more minutes, Vinny's body feeling full of brilliant fire. Reina used Vinny's underwear to wipe herself, then threw it back on his face.

"Come on, time to freshen up," she said. Vinny took a few seconds to explore her undercarriage with his fingers, finding his way back across familiar landscapes. They both got up, showered quickly, and changed into designer sweat suits.

"So," Vinny said, "where is—?"

A car pulled into the driveway just at that moment. "I called my mom while you were showering. Here they are."

Reina's mother pulled up in a new black BMW, and Vinny raced to the door—it was faster than he'd ever moved. The car had barely pulled to a stop when the passenger door opened. Out came an eleven-year-old kid, tall and thick like a linebacker, but with Reina's skin and Blaze's brow. And those fucking dimples. But the eyes, the shape of the face, that was all Vinny Bruno.

Vinny choked back a tear.

"*Esa es mi alma. Y tu eres mi corazón.*"

"*Y tu eres mi vida,*" Vinny said, "*siempre.*"

The son that Vinny had never seen burst through the door and into Vinny's arms. "Daddy, Daddy." Vinny Junior shouted and hugged him and wouldn't let go. Vinny couldn't believe that the kid had no qualms, no reservations, about meeting his father for the first time. Vinny looked at Reina.

"You've never been gone from this house, *amor*. This is how it's always been."

"And this is how it's always going to be," he said. He kissed the top of Vincent Junior's head and then leaned over to kiss Reina. She pulled back her hair. There were the diamond earrings. And below her right ear, just next to the hairline, was a tattoo Vinny hadn't yet seen. An infinity symbol.

The End

About the Author

Anthony Bucci, convict/wiseguy, inmate number 21416-038, was a captive of the federal bureau of prisons while serving a 21 year bit. At the onset of his sentence Anthony was bitter and trouble was no stranger to him. He spent a lot of time in solitary confinement. It was in solitary confinement, in his darkest hour, that Anthony had a spiritual awakening and started writing his masterpiece Infinity Crew. Infinity Crew means the world to Anthony. It should, it saved his life.

Upon his release from solitary Anthony completely changed from the street thug he had once been. Compassion became his motivation and strength. Anthony enrolled in and completed over fifty educational courses, volunteered and took care of sick and terminally ill inmates, trained service dogs for the handicapped, and was the first inmate in the country to be granted a parental compassionate release to care for his handicapped mother.

Since his release in October 2019 Anthony is living a compassionate, animal cruelty free, sustainable lifestyle in Boston, Massachusetts. He cares for his mother and is rebuilding relationships with his children and loved ones. Anthony has launched "The Convicted Vegan Wear" apparel line. He is led by his dreams and is on a mission to show the world that anything is in the realm of possibility if you work hard and live your life by the law of good karma.

Anthony was at rock bottom and has faced his demons. He makes it a point to be available to talk to anyone down and out. Anthony lives by the belief without you there is no me. Anthony is staying convicted to being someone nobody thought he could ever be. He is living the story he has always wanted to tell, and would be honored if you would be his audience for years to come.

Facebook/ The Convicted Vegan

Instagram @theconvictedvegan

Twitter @theconvictedvegan

https://theconvictedvegan.com